Double

Crossing

By Meg Mims

DOUBLE CROSSING

Copyright © 2011 MEG MIMS

ISBN 13: 978-1466223202

ISBN: 1466223200

Cover Art Designed by Elaina Lee

Edited by Audrey Jamison

I thank God for this blessing. All my love and heartfelt thanks to my daughter and husband for their patience and support over the years. Mom, you taught me true dedication with your artwork – although I chose writing, I have tried to follow in your footsteps. Dad, thanks for all your encouragement and fostering my love for history. To my sisters, brothers, extended family and friends – your support has meant so much to me. And I have to thank the Crabs, the OFE, the Wonsies, Savvy Authors and the SHU peeps – no way could I have done this without youse guys! To Sharon and Amanda – special thanks for all the laughter, the logic help and the brainstorming. Thanks to Stephanie and everyone at Astraea Press also for this wonderful opportunity.

"...whatever you do, do it all for the glory of God."
1 Corinthians 10:31

'The Lord is my strength and my shield; my heart trusts in him...'
Psalm 28:7

Chapter One

Evanston, Illinois: 1869

I burst into the house. Keeping the flimsy telegram envelope, I dumped half a dozen packages into the maid's waiting arms. "Where's Father? I need to speak to him."

"He's in the library, Miss Lily. With Mr. Todaro."

Oh, bother. I didn't have time to deal with Emil Todaro, my father's lawyer. He was the last person I wanted to see—but that couldn't be helped. Thanking Etta, I raced down the hall. Father turned from his roll-top desk, spectacles perched on his thin nose and hands full of rustling papers. Todaro rose from an armchair with a courteous bow. His silver waistcoat buttons strained over his belly and his balding head shone in the sunlight. I forced myself to nod in his direction and then planted a quick kiss on Father's

1

leathery cheek. The familiar scents of pipe tobacco and bay rum soothed my nervous energy.

"I didn't expect you back so early, Lily. What is it?"

With an uneasy glance at Todaro, I slipped him the envelope. "The telegraph messenger boy caught me on my way home." My voice dropped. "It's from Uncle Harrison."

Father poked up his wire rims while he pored over the brief message. His shoulders slumped. "I'll speak plainly, Lily, because Mr. Todaro and I were discussing this earlier. My brother sent word that George Hearst intends to claim the Early Bird mine in a Sacramento court. Harrison believes his business partner never filed the deed. He needs to prove our ownership."

"Hearst holds an interest in the Comstock Lode, Colonel." Todaro had perked up, his long knobby fingers forming a steeple. The lawyer resembled an amphibian, along with his deep croak of a voice. "His lawyers are just as ambitious and ruthless in court."

Father peered over his spectacles. "Yes, but I have the original deed. I didn't plan to visit California until next month, so we'll have to move up our trip."

"Oh!" I clasped my hands, a thrill racing through me. "I'm dying to visit all the shops out there, especially in San Francisco. When do we leave?"

"We? I meant myself and Mr. Todaro."

I stared at the lawyer, who didn't conceal a sly smirk. "You cannot leave me behind, Father. I promised to visit Uncle Harrison, and what if I decide to go to China?"

"Lily, I refuse to discuss the matter. This trip is anything but a lark."

"It's a grueling two thousand miles on the railroad, Miss Granville. Conditions out west are far too dangerous for a young lady," Todaro said. "Even with an escort."

"The new transcontinental line has been operating all summer. Plenty of women have traveled to California. I've read the newspaper reports."

"I'm afraid the Union and Central Pacific cars are not as luxurious as the reports say. You have no idea. The way stations are abominable, for one thing."

I flashed a smile at him. "I'm ready for adventure. That's why I've considered joining the missionary team with Mr. Mason."

Father scowled. "You are not leaving Evanston until I give my approval."

"You mean until you dissuade me from 'such a ridiculous notion.'"

"Need I remind you of the fourth commandment, Lily?"

"No, Father. We'll discuss this later."

My face flushed hot. Annoyed by being reprimanded in front of Todaro, I ignored the rest of the conversation. I'd always wanted to see the open prairie and perhaps a buffalo herd chased by Indians, the majestic Rocky Mountains and California. California, with its mining camps, lush green meadows and warm sunshine, the cities of Sacramento and San Francisco that had to be as exhilarating as downtown Chicago. I'd pored over the grainy pen-and-ink drawings in the *Chicago Times*. Uncle Harrison, who'd gone west several years ago to make a fortune and succeeded, for the most part, would welcome me with open arms. I plopped down on an armchair and fingered the ridges of the brass floor lamp beside me. Somehow I needed to persuade Father to allow me to tag along on this trip.

When Mr. Todaro's bulky form disappeared out the door, Father glanced at me. "All right, my dear. Let's discuss this business about California."

Heart thudding, I stood up. "Why do you need Mr. Todaro, Father? I don't trust him one bit. Uncle Harrison has a good lawyer in Sacramento."

"He insisted on accompanying me. Emil has a quick mind in court."

"Maybe so, but—"

"I wouldn't be alive if not for his help. He pulled me out of a heap of bodies at Shiloh, remember. I know you don't like him, Lily, but I will keep him as my lawyer."

Frowning, I swallowed further protest. True enough, I disliked him. Something about the bulbous-nosed, oily man sent shivers up my spine. I crossed to the window, remembering the time I'd seen Todaro aim a kick at my pet lizard in the garden. Telling Father about the incident now would make me sound childish and petty.

Etta carried in a silver tray of refreshments and set them on the table between the desk and the leather sofa. I sank into the soft cushion with a whoosh. My feet still hurt from my downtown shopping venture and several hours of errands.

"I bought the handkerchiefs you wanted, Father, and that brass letter opener. I found a pearl brooch at Marshall Field. The silver setting looked inferior, though." I plucked up a golden-crusted pastry filled with creamed chicken and dill. "My seamstress had no open appointments today, and I couldn't find one straw hat that I liked at any of the millinery shops."

"If you're serious about China, you'll have to give up your notions of fashion."

"I suppose," I said, licking a spot of gravy from my thumb.

"That young man has filled your head with nonsense, in my opinion."

"Charles is dedicated to God. The China Inland Mission has accepted him, did I tell you? Now he's raising funds for his passage."

"You've never been dedicated to working in Chicago among the poor. Charity begins at home," Father said. "Your mother was devoted to the Ladies' Society at church."

"Her charity circle sewed clothing and quilts. I can't even thread a needle."

"So we agree." Father snagged a handful of candied almonds. "You need to gain valuable skills here in Evanston, or at a finishing school, before you run off to China."

"I'm too old for school! I'll be twenty in a month—"

"Ripe for marriage, then, and giving me grandchildren. I'd rather dandle a baby on my knee than read letters about you starving in a foreign country. I'm not going to allow you to wed Charles Mason, either. He might be full of the Spirit, but he's more interested in using your inheritance for his own purposes. I never detected any love in him for you."

His final words stung. I couldn't protest much, either. Charles was a decent man, a hard worker, dedicated to his calling, but admiration wasn't the best foundation for a love match or a lasting marriage. Father might be right about Charles' interest in my inheritance, too, which nettled me. I changed the subject.

"Tell me about the Early Bird mine, Father. Is it like the Comstock Lode?"

"Not quite. Your uncle is set on new technology, hydraulic mining. It uses high pressure jets of water and quicksilver. It's quite expensive. He knows more about it than I do."

I chose a toast point topped with cheese, tomato and spinach. "Then I'd better travel with you to California so I can ask him myself."

"You need to stay here where it's safe."

"But you cannot protect me from the world forever, Father. I must choose a path—"

"Keep praying, Lily. The Lord will show you the way." Father bit into an apple cinnamon tart. "If you truly loved Charles, you'd have accepted his marriage proposal right away."

After gulping some chilled lemonade, I set down the glass. I'd prayed on my knees every night and morning, waiting for some sign, but nothing changed. I didn't love him, and didn't share his missionary dream. If I rejected him, I might be stuck in a loveless marriage to someone else. If I married Charles, perhaps my inheritance money would come to good use once I turned twenty-one. But I'd be thousands of miles away from home, among foreigners, and might never see Father again. Neither choice led to happiness.

Tiny dust motes danced in a ray of late sunshine beaming through the window's lace curtain. Cicadas droned outside among the trees. The mournful sound, buzzing low and then high, sent a shiver down my spine.

Waiting for an answer to prayer led to frustration, but perhaps that was best. For now. "My pet lizard lost another clutch of eggs a week ago to a badger. I shot the creature—"

"With what?"

"Your Army revolver."

"Good heavens, child. That weapon has a nasty kickback," Father said grimly. "It might blow your hand clear off. Promise me you won't handle it."

I didn't want to admit that I had lost my grip on the revolver, and gagged on the rank smell of gunpowder. I'd also been shocked by the tremendous bang that deafened me for several days. Still, I was reluctant to promise anything in case of any future predators harming Lucretia or her eggs. Rising to my feet, I rocked back and forth on my heels.

"Did you forget about my early birthday present?"

"No, but don't think you're going to distract me about that revolver."

"I will promise not to touch it, but only if you hire a different lawyer."

Father coughed hard, his mouth full of tart, and swallowed. "No, Lily! I will not bargain with you. This notion you have about Mr. Todaro is foolish. Don't worry your pretty little head about the Early Bird mine any further."

My chest tightened. We'd never quarreled over anything this serious before, not even Charles. Father had often given in to my whims. Something about Emil Todaro soured my stomach. Perhaps that was the Spirit at work in me. I decided to stand firm.

"I'm sorry, Father, but even Uncle Harrison said Mr. Todaro is not trustworthy—"

"I refuse to hear another word on the matter."

Scowling, he returned to his desk and barricaded himself behind a flimsy newspaper. His stubbornness matched my own. I paced the library, slowly perusing the crammed bookshelves, and traced a finger over the globe's continents and oceans. The sphere spun on its stand with a low hum. I stole a glance at Father. He rustled the thin pages, as if awaiting my apology. No doubt he was unhappy with me, but my feelings intensified about Todaro. I could not shake my conviction despite the commandment to honor and obey a parent.

Tired of counting the sofa's brass tacks, I toyed with some wilting flowers in a vase. Silence reigned. I breathed out a deep sigh and moved to the window again. Twilight made it easier to study Father's reflection. At forty-six, he was too young to be widowed. Mother's unexpected death had stunned him so soon after his return from serving the Union in the War. A sore hip bothered him on occasion, brought on by bone-chilling winter nights, damp or soaked tents, marches over difficult terrain or long horseback rides. Deep worry lines tracked his face, iron gray streaks in his hair and beard made him look years older. We shared the same pride, loyalty and tolerance of faults in others.

Emil Todaro was an exception.

Drumming my fingers on the window, I heard the parlor clock strike half past six. "When are you and Uncle Harrison due in court in Sacramento?"

"He didn't mention an exact day or time in that telegram."

"How long will you be gone?"

"A week or two, I suppose. We leave in three days." As if sensing a truce, Father pulled a desk drawer open. "Here is your birthday present, Lily."

I kissed his cheek again and accepted the package. Slipping aside the silky ribbon, I tore the wrinkled rose-scented tissue to reveal a beautiful red leather-bound sketchbook. The cover had stamped golden scrollwork. Each creamy watermarked page begged for sketches or soft watercolors. Remorse filled me. I shouldn't have caused him so much heartache.

"Thank you, Father. What's this?"

A brief inscription filled the inside cover. I read in silence, my throat constricting with more guilt. *Presented to Lily Rose Delano Granville. Treasure all that is precious to you, and you will have treasure for years to come. From your Dudley.*

"Why did you sign it that way? I haven't called you Dudley in years."

"You scrawled it on all the sketches your mother sent." His voice gruff, he tugged at a loose strand of my curly blonde hair when I leaned to kiss his cheek. "You remind me of her so much. She sent your drawings with her letters. They cheered up the men in my regiment, too, whenever I shared them. Forgive an old man his memories."

"You're far from old age. Perhaps I'll go sketch in the garden. I'm expecting Charles to call today or tomorrow."

"He hasn't come to ask my advice, or for my blessing."

"I think he's afraid of you—"

"How can he face heathens then, in a foreign country? You ought to meet other men in the world. Better men, who have a fortune of their own."

I raised an eyebrow. "Perhaps you'll meet better lawyers in California."

"Don't be impertinent." Clenching his pipe in his teeth, Father picked up his newspaper once more. "That won't serve you if you're serious about becoming a missionary."

"Would you rather I follow Aunt Sylvia on stage?"

"Harrison and I disowned her, in case you forgot!" Father knocked pipe ash over his papers and spluttered with anger. "I would lock you in a nunnery if you ever disgraced yourself that way—don't you dare say we are not Catholic, either."

Heat flared in my cheeks. He knew me too well, since I'd almost lobbed that volley. Guilt seared me again when he picked up his paper with shaking hands. I hadn't meant to upset him like this. We both needed some time to recover, so I fled to the garden. The French doors rattled shut behind me. Crossing the flagstones, I clenched my fists around my new sketchbook. Father would recover his good humor before bedtime. I tiptoed past the kitchen window. The clink of china and flatware drifted to my ears along with their low voices while Etta and Cook prepared the evening's meal. My heels sunk into the soft grass. I passed the rose-covered trellis and then perched on an ironwork bench, the metal warm under my fingers. Lucretia scurried out from a hedge's thick foliage, eyes blinking. She froze, staring at me, when I opened the book to the first page and slid a pencil stub from my pocket.

I needed something to make me forget the argument with Father. Capturing the lizard's familiar form, I filled it in with dark cross-hatching and smudges. What a beautiful creature. My friends kept Persian cats or lapdogs, but lizards held a special fascination for me. Exotic, alluring with their patterned skin texture and independence from humans. Lucretia flicked her tongue and scuttled away, alarmed by some noise in the distance. The setting sun glowed dull red and orange past the shadowy trees, casting golden beams over the garden. The aroma of roast chicken, thyme and sage reminded me of dinner.

Rising to my feet, I groped for my mother's necklace which held the tiny watch that Charles had given me. I must have left it upstairs on the dressing table. Tinkling water spilled from a cherub's pitcher into the fountain. I sat down on the bench again and added ferns and shadows to my sketch.

Minutes later, a loud crack echoed in the air. The odd sound lingered. It reminded me of the revolver's shot when I'd killed the badger. Had it come from the house? Closing my book, I hurried through the garden. Two shadowy figures slipped off the side porch and fled toward the street. The taller one wore dark clothing. I recognized the shorter man as Emil Todaro by his frog-like gait. Rushing after them, I witnessed their mad scramble into a waiting buggy. The team shot forward under a whip's cruel lash.

Why had the lawyer returned? What did they want?

I climbed the steps to the side door and found it locked. Scurrying around to the back of the house, I tried the library's French doors but they didn't budge. My heart jumped in my throat. I picked up my skirts, raced around to the front door and flung it wide.

"Etta! Etta, where's Father?"

The maid poked her head out of the dining room. "In the library."

"I saw Mr. Todaro leaving with another man. Did you let them in?"

"No, Miss Lily. I did hear the Colonel talking to someone, though."

"Didn't you hear a loud bang?"

"I did, but I thought it was Cook with her pots. I was in the cellar fetching more coal." Etta trailed me through

11

the hall. "Is something wrong?"

"I'm not sure." The library's doorknob rattled beneath my fingers when I twisted it open. I peeked inside the dim room. "Are you all right, Father?"

An odd smell tickled my nose—gunpowder. I swallowed hard, my throat constricting, staring at how Father was sprawled over his desk, head down, one arm dangling over the edge. My head and ears thrummed when I saw papers littering the floor. The safe door stood ajar, the drawers yanked open every which way. I took a step, and another, toward the pipe that lay on the plush Persian carpet. His crushed spectacles lay beside it. Father's hand cradled the small derringer he'd always kept in his desk drawer. Its pearl handle gleamed above a stack of papers, stained dark crimson.

A fly crawled over Father's cheek. Etta clawed the air, one hand clamped over her mouth. I saw a tiny blackened bullet hole marking his temple, and wet blood trickling downward. Frozen in place, I heard a shrill scream—my own, since pain raked my throat.

Everything swirled and a dark void swallowed me whole.

'I am troubled... I go mourning all the day long...' Psalm 38:6

Chapter Two

I spent the night in a haze of grief. Etta told me later that she stopped all the clocks to the moment we walked into the library. She'd assisted the undertaker the next morning to wash, shave and then dress Father's body in his freshly pressed uniform, polished the ceremonial sword and laid it with the leather scabbard by his side. After placing huge black wreaths on the front and side doors, she draped dull black crepe over paintings, windows curtains and mirrors throughout the house. Etta even sent notices to the local newspapers and telegrams to California and New York. I did nothing but weep.

In bed, in the bath until my skin shriveled, curled on the window seat, or in Father's parlor armchair. Guilt oppressed me like a monolith crushing my chest. I blamed myself during that long crying jag. At last I slept, exhausted, grateful for the oblivion in darkness.

The following day, I crept from my room and helped Etta place two tall floor lamps on either side of the mahogany coffin. She had mended and sponged the dull black mourning dress I'd worn for Mother's funeral, but the fabric itched in the heat. My chest ached, my eyes burned. Another stab of guilt brought fresh tears that wouldn't end. Etta petted and fussed over me, but nothing she said helped.

"It's all my fault! All my fault—I want to die!"

"And what would the Colonel say about that?"

I pushed away from her comforting embrace. "I quarreled with Father. I never apologized before he died, and all because of that toad! I saw him leaving the house with another man, right after I heard the gunshot."

"Who, Miss Lily?"

"Mr. Todaro. They killed Father and stole the deed to the gold mine. The safe was open, and I searched everywhere. It's missing. The police refused to believe me yesterday."

"They didn't have a whit of patience, for you or me or Cook." Etta clucked her tongue. "Well, the visitation begins soon. Neighbors have filled the house with food, so you must eat something. Come along to the dining room."

"I'm not hungry."

Pinching myself for the hundredth time, I knew this was no nightmare. Was God punishing me for some sin? I shook that off. Father's murder was cold-blooded and unjust. Emil Todaro and his colleague had arranged the scene to look like a suicide. The police ruled it as such and sent a message today to verify that the lawyer was nowhere to be found in Evanston or Chicago. I knew then for certain that Emil Todaro had stolen the deed to claim the Early Bird mine.

My thoughts tumbled in my mind like water churning through a rocky streambed. If only I'd stayed by Father's side in the library. If only I'd waited to deliver Uncle Harrison's telegram in private. Todaro wouldn't have known that Father had the deed. He and his colleague must have used the side door to gain admission. Father was alone, vulnerable and unsuspecting. If only I'd stayed in the house. I knew that Todaro was a liar and a thief.

But I never thought he was capable of murder.

The black bombazine dress cinched me so tight I panted for breath. The skirt fell short of covering my shoes, despite Etta's quick work of letting down the hem. I cared nothing about my reddened eyes or my ill-fitting dress. One thought ruled me.

Revenge.

I'd been taught that revenge was the Lord's, but that smug look I saw on Emil Todaro's face the other day was too much to bear. If nothing else, I would see him hang.

"What a shame we can't have a proper funeral," Etta said. "This miserable heat won't allow that. People are already gossiping that the Colonel shot himself."

"We know the truth. I don't care what people think."

Despite my bravado, I did care. Deeply. I followed Etta into the garden, stripping all the red flowers from their stems. Cook had filled half a dozen vases with water by the time we carried in armfuls of roses, zinnias and salvia. The crimson arrangements helped to mask the scent of death, of decay, of finality. By the time visitors arrived, my stomach jitters increased. Drained of energy, numb from the preparations, my voice cracked while I stood beside the coffin and received neighbors, friends and Father's business associates. Visitation required strict etiquette, and I couldn't fail my father. Not after I'd failed him two nights ago.

People greeted me with subdued sympathy. I thought long and hard to recall the tall, thin man I'd seen with Emil Todaro, in case he'd come to pay his respects. I had not caught sight of his features or heard his voice.

One image had burned all else out of my mind— seeing Father slumped over the desk, the blood-soaked papers beneath his head, the silver gun cradled in his hand.

"Mr. Mason is here, Miss Lily," Etta whispered in my ear, "with his sister."

I whirled to see Charles escorting Adele through the crush of people. She reached me first, eyes properly moist, her dove gray suit matching her gloves and a veiled hat. I accepted her murmured words of comfort and then turned to Charles. His boyish plump cheeks flushed red below his thinning fair hair, and his brown eyes reflected kindness and compassion. A black armband encased his suit's sleeve. I didn't expect him to embrace me, however, in full sight of everyone. Shocked, I pulled away in embarrassment.

"Please accept my condolences, Lily—Miss Granville. I wanted to call yesterday," he said in earnest. "I am so sorry for your loss."

"Thank you, Mr. Mason."

"Perhaps it is God's will. We can marry and go to China without any ties to this place." His eyes flickered to Adele when she hissed a warning. Charles shifted from one foot to the other. "I've raised half of the money we need. Say you'll marry me, Lily."

Speechless, I swallowed hard. This was the last thing I needed—to be railroaded into making a hasty decision.

"I'm sorry, Charles, but I believe my father's lawyer murdered the Colonel. You must understand that I want him brought to justice."

Charles stepped back in surprise. "What about the police? Have they arrested him?"

"Mr. Todaro fled to California from what I heard. I'm leaving as soon as possible to follow him. I must recover what he stole."

"Then I'll chaperone you across the country. Adele could accompany us," he amended, his cheeks reddening, "to keep propriety, of course."

I stifled a laugh at his sister's horrified expression. "Let's discuss the matter later." Etta tugged at my elbow, clearly flustered, her eyes wide and cheeks pink. "What is it?"

"Miss Lily, your aunt has arrived."

Stunned, I blinked twice. "Aunt Miranda, Mother's sister? She sent a telegram from Boston with her condolences."

"No, miss," Etta said, her mouth near my ear. "The lady said to give you this."

I took the ivory-colored calling card Etta held out and read the words 'Lady Sylvia Stanhope' printed in simple script. My mouth went dry. Aunt Sylvia? Father's sister— whose name Father had forbidden me to speak. I froze, unable to prevent a sudden invasion when a woman swathed in black swept into the parlor. A veil shrouded her features. Booming yet melodious, her voice stopped the crowd's hushed conversation.

"My dear niece, what a horrible tragedy!"

With that, she embraced me. I fought against her overpowering scent of gardenias and stiff bodice. A

17

runaway horse wouldn't stand a chance if Aunt Sylvia caught the reins. I wadded my black-edged handkerchief between damp palms.

"Indeed—but Father told me the family disowned you."

"Oh, I gave up the stage long ago. Although my brothers never approved of my career, I've come to mend fences. Dearest Lily! Who doesn't need assistance in handling things at such a difficult time? You must be at your wit's end."

For the second time, I was crushed against her formidable bosom. I could not break her hold when claw-like hands sunk into my shoulders. Aunt Sylvia inspected me from head to toe with shrewd eyes.

"What is that awful dress you're wearing, child?"

"I beg your pardon?" Stunned, I glanced at Charles who had stepped back at least a foot. He seemed appalled by my aunt. I couldn't blame him. Stammering, I introduced them. "Uh, this is Mr. Mason. Mr. Mason and his sister, Miss Mason—Mrs. Stanhope."

"Lady Sylvia," she corrected. "My husband, Sir Vaughn, had urgent business this evening. I haven't seen you in years, Lily. You're still scrawny as a chicken."

My face flushed hot. I stared when she lifted her dark veil to reveal glossy brown hair, a swan-like neck, luminous skin and deep set eyes, plus full lips. Steeped in poise and confidence, Aunt Sylvia's stage-worthy presence trumped even Adele's delicate beauty. My teeth remained clenched from her insult.

"The moment I learned the news, I rushed here to be by your side." Aunt Sylvia dabbed at her dry eyes. "Family is important. I'll be here when you falter."

Annoyance filled me at her use of 'when' and not 'if.' Charles and Adele gave a hasty excuse and escaped. I simmered at their abandonment. Was it my fault that Aunt Sylvia had barged into my life? I couldn't order her to leave. Father might be rolling in his grave, but paying her respects as a sister was proper. I scanned the surging crowd, most strangers now. People from Chicago had flocked here in morbid fascination. My father had been loved in Evanston by neighbors and friends, and hailed as a hero upon his return from the War of Rebellion, but his businessmen friends had dwindled.

Still, Colonel John Granville did not deserve scandal surrounding his death.

"Ignore any questions. People may twist your words," Aunt Sylvia whispered in my ear. "Be gracious and above all, remember to thank people for coming to pay their respects."

I'd been doing that before her sudden arrival but held my tongue. It took real effort not to shout the truth aloud, stamp my feet in rage that Father had been murdered in cold blood. Fresh rumors of gold speculation on Wall Street swirled among the visitors, along with tales of the fire on a Chicago wharf and the Prohibition Party's rise to power. My world had narrowed to this black-shrouded parlor. I cared for nothing else.

Father would expect me to show dignity and poise. No matter what people said, no matter what they believed of him or of Aunt Sylvia. She gushed and preened if anyone mentioned her theater career. Her warning to maintain decorum was hypocritical considering her own behavior. Some things would never change.

"Miss Granville? May I express my deepest

19

sympathy." The gentleman with a clipped British accent bowed over my hand. My aunt rushed to join us. "Forgive my late arrival."

"Lily, may I introduce my husband, Sir Vaughn Stanhope. He's a baronet with an estate in Derbyshire, England. I expected you to arrive later than this, my lord."

"My business was concluded early, my lady."

Sir Vaughn held a silver wolf's head-topped cane in one beefy palm. I stared at his oiled graying hair, the baggy pouches under his dark eyes, the gold-rimmed monocle dangling across his black silk waistcoat. Aunt Sylvia brushed my sleeve with a fussy hand.

"You cannot wear this for the funeral service, Lily. I have just the thing."

My aunt dragged me like a mother hen to the hallway, past the last stragglers to the visitation. I saw valises, hat boxes, carpetbags and a small leather trunk piled by the steps. The gardener hefted a full-size trunk on his back up to the second floor, grunting with each step. By the looks of all the baggage, I assumed that Aunt Sylvia and her husband intended to move in—lock, stock and barrel. Someone tapped me on the shoulder. Weary, I greeted a thin man in a tweed suit, his rheumy eyes attesting to illness. He cleared his throat before he spoke.

"Miss Granville?" He clasped my hand and bowed. "Marvin Norris. I served with the Colonel in the war. Please accept my condolences on your loss."

"Thank you, Mr. Norris."

"He was a gallant leader and courageous. Such a sad end. I didn't realize he'd been so despondent in the last few months."

"He didn't kill himself," I said in my firmest voice.

"He was murdered."

"Lily, please," Aunt Sylvia said, sounding shocked. "Forgive my niece, Mr. Norris, and thank you for coming. Now, child, you need your rest—"

"I am not a child. It's true Father was murdered."

"The police disagreed." Aunt Sylvia dragged me toward the stairs. "I have a costume that will be more appropriate for the funeral tomorrow."

Shocked, I broke her hold. "A stage costume?"

"No, of course not."

Sending a prayer for patience heavenward, I marched up the steps after her to the third bedroom. Aunt Sylvia unfastened the large trunk and pawed through silk and satin gowns. At last she shook out a plain black dress. Black-hemmed petticoats and a black corset followed, along with stockings, shoes and black lace mitts.

"I wore these for my first husband's funeral," she said and thrust the bulk in my arms. "So long ago, I can't even remember the year. I was eighteen, a girl much like you. My husband was twenty years older, an actor, and still in his prime. Unfortunately, he fell off the stage during rehearsal one night, dead drunk, and broke his neck. Such a tragedy."

I'd heard a glimmer of this story at my mother's funeral, but always wondered if it was true. "The dress I have—"

"Will not do at all, child. Try on everything, because your maid will need time to make any adjustments. I'll need her help in unpacking, too."

Aunt Sylvia shooed me out the door and shut it in my face. Fuming, I marched to my own bedroom and hurled everything over the bed. What an insufferable and overbearing woman! No wonder Father had cut off all ties to his only sister. A sudden rush of dread washed over me. The visitation had been difficult enough, and tomorrow was the funeral. Charles seemed willing to escort me to California, but would no doubt pressure me to marry him during the trip. With or without an escort, I had to leave.

Taking up my sketchbook from the bedside table, I stroked the leather cover and opened it. The inscription, written in Father's strong script, blurred together as tears filled my eyes.

Treasure all that is precious to you...

I doubled up, my stomach clenched tight, and wept until nausea overcame me. No comforting Scriptures came to mind. I had prayed and begged God to heal my mother during her illness to no avail. Now Father was dead too. Had God Himself abandoned me?

Sinking to my knees, the sketchbook in my arms, I wept bitter tears. The long hours of loneliness, of not seeing Father's smile at meals or hearing his gruff voice, all of it crashed down upon me. He was gone forever. He'd wanted to see me wed and surrounded by children. A lost dream now. A husband, whether Charles or anyone else, would not comfort me or take his place. I'd lost the chance to beg his forgiveness.

In despair, I plucked the scissors from my sewing basket. Raising my head, I glimpsed my blotchy face and reddened eyes in the dressing table's mirror. The black crepe bow in my hair sparked rebellion. I tore it off and trampled the bow underfoot. Then I pulled out all my hairpins until my honey-blonde curls fell in a riotous tangle to my waist. I hacked it free at shoulder length and clutched the mass in my hand. Then I crept downstairs.

Aunt Sylvia's booming voice echoed from the kitchen. I dashed across the hall and inside the stuffy parlor. Despite the suffocating heat and cloying scent of roses, I tiptoed toward the coffin. Soft lamplight flickered on either side. Father's cheeks looked pasty, the skin wrinkled, his eyes already sunken. I'd never laugh with him or feel his embrace again. Fresh tears trickled down my cheeks as I tucked my hair beside the body and hid it with a fold of the satin lining.

"You treasured this, take it with you," I whispered. "Forgive me, Father. Please."

I fell on my knees, my hands clasped together, and rested my head against the wood. Why couldn't I turn back time? I wanted to shoot Todaro myself, even if that condemned me for eternity. I had to find my father's killer. No matter what the dangers and hardships on the train, no matter what the cost. I could do nothing less.

I owed Father that much for failing him.

'...*Grant me justice against my adversary.*' Luke 18:3

Chapter Three

I suffered a series of terror-filled nightmares that night. I'd heard screeching metal on metal and fallen into a dark abyss before waking up, sweating and panting for breath. Etta brought strong coffee long after I donned my aunt's stifling dress.

Once she left, I packed a small trunk. My traveling suit, two shirtwaists, a nightgown, plus several hats and my parent's framed photograph barely fit inside. I strapped it shut and then stuffed spare clothes, a nightdress and under garments in a valise, plus a toothbrush and powder, hairbrush and other essentials. My spare leather boots held a rolled wad of cash, over a hundred and fifty dollars, in one toe. Crumpled tissue beneath the bed caught my eye. I leaned over to retrieve it along with the leather sketchbook Father had given me.

Fighting an urge to leave it behind, I pushed it into

my pocketbook along with a handful of pencils. One slim novel fit beside it. I hurried into Father's bedroom and rummaged through his wardrobe. At last I found his gold watch in his suit pocket and pulled out a small scrap of paper with it. I shoved them both in my pocketbook and then retrieved his Army revolver from behind his shoes.

I'd promised not to handle it, but knew I needed something for protection. Charles wouldn't be able to face a killer or a wild Indian.

Back in my room, I shoved the weapon beneath my boots along with a box of ammunition and fastened the bag. Then I stored it with the trunk under my bed and hurried downstairs to breakfast. Aunt Sylvia had a ranting fit over my hair. I'd pinned it up, but stray wisps escaped and it did look awful. She jammed a heavy veiled bonnet on my head and dragged me out to the buggy. Sir Vaughn looked bored during the drive to the cemetery.

Few people attended the graveside service. Charles and Adele stood beside their father, aloof in the shimmering heat. Dry leaves scuttled past my dust-coated shoes. Reverend Hanson offered prayers and scripture verses, but even the beloved twenty-third Psalm failed to offer any comfort. Only Psalm eighteen, my Father's favorite, calmed my rebellious anger.

"'The Lord is my rock and my fortress, and my deliverer; my God, my strength, in whom I will trust....'"

I watched the casket lowered by creaking ropes into the ground. What an ignoble end for a courageous man. Father had faced death on the battlefield, never expecting it would creep upon him in the safety of his beloved home. Betrayed by a friend he'd trusted, a friend who saved him at Shiloh. A friend who succumbed to pure greed. Aunt Sylvia and Sir Vaughn both gripped my arms tight, as if they expected me to hurl myself into the yawning hole. Instead I pictured Father sitting in the library, pipe clenched between his teeth, newspaper in hand.

I'd give anything to have him back again. Safe and alive.

I opened my hand and let a handful of dirt rain upon his coffin. "I will find your killer, Father. I promise," I said aloud, and then headed straight for Charles. "Have you considered our conversation yesterday?"

He grasped my gloved hands in his and then left, following his father and sister toward their buggy. I realized he'd thrust a small slip of paper between my fingers. Had Aunt Sylvia and her husband noticed? I tucked it away in a pocket and returned to the carriage.

"Who was that young man?" my aunt asked, her eyes narrowed.

"My neighbor, Mr. Mason. You met him last night."

"You must realize your position now." She climbed into the enclosed Brougham and settled against the opposite seat. "You'll inherit the Granville fortune when you turn twenty-one, Lily. Many men will try to influence you into courtship and marriage. You'll have no control or say after that."

"I realize that, Aunt Sylvia—"

"You must address me as 'Lady Sylvia.'" She paused, as if to gauge my compliance, but I refused to reply. "You ought to realize that men will first consider your inheritance before your looks or manners."

I'd learned enough about what sparked a man's interest. I saw right through her advice, however. She seemed more worried about losing her own influence over me than anything else. And I refused to call her 'Lady Sylvia.'

"Charles is a strict Christian."

"That does not matter, Miss Granville." Sir Vaughn sniffed. "You'll be in mourning for a year. That will preclude any courtship or social events."

"You'll be six months in mourning for a dear brother." I noted the quick flash of displeasure in Aunt Sylvia's eyes. Sir Vaughn merely adjusted the black band on his sleeve.

"Lily, you must tame that impertinence," she said, "because no man will tolerate such boldness. 'Her voice was ever low, gentle and soft.'"

"I prefer the Shakespeare quote, 'Do you not know I am a woman? when I think, I must speak.' *As You Like It* is one of my favorite plays."

"That is perfect proof you'll remain a spinster."

I gazed out the window, aware now that she would always have the last word. I had one saving thought in mind. The minute we arrived home, I raced upstairs with a hasty excuse, shut the door and rested against the solid wood. I unfolded the paper Charles had given me.

Tonight, nine p.m., behind the stables. Minimal luggage.

My heart soared. Charles hadn't failed me after all! I wished we could leave now, but that would raise suspicion. Aunt Sylvia might send the police to stop us in Chicago. We'd bide our time and slip away in the dark. I only needed an excuse to retire early.

Downstairs, Etta and Cook had set out a lunch buffet of cold beef tongue, chicken, roast pork, a variety of salads, fresh bread, pickled beets and onions, apple dumplings and cheddar cheese. My appetite failed as Sir

Vaughn and Aunt Sylvia fell to the meal as if they hadn't eaten in weeks. I excused myself and fetched a straw hat and gloves, too restless to stay cooped in my room. I wandered over to the Rose of Sharon bush, then sat on the bench beneath its shady oak. Perspiration trickled down my face in the heat.

Soon I'd be in Chicago with Charles, taking a late train heading west through Illinois and Iowa to Council Bluffs. Deep sadness filled me. Would I ever see these gardens again? Todaro was a dangerous man, and he might strike back like a deadly snake.

I prayed again, this time with more sincerity, for protection and guidance. It seemed as if Charles Mason had only one thought—to leave America for China. Had he agreed to escort me to California in order to whisk me onto the first boat leaving San Francisco? I needed to be careful. Despite his strict faith, he might force me into a compromising situation. I'd have no other choice but marriage.

My pet lizard scuttled out from a bush and then vanished. "Lucretia, where are you—oh!" I jumped when Sir Vaughn emerged from behind the oak. "You startled me. I wasn't aware you were walking in the garden."

"Miss Granville, you must learn the proper title for a titled English baronet." He inserted his monocle and stared at my dress, my hat and my face. "Begin again."

Resentment seethed inside my chest. "I-I wasn't aware you were here, sir."

"'I was not aware of your presence, Sir Vaughn.'"

"It's not proper to sneak up on a lady, Sir Vaughn," I said, gritting my teeth.

His eyes flashed with disapproval. "Colonel

Granville is not even cold in his grave, and yet here you are acting a willful child. Again."

"I needed some fresh air—"

"All well and good, considering your other odd behavior." Sir Vaughn flicked a gloved finger at a short strand of hair that escaped my hat. "Lady Sylvia has decided to send you to a finishing school. I quite agree you are in dire need of polished social skills."

That irked me, but I kept my temper. "She is not my guardian to make—what are you doing?" Alarmed, I backed away from the cane he held out like a divining rod. Sir Vaughn jammed the end into the foliage behind him in several places. "What is it?"

"A loathsome creature." He flicked a button to retract the small blade that had shot out from the cane's bottom. "I must have been mistaken, forgive me. Your aunt has your best interests in mind, child. You will obey her wishes."

I sat. "I am skilled in running a household, keeping accounts, acting as a dinner hostess, speaking French, discussing history, mathematics, literature and art."

His dark gaze had strayed beyond me, so I twisted around on the bench. Aunt Sylvia hurried along the garden path with her skirts swirling around her. Mouth pinched, her thick eyebrows narrowed toward the bridge of her nose, she scolded me in a shrill voice.

"That hat! Your hair is so untidy—I will never understand why you cut it. You ought to be inside, dwelling on your loss, and then preparing for dinner."

I ignored her criticism. What was the use? Neither of them would understand. "I'm not hungry," I said, avoiding Sir Vaughn's stern gaze.

"You will join us, child."

Aunt Sylvia's demanding tone annoyed me further. "As I reminded your husband, you are not my legal guardian. You cannot force me to do anything, whether to eat or attend school, or even leave this house. Only Uncle Harrison can do that. Now if you'll excuse me—"

Aunt Sylvia's sudden scream froze my blood. She scrambled to climb on the ironwork bench and I snatched my hand away from her boot. "Lord have mercy, kill it, kill it! Ugh, how horrible," she said and shivered. "What was that thing?"

Lucretia had skittered to safety into a hole before Sir Vaughn could stab her to death. "She's my pet lizard! Don't hurt her," I said, tugging at his arm. He shook me off, continuing to hunt through the ferns and piles of old dead leaves. "I've sketched her and many other animals in the garden—squirrels, rabbits, birds. Please."

"A pet lizard." Aunt Sylvia gripped my shoulder and climbed from the bench with shaking hands. "To think a young lady would keep such a nasty creature. You ought to confine your illustrations to flowers or trees. Come inside at once."

She marched me straight to the house. Etta's gaze held sympathy as she served dinner. Sir Vaughn had claimed my mother's chair, but I resented Aunt Sylvia far more when she sat at the head of the table. Too upset to eat, I sat in stony silence between them. Like a harpy, Aunt Sylvia ripped into my lack of a proper education, my inappropriate comments and my boldness in speech. I fled at last, unwilling to tolerate any further criticism.

I halted at the top of the landing when I heard my name. They must have been unaware that their voices drifted this far. I could hear Cook's rattling pots and pans as well. I stooped low and leaned forward, head cocked to one side.

"My niece will be trouble."

"Let me assure you, dearest. Once the doctor administers a calming sedative, we shall take her to Bellevue." Sir Vaughn sounded smug. "The staff exercises the utmost discretion. Dr. Patterson confines the most difficult patients to the third floor."

I'd bitten a knuckle so hard I tasted blood. Bellevue! It didn't sound like a finishing school at all, not if sedatives and patients were involved. So that was their game. They'd imprison me in a sanitarium, perhaps live here in this house or sell everything. I hurried upstairs and into my father's bedroom. The familiar scents of cigars and bay rum brought tears to my eyes, and I ran a hand over the armchair in one corner. I didn't trust Aunt Sylvia. I had to reach Uncle Harrison. He had yet to reply to my urgent telegrams over the last few days.

My own wits would have to serve me in surviving this nightmare.

I fled to my room and wedged a chair beneath the door knob. Quickly I changed into my riding habit's dark navy split skirt and jacket, leaving my aunt's hateful black dress, petticoat and corset in a heap on the floor. I dragged out my trunk and carpetbag, then kicked the bombazine mass along with the petticoats and black corset under the bed. Father would understand. I would resume proper mourning attire once I reached California.

At half past eight, I slid open the bedroom window and prayed no one had heard the creak downstairs. Twilight deepened, crickets chirped in the garden and the smell of

31

wood smoke from a campfire tingled the inside of my nose. I fought a sneeze while I lowered my trunk by rope to the ground, where it rested within dark shrubbery. The trellis groaned under my weight, but somehow I scrambled out with my pocketbook jammed inside my jacket and my carpetbag slung around my neck by a length of muslin. It nearly strangled me. My skirt hem caught on a loose nail, but I ripped it free. One end of the knotted muslin came loose and my carpetbag tumbled to the ground. Once I reached the grass, I sent a prayer of thanksgiving heavenward. Retrieving my trunk and carpetbag, I scurried away from the house.

My eyes adjusted to the growing darkness by the time I reached the stables. No alarm had been raised by any servants. I stopped, my heart in my throat, when a shadowy figure emerged.

"I wasn't sure you read my note. Are you ready, Lily?"

I relaxed at Charles's voice. He gripped my gloved hand, yet another reassurance of his friendship. "Yes, I'm ready. We must hurry—I think Aunt Sylvia plans to send me to an institution. No doubt to gain my inheritance without my say."

Charles grasped my elbow. "Then we'd better go. I have a buggy waiting to take us to the Chicago train station."

He guided me around the stables. Soft whickering noises from horses and the rush of bats startled me. I stopped when I saw a second shadowy figure waiting by the buggy, my heart in my throat. The man loomed before me, his voice gruff, and took a coin from Charles.

"Here you are. Leave the buggy at the nearest

livery."

Relieved, I allowed the stranger to boost me into the buggy. Charles followed. Within the hour, we stood on the platform of the Chicago and Northwestern train waiting for the last departure. Steam plumed from its smokestack, and people jostled and shoved their way forward. Soon we'd arrive in Omaha and book our Pullman tickets at the Union Pacific's eastern terminus. Despite my jacket, I shivered from excitement. Once inside the first class car, I sank onto the high-back seat. The engine blew its final whistle. The gritty waterfront, the tall buildings, Marshall Field's and other favorite shops, the city I knew as well as Evanston faded in the distance.

Well out of Aunt Sylvia's reach, I left all doubts behind and looked forward to the seeing Emil Todaro hang for murder.

'...*forgetting those things...I press toward the mark.*' *Phillippians 3:13-14*

Chapter Four

Like a bird freed from its gilded cage, I reveled in my newfound independence. I'd slept with my head pillowed on Charles' shoulder that long night. I woke fitfully at times. But I was content that every mile took me farther away from Aunt Sylvia's reach.

We walked the aisle the next morning to stretch our limbs. Charles bought fruit, bread and cheese, plus several day-old newspapers from the train butcher. He buried himself behind the flimsy sheets, his valise between his feet. I immersed myself in Jane Austen's polite world, but I set the book aside when a widow in dull black, with a touch of white at her collar, walked past. My mood plummeted. I didn't regret leaving Evanston, but my guilt returned. I would wear proper mourning attire the moment I reached my uncle's house in Sacramento.

Plumes of steam billowed past the window. Farmland and small villages popped out of the immense stretches of wilderness and then disappeared. Creeks wandered through thickets or dense forests. I wrinkled my nose at the scent of scorched grass. Blackened earth stretched far beyond one side of the track, no doubt set afire by stray sparks.

A flash of bright light hurt my eyes. The conductor's brass buttons winked in the fading rays of sun while he punched our tickets and then headed down the aisle. We stopped often for passengers, leaving behind quiet main streets with clapboard houses squeezed between clusters of shops. One young woman about my age sat several seats ahead, facing me. Lonely, homesick for the familiar routine and seeing Etta and Cook at their duties, I beckoned her to the empty seat across from us. She rose, her cheeks flushed pink, and slipped past Charles with a grateful smile. He lowered his newspaper.

"I'm traveling to Sacramento. This is my cousin, Charles Mason," I said. He looked surprised at my words.

"How do you do, Miss—"

"Kimball. I'm joining my fiancé in Cheyenne," she added. "Sacramento? I've always wanted to see California."

"As I have. My uncle is expecting us. I'm Lily Granville, but please call me Lily."

"Then you must call me Kate. Robert—he's my fiancé—works as a bank clerk." She laughed, a lovely tinkling sound that brightened my spirits. "He said I shouldn't expect much in Cheyenne. The railroad was built through there a year ago."

Her creamy skin contrasted with thick blue-black hair. The darling straw hat she wore held a tiny bluebird, complimenting the blue-and-white striped suit that showed off a perfect hourglass figure. I looked stick-thin in comparison, since I often forgot to eat. I could pledge to gain twenty pounds, but the weight would refuse to settle in the right spots. My bosom had never drawn any man's attention before. And I refused to stuff horsehair inside my corset, like some young women I knew who wanted to enhance their curves.

While Charles resumed reading his newspapers, we exchanged pleasant conversation about her wedding plans, her trousseau, her hopes for making friends and starting a family soon after her marriage. I sensed Kate's curiosity when I adjusted my sketchbook.

"I enjoy drawing." When she asked to see it, I handed it to her with reluctance. "I'm hoping to see buffalo, the mountains and maybe a native Indian or two."

"What a beautiful lizard. I've only seen farm animals besides snakes, toads, raccoons and a wildcat once. I'm from Indiana." Kate glanced outside and squinted from the brighter sunshine. She shaded her eyes. "I wonder where we are now?"

"We passed Cedar Rapids," Charles said from above our heads. I hadn't even noticed his absence until now. He plopped down beside me. "I brought lunch."

"Thank you so much, cousin," I said sweetly and surveyed the box filled with a variety of sandwiches on crusty bread. I chose one and urged Kate to do the same. "I'm starved."

"It's not yet noon, but we didn't have much choice of breakfast. I asked when we'd arrive in Council Bluffs, but the porter wasn't certain," he said and claimed the last sandwich.

I savored the spicy mustard's bite and the tender roast beef. "I ought to send a telegram to Uncle Harrison. I— we might have a waiting message at the next telegraph office."

"Trains, the telegraph, what's next?" Kate asked, nibbling hers. "Flying in the air?"

We laughed. "100 years ago someone did fly a hot air balloon," Charles said. "But they'll never achieve the same distance as this train. Perhaps someone will figure out a way to power a buggy by steam. That would be interesting."

"And what would all the livery stables do?"

"Yes, and the dung collectors," I said.

Kate's infectious laughter helped me regain my sense of adventure. Charles dodged subtle questions about himself, however, and deferred to me whenever the topics of conversation strayed to my home, family and travel plans. I kept my answers minimal and decided not to share the facts of Father's murder. Charles took the waxed papers once we finished our lunch, along with the box, and headed to the smoking car. I joined Kate on her seat to avoid the noon sun's hot rays and the increased dust that invaded the car.

"Tell me more about your fiancé in Cheyenne."

"We had a 'whirlwind courtship,' or so my aunt called it. I met him in Rockford while I was visiting. I think Aunt Zoe pushed me into accepting Robert or going back home. She said I talked enough in one day to fill a month's worth of chitchat."

I had to laugh, since she had done most of the talking over lunch. But I didn't mind listening to Kate's description of her mother's wedding dress with hand-tatted lace, the muslin sheets she'd embroidered, the feather pillows and quilts packed in her trunk.

Yawning, I stretched my limbs. "I slept a little last night. I'll be glad to get a proper night's sleep in a Pullman berth."

"Yes, I'm looking forward to that. This might be the one chance I have to travel," Kate said. "I'll be too busy with a husband and family, I'm sure."

Excusing myself, I headed to the Ladies' washroom. I scrubbed my face and hands pink The water turned black from all the smoke and soot. Avoiding the soiled roller towel, I dried off with a clean handkerchief. Then I brushed out my hair and pinned stray curls into place near the small knot behind my head. Homesick, I yearned to see Etta scurrying back and forth from the kitchen where Cook would be scowling over the hot stove. And Father, sitting in his armchair, his newspaper and pipe in hand.

"Those days are gone forever," I said aloud. "I'm starting a new chapter in my life."

My confident tone failed to mask my lingering heartache. How silly, talking to myself that way. I left the washroom and slipped out to stand on the open platform between the swaying cars. Gripping the rail, the track a blur below my feet, I enjoyed a dizzying sense of danger and excitement. I'd never been alone more than a few hours of shopping in Chicago. Eastern Iowa's trees reminded me of the thicker stands of stately tall elms, dense oaks and poplars back home, but now swaths of prairie dominated the landscape. Menacing clouds brewed far north of the track, with flashes of lightning and dark curtains of rain. Not a drop fell from the sky, though. I returned inside the car, wishing for cooler air.

Within the hour Charles strolled down the aisle and

sat across from us. His spectacles glinted in the sun. "We'll be in Council Bluffs in twenty minutes," he said and stretched. "I hope we can get Pullman tickets. There's a lot of people going on to California from Omaha."

"We'll get them." I refused to believe we'd sleep sitting up for the next four or five days. The tiny watch still ticked in my ear as I held it close, and then tucked the necklace inside my collar. "What time does the Union Pacific train leave? I hope we won't miss it."

"You must have seen an outdated timetable," Kate said. "It won't leave until tomorrow morning, I'm afraid."

Charles and I stared at each other across the aisle. "We could always find a church, Lily. You promised to think seriously about marriage."

"Two hotel rooms would be easier."

"But not cheaper."

I frowned. "In the long run, it would be."

"Marriage?" Curiosity gleamed in Kate's blue eyes. "I thought you were cousins."

"Charles is intending to travel to China," I said. "He needs to raise funds to support several years of missionary service. And prayers, of course."

"Perhaps I ought to pray for patience," Charles said, his tone sour, and brushed ashes from his sleeves. "And we are quite distant cousins, Miss Kimball."

I leaned back and watched the scenery outside. "More distant than you think."

He looked flustered at that and fell silent, a habit when he couldn't think fast enough to reply. I fought back a smile. Charles would have to pray hard if he thought I would marry him—in church or under a revival tent—before we reached California.

Perched high above the muddy Missouri River, Council Bluffs had a sweeping view of Nebraska's rolling prairie stretching west far and wide. Ten thousand residents chose the high bluff. Twenty-four thousand favored the western riverbank, where Omaha's shops, houses, lawns, flowers, shrubs and trees stood where bare prairie once reigned. I drank in the clusters of airy cottonwoods, the sun-washed buildings of brick and frame and the crowd of passengers heading from the train to the omnibuses near the riverbank.

"I thought they finished that bridge over the Missouri by now. I don't like ferries," Kate said and shaded her eyes. "Or boats. I almost drowned once."

Men, wagons and horses swarmed below near the river. Sturdy iron supports jutted from the brownish water. "We'd better follow everyone else or we'll have to swim across," Charles said, ushering us like a mother hen. "Now I know why they call it the muddy Missouri."

Once we joined the other passengers, teams of horses pulled the omnibuses along a steep, hairpin path down the bluff to the river. Men guided each omnibus onto a flat-bottomed ferry that soon headed into the river. The shallow boat pitched and swayed during the crossing. Several women fainted and Kate looked queasy. My knuckles white, I clung to the seat ahead of me and hoped we wouldn't tip and drown. Fresh horses drew the omnibus off the grounded ferry and toiled up the steep riverbank. Their harnesses strained over sweaty flesh, and their tails swished at huge flies. Kate and Charles both mopped their damp faces and necks.

"Hurry, we have to get in line at the ticket office."

"I already have a ticket," Kate said. "Robert sent it to

me."

"Is it a Pullman ticket?" I waited while she scrounged in her bag and then examined the heavy cardboard. "First class, but it can't be that expensive to convert to a berth. My treat. I'd love your company from Omaha to Cheyenne."

"Oh, but I couldn't expect—"

"Hush. My cousin can be so dull," I said and flashed a smile at Charles. He glowered in return. "We'll have more fun chatting, and it's only one night on the train."

I led the way to the grilled window fronting the clapboard building. We waited fifteen minutes before we secured our Pullman berths. My worries returned, however, when I found no messages from Uncle Harrison at the telegraph office.

"Now for a hotel room. You'll share with me, won't you?" I asked Kate. She looked relieved. "I promise not to hog the bedcovers. Let's try the Herndon. My uncle stayed there when he traveled to California, from what Father told me."

"I'll join you later," Charles said and marched off without another word.

"He's serious-minded," Kate said, "but I admire your cousin for that."

I didn't dare tell her the truth that Charles was not related at all. Where had he gone off to now and why? Maybe he did want to find a church. Tired of sitting so long and anxious to walk, Kate and I walked several blocks uphill and at last found the Herndon Hotel. By the time we climbed the stairs to our room, I claimed the chair nearest the door and fanned myself in relief.

"Thank goodness." Two inches of mud caked my

riding skirt's hem and my boots. Even my valise had spatters. "Look at all this filth. How much water is there?"

"Not enough."

"There ought to be a public bath house somewhere."

Kate protested that idea. "You can't set foot in such a place! If I have to fetch water from the river, I will."

She brought four tin buckets with a maid's help. Once we freshened up and sponged our clothing, I donned my green wool suit and gloves. My straw hat was an odd match but all the other hats had been packed in my trunk. I knew it would be safe at the Union Pacific depot, awaiting our departure tomorrow. The hotel room seemed cozy with clean muslin sheets on the featherbed and soft pillows.

"I need a long nap," Kate said, yawning wide, and crawled onto the mattress. "I couldn't sleep a wink last night, I was so excited."

"I need a few things I forgot to pack. I'll be back soon. Meet me downstairs at half past seven for dinner."

She fell asleep before I left the room. Would Emil Todaro have stayed here on his way to California? I hurried downstairs and asked the clerk, but a quick scan of the registry didn't produce that name or any other in the lawyer's familiar scrawl. Disappointed, I headed out to the street. My goal: the nearest general store. I made a mental list of useful items as I walked north on the sloping walkway. Gentlemen in tailored suits tipped their hats as I passed. A team of bays, muscles heaving, pulled a heavy wagon up the hill. Workmen in soiled collarless shirts and denims unloaded crates in an alley. A woman herded a group of squealing children, while a horse car's driver sang out upcoming destinations: Howard Street, the Courthouse, Henry Street. Two wagons clattered past, raising a cloud of dust.

I clamped a handkerchief over my mouth but Omaha's black dirt still choked me. My hard sneeze left a ringing in my ears. There had to be a general store somewhere with needles and thread. Stray sparks from the Chicago and Western's smokestack had burned tiny holes in my split skirt and jacket, and I was desperate to repair them both.

At last I found a shop. A bell jangled above my head when I entered. The bulky proprietor laughed and joked with several customers while he filled orders at the polished walnut counter. I meandered down each crowded aisle. Scents of dill, chives and cinnamon tickled my nose. Potatoes with earthy skins and papery onions filled open barrels. Small jars of pickled beets and corn relish, tins of fruit and baked beans lined the shelves. Huge burlap sacks of flour, sugar, salt, coffee and beans lay near the door, and wheels of cheese had been stacked above crates of smoked fish and salt pork.

Seeing the flatirons, hoes, plows and other tools all around brought a sense of normalcy back to my life. I realized I'd been wandering in a haze since Father's funeral.

I soon found the rack of notions. "Closing in half an hour, miss," Mr. Porter said with a friendly smile. "Like to see my bolts of silk? I got pattern paper too."

"I need a travel sewing kit, if you have one."

Armed with a clever box crammed with thread, needles and a tiny pair of silver folding scissors, I wandered the back aisles. A leather money belt caught my eye, with firm stitching and eight compartments. Dodging a row of sturdy butter churns and stacked washboards, I placed the belt on the counter along with an oilcloth cape and several green apples.

"Two dozen peppermints also, please."

"Certainly, miss."

Once I paid the bill, I scurried to a quiet corner away from the few remaining shoppers. Shiny snaps on the wide belt secured each compartment. I adjusted it around my waist and tugged my suit jacket to hide its bulk. Perfect!

I glanced around for a mirror and then froze, staring at my feet and then behind me. My pocketbook was nowhere in sight. I thought I'd wedged the leather two-handled bag between the crates of saltines at my elbow. Frantic, I searched the entire corner and each aisle of the shop in vain. Fear gripped me in a stranglehold. My expensive Pullman ticket, stolen! My hands shook and I had trouble thinking straight for a full minute.

I raced back to the counter. I waited until Mr. Porter finished a customer's transaction. "Sir, did I leave my pocketbook here? I paid my bill not five minutes ago. The money belt, sewing kit, peppermints—"

"Sure I remember, miss." Mr. Porter reached beneath the polished wood and planted my bag on top. "A gent brought this to me. Said he found it on a barrel."

I stared at him. "What did he look like?"

The storekeeper shrugged. "Wore a suit and derby hat, like every other man passing through town."

I opened the pocketbook's clasp and glanced inside. Everything was intact, even my precious Pullman ticket and all my money. I murmured a prayer of thanks until realizing that my sketchbook was wedged upside down, on the wrong side. My black-edged handkerchiefs were crumpled on the bottom as well. Someone *had* searched the contents.

Someone who followed me from the hotel. Some

stranger from the train, or Emil Todaro himself? A shiver raced up my spine. It couldn't be possible. Or could it? Had I underestimated him again? Instead of being the hunter, was I now the prey?

That thought infuriated me.

****

Half a dozen black flies, the ones that pestered and bit, crawled on the beehive-shaped screens shielding platters on our table. The greasy potatoes soaked up blood from the close-to-raw beefsteak. The limp pale cabbage wedge also curbed my appetite. Charles and Kate discussed the springtime ceremony that had united the Union Pacific railroad with the Central Pacific in Utah, but my mind dwelled on Porter's store. Had it been my imagination? Perhaps a good Samaritan had found my bag on a barrel after all. Maybe I'd been too quick to judge.

I jumped when Kate poked my arm. "You're so distracted, Lily. You haven't heard a word we've said to you. Is something wrong?"

"I'm worried about my uncle, and this suit is too hot to wear on the train." I poked the mess on my plate. "I also don't like beef that looks fresh from the cow."

A maid carried soiled plates to the kitchen and returned with a pot of coffee. Hotel guests devoured their meals as if they didn't expect to get another decent meal until reaching California. My head throbbed from the chatter that mingled with rattling wagons, horse cars and pedestrians outside.

"Lily Granville, I shall never forgive or forget this trick!"

All the noisy conversation died at that trumpeting

voice. Heart in my throat, I turned to the doorway and stared along with everyone else at Aunt Sylvia. Like a steamship plowing the ocean waves, she surged through the crowded room with Sir Vaughn following. Kate stared at me, blue eyes wide. Charles looked dumbfounded. Aunt Sylvia loomed over us in dull black, her thick veil pulled away, her expression livid. Sir Vaughn sniffed the air in disdain.

"I say, this reminds me of an Irish pub."

"Uh—won't you join us?" Charles had scrambled out of his chair and pulled two empty seats from an adjoining table. I stood as well, my fists clenched.

"Miss Kimball, this is my aunt, Lady Stanhope and her husband."

"Sir Vaughn," he said and inserted his monocle. The Englishman peered at Kate's bosom with appreciation before he addressed me. "My dear Miss Granville, you have no idea how worried we've been. Lucky for us that Miss Mason knew your plans."

I bit down on my lip. "Adele told you?"

Charles mouthed an apology to me, but Aunt Sylvia shoved him aside and plopped down on the chair. "First, you left Evanston without a proper chaperone," she said, and began ticking off numbers on her gloved fingers. "Second, it seems you forgot you're in mourning for your poor father. Third, you left without my permission—"

"I'm going to California to find Uncle Harrison, my legal guardian," I interrupted.

"Fourth, you didn't consider the possibility of scandal at all. Mr. Mason hasn't even proposed to you, according to his sister."

"If you'll excuse me," Kate said and fled the dining

room before I could protest.

My face burned. I gritted my teeth, aware of the curious diners' hushed whispers around the room, and lowered my voice. "I overheard your plans about Bellevue. Did you think I'd allow you to shut me away in such a place?"

She gave a dismissive wave. "We only have your health in mind."

"I'm in perfect health. You'd better take the train back to Chicago, Aunt Sylvia, because I already bought my Pullman ticket."

"You cannot travel alone with Mr. Mason. You're not engaged."

"Uncle Harrison is expecting me."

I ignored a twinge of guilt while the fib hovered between us. Her mouth pinched tight, she drummed her fingers on the tablecloth. Charles stood quiet, his face beet red, one hand smoothing back his fair hair, the other adjusting his collar and tie. Angry yells and shouts drifted through the window panes from the street, drowning out the resumed conversation around us, the clatter of plates and flatware. Outside, I caught sight of several men who fought with bare fists. They kicked, bit, scratched and pummeled each other. Sir Vaughn glanced out the window and then sat across from my aunt. He waved a hand.

"Common ruffians. These rustic surroundings breed a lack of manners."

"Lily, you have no idea of the dangers. My husband traveled to Nevada earlier this year," Aunt Sylvia said. "Neither you or Mr. Mason have considered the impropriety of this."

"He's a gentleman for escorting me."

"I can see for myself what you both are—"

A blood-curdling yell, similar to what I'd read about an Indian war cry, stopped her cold. The moment I glanced up, the window exploded. Shards of glass rained on us and a man rolled over the table. Scattering plates, flatware, cups and teapot, before he crashed onto the floor—unconscious, and half-draped in the tablecloth among the broken china and glass.

Mere inches from my feet.

'My God hath sent his angel, and hath shut the lions' mouths...'
Daniel 6:22

Chapter Five

Horrified, I stared at the young man on the floor. Bright scarlet blood streamed from a deep cut above his left eye. I grabbed a clean napkin from a nearby table and knelt to staunch the heavy flow. Tossing the soaked linen aside, I grabbed two others.

"Good heavens, Lily, you'll ruin your suit," Aunt Sylvia chided. "Get up this instant."

Ignoring her, I untwisted the young man's arm behind him but he failed to wake. "It's obvious he needs help. It's my Christian duty. And yours, Charles."

"He may be a criminal for all we know," he said, but handed me more napkins.

Sir Vaughn huffed. "Quite right, Mr. Mason. He's bleeding all over your skirt, Miss Granville, so leave him be. The proprietor will carry him out to the street."

"He's waking up."

I surveyed the young man's calloused palms and fingers, his blood-stained knuckles, the sawdust in his tangled dark hair which needed a barber's clippers. The crack of one boot sole proclaimed a man down on his luck. He smelled of sweat, leather and tobacco. Stubble on his cheeks and square jaw added to his gone-to-seed appearance. He opened one blue eye.

"Oof." Wincing, he raised a hand to his head in slow-motion, and then let it fall back against his shoulder. Fresh blood stained his shirt. "What the—"

"Shh. You're hurt."

He rolled to one side as if he hadn't heard me, groaned and then sat up. "That stinkin' muleskinner packed a punch. Well, I'll be da—"

"Watch your language," Sir Vaughn said and prodded him with his cane. "There are ladies present. Now take your leave or we shall send for the local sheriff."

"I hope someone sent for a doctor." I pressed the bloody napkin against his cut. "You'll need stitches to close this."

"I been hurt worse in plenty of fights before." The young man swiped at his temple with a sleeve. "Run on home, little lady."

"I am a guest here at the Herndon, and a passenger on the Union Pacific railroad," I said. "But if you prefer bleeding to death, that's your prerogative."

The young man squinted at me, at Charles who stood in shocked silence, at Sir Vaughn and then Aunt Sylvia. She backed away as if he had the plague. I met the young man's oddly mismatched eyes, one blue and the other hazel with flecks of dark gold. He flashed a sheepish grin while taking in my own face and figure.

"Sorry, miss. Looks like I ruined your pretty dress—"

"What in tarnation is going on here?" The hotel manager had arrived and surveyed the mess on the dining room's floor. "Ace Diamond, I should've known you'd be causing trouble. What have you done this time?"

"Ain't my fault. I didn't start the fight." Ace staggered to his feet and stood, but then careened against me. "Whoa."

He arched like a cat and plucked the handkerchief that Charles offered. The moment he stepped away, I froze at the sight of his gleaming belt buckle. Military in style with the Lone Star of Texas, it screamed of service as a Confederate soldier. Loyalty to my father welled up inside my heart, so I stepped away when he brushed bits of broken glass from his filthy shirt. Ace Diamond had made a quick recovery from his injuries. Perhaps his boast of suffering worse in previous fights was true.

"Go on, be off with you," Sir Vaughn said and shook his cane. The Texan snorted in contempt and ignored him.

"So, miss, you're heading to California?"

"Yes. To Sacramento."

Ace squinted. "I'm fixin' to get there myself one day. What's this?"

"My sketchbook!"

I bent to retrieve it but he snatched it first, wobbling on his feet. Ace dusted the leather cover with his hat before he handed it over. Then he began swaying, eyes closed, and sagged against my shoulder. Charles glared when the Texan slipped an arm around me. Aunt Sylvia jumped from her chair, but Sir Vaughn blocked the path.

"Much obliged if you'd help me out, miss. To the street," Ace mumbled.

"Of course."

Ignoring the gawking crowd, I supported him out the door and past the hotel lobby. Ace staggered against me, almost dead weight. Once we reached the street, I breathed in fresh air. He straightened up and plopped his hat on his disheveled hair. Flexing his shoulders, he swiped a forearm against his face and squinted at the fading sunset beyond Omaha.

"Can't thank you enough, miss—I didn't catch your name."

"No, you didn't. Good day, Mr. Diamond."

"Hold your horses." Ace tugged me into an alcove beside the hotel's brick entrance and glanced back. He lowered his voice. "That man, the one with the fancy eyeglass and cane. How well do you know him?"

I folded my arms under my bosom, aware of his roving eyes. "Do you mean Sir Vaughn? He's married to my aunt. From what little I know, he's a titled Englishman."

"Fat chance." Ace rubbed his jaw. I could count each whisker, he stood that close. "I'm sure I seen him in St. Louis three months ago, acting on stage. Had the same fancy duds, eyepiece and cane. And your aunt, is she an actress too?"

His curious Texan drawl and pronunciation of 'Looey' registered in my brain before the importance of his words. Ace seemed to wear dirt and blood as a badge of honor. He was so different from the men I'd met at home, all well-educated with careful manners, buffed nails and tailored suits, their hair brushed and smelling of citrus or bay rum. This man with his odd eyes and rough clothing was intensely male, honest in an overripe scent of musk and leather, horses and tobacco. Flustered, I had to think hard for a reply.

"Aunt Sylvia abandoned her career years ago, so she said—"

"She was up on stage with him, big as life."

I bit my lip, considering his information. "Acting the part of his wife?"

"Dunno about that. I didn't pay much attention since I was drinkin' with friends and throwin' peanuts." He flashed a devilish grin. "I bet you a gold tooth that fancy accent is no better than a plugged nickel. One good turn deserves another. That's why I'm warning you to be on your guard. Whoa, mister! Back off or you might get a fist."

I heard Charles mutter something under his breath before I whirled to see him at my shoulder. "Oh! He's—my friend, Mr. Mason. From Evanston."

"Soon to be fiancé," Charles said with righteous indignation and brushed his lapels. Miss Granville, are you all right?"

"Yes." Annoyed at his interruption, I glanced at Ace. "Thank you for that interesting information, Mr. Diamond. I—I am grateful."

"Miss." He tipped his hat. "You need anything else, let me know."

Ace ambled off across the street, not at all unsteady. Curious, I watched until the Texan reached a boardinghouse, its windows alight in the growing dusk, about three blocks north. He soon disappeared into the shadows. He'd faked his need for support to tell me that tidbit about Sir Vaughn in private. I pondered his story while Charles escorted me back inside the hotel. Why would Ace make that up? My anger swelled at Aunt Sylvia, who had reason to lie to me. This nightmare worsened at every turn, given the incident at Porter's store.

"I thought he'd take advantage of you, Lily," Charles said, letting go of my arm. He sounded forlorn, as if I'd neglected to pet a wriggling puppy.

"Mr. Diamond acted a gentleman, contrary to his appearance. You of all people ought to know not to judge a person that way."

"Uh—yes, I suppose so. Shall I fetch a maid to clean your suit?"

"I'll take care of it. It's late, Mr. Mason, so if you'll excuse me."

I brushed my skirt's stiffness, far more aware of the man who'd marked me with his blood. His information made one thing certain. I had to confront Aunt Sylvia.

Charles tagged after me, In the upstairs hallway, I stopped dead. My aunt and Sir Vaughn blocked the way along with several other curious hotel guests. They parted when I rushed forward. Kate stood in our room's doorway, handkerchief in hand, her face streaked with tears.

"What happened? Are you hurt?"

"Oh, Lily, I know I locked the door! I left to—well, you know. And by the time I got back, I found our room like this."

She stood aside. I peeked around her shoulder and gasped at the mess. All my belongings had been strewn across the bed, the dressing table and the polished oak floor.

****

Together Kate and I repacked. I'd been angry after Porter's store but this invasion scared me. First my pocketbook, and now my hotel room... It wasn't imagination

54

after all. Someone was following me. Emil Todaro , or someone in league with the lawyer. Someone who accompanied him the night of Father's murder. I shivered. Rubbing my arms, I pondered what to say to Kate. She was innocent of all this and didn't deserve being left in the dark about my danger.

"I'm sorry."

"It's not your fault." Kate squeezed my hands. "Is anything missing, Lily?"

"No." I squeezed back, grateful for her unexpected friendship. Then I sat her down and explained the whole story, from Father's murder to the stolen deed and my decision to track his killer. "We can wedge a chair under the doorknob tonight. We should be safer that way."

"Whoever it was must have been watching for me to leave."

All the pent-up tension from today's troubles drained away and left me exhausted. So much had happened since we reached Omaha. Shouts wafted through the open window from the street below and reminded me of Ace Diamond.

"You missed the best part, you know, leaving right after my aunt's arrival."

"I'm glad you explained everything. What a tragedy about your poor father," Kate said and stooped to pick up my sketchbook. "But what did I miss?"

I told Kate about Ace Diamond, but left out his story about St. Louis. Not that I didn't believe him about seeing my aunt and 'Sir Vaughn' on stage together. I could believe the clipped British accent and his need for a cane might be props, together with his wardrobe. I didn't care. Aunt Sylvia could plot all she wanted, but she would not stop me from going to California. Nothing would, not even an intruder into our hotel room.

I faced my fears, though. Who else but Emil Todaro would track me? I needed protection, more than what Charles' presence could offer. Resolute, I faced Kate. She held out my tweed jacket, the seams ripped and sleeves turned inside out.

"I found this under the bed. To think someone would be so spiteful, Lily," she said. "But why would a thief go through your bag and not mine?"

I fingered the jacket. "It looks like he was searching for something," I said, half to myself. He hadn't taken Father's gold watch, though. Just the Army revolver and ammunition. That left me feeling vulnerable. "It wasn't money either. Someone searched my pocketbook at Porter's store, and now my room. If you'd rather not stay here, Kate—"

"Oh, Lily, I couldn't leave you alone now." She snatched up my jacket. "Let me sew this for you. The seams aren't frayed, so it won't take me long."

"Thank you. I can't even thread a needle." I chewed my pinky finger and mused aloud. "What is he looking for? What could I have brought—oh, my goodness. Maybe Emil Todaro didn't steal the deed to the gold mine. Maybe they think I have it!"

"Do you think so?" Kate stifled a cry of pain. "Ouch! Don't tell me any more until I'm done with this mending."

Deep in thought, I searched every nook and cranny in the entire room but the ammunition and revolver were missing. I felt violated by Todaro's pawing through my personal things. My life was being peeled away, layer by layer like a common onion. I'd chosen this task, however, and I had to stop being so naive. He'd killed Father, after all. He wouldn't stop at anything to get that deed, if that's what he wanted.

Todaro was a killer.

Kate had finished my jacket and now slipped behind the screen to change into her nightdress. "I'm worried, Lily. Once I get to Cheyenne, what will happen to you?"

"Charles will be with me."

Not that the thought gave me any comfort at all. He'd grown up in Evanston like me, sheltered from the world, with a dream of being sent to China for missionary work. I doubted if Charles understood the sacrifices, the hardships, the dangers he'd face there. He had heard the same lecture I had, in a revival tent back home, listening to a rugged, ranting preacher urging young people to take up the cross and head to heathen lands—much like the Crusaders had long ago. I hadn't been moved. His wife, haggard and pale, clutched a Bible in one hand with downcast eyes. I'd learned afterward that the missionary couple had buried all but one of their seven young children in China.

I didn't want that legacy.

"We both need sleep," Kate said in a firm voice and handed me my nightdress. "It's half past ten and I'm so tired I could sleep on a rock. Things can't get any worse."

I hoped she was right. I tried to pray for guidance and help, shifting on the mattress, but the right words failed me. Kate slept through all my tossing and turning. I stared into the dark, trying to remember the Bible verses I'd memorized as a child. That didn't help either. Was Emil Todaro searching for the Early Bird deed? Did he intend to kill me? Would Charles be of any help in another crisis?

Kate rolled over, taking the sheet with her. I sat bolt

upright in bed and hunched my shoulders. Mother always said God worked in mysterious ways. Ace Diamond was the last man I'd ever consider an angel of mercy.

With my luck, he might have already left Omaha. If not, then I'd take that as a sign of divine intervention. His fists might come in handy if I hired him to protect us on the long journey west.. He knew far more about weapons and fighting than I did. An ex-Confederate soldier, a Texan no less, who engaged in street brawls.

Then again, beggars couldn't be choosers.

'And if one prevail against him, two shall withstand him; and a threefold cord is not quickly broken.' Ecclesiastes 4:12

Chapter Six

The next morning, I rushed Kate out of the Herndon Hotel. I had no idea if Aunt Sylvia and her so-called husband would return to Chicago, and no intention of arguing with them about continuing on to California. The crisp summer breeze and warm sunshine revived my spirits. If Ace Diamond couldn't help, then I'd have to rely on Charles. Maybe I could bribe the Texan with a free ticket. He'd given me the impression of a mercenary.

"Lily, this isn't the way to the depot." Kate bumped into a portly gentleman, who tipped his hat and hurried on toward a nearby hardware store. "Where are we going?"

"I have a plan," I said and stopped before a trim, white-painted boardinghouse. Red geraniums marched along the picket fence. A sign hung over the front door proclaiming, 'Burkett's Boardinghouse: Reasonable Rates,

Inquire Within.'

"Who do you know staying here?"

"That man I met yesterday, the one who crashed through the window. I'm going to hire him for protection. I expect we'll have trouble on the Union Pacific after yesterday."

A maid in a stiff white apron and cap answered our knock. "Good morning, may I speak to the landlady?" I asked. After she ushered us into the hallway, all the men around the dining room table scrambled to their feet. "Please, don't mind us."

"Cup of coffee, miss? You're welcome to join us," one man said and shoved aside the next man who stood to offer Kate his seat.

"Oh, no, but thank you so much, gentlemen."

They couldn't hide disappointment but returned to their hearty spread of bacon, eggs, biscuits and gravy, griddle cakes and enticing maple syrup. Tempted by the delicious smell, I pulled Kate out of the doorway. The maid brushed past us with a peach pie and fresh coffee. A woman in a severe navy dress and white apron emerged from a back room, her hair pulled in a bun, and nodded at us with a stern gaze.

"I am Mrs. Burkett. I'm afraid I have no rooms available at present."

"We'd like to speak to Ace Diamond, if you please." I caught the quick frown on her face. "I believe he boards here with you?"

"He's out in the stables. That way," she added, gesturing down the hall, "and perhaps you can rid me of him for good. Nothing but trouble."

"How long has he worked for you?"

"Close to a month. Too long as far as I'm concerned."

"I see," I said, aware of her thinly veiled irritation. "You say he's been trouble. Is he unreliable in his work?"

"Reliable if he wants to be. He fought off a horse thief once," she added grudgingly, hands on her hips. "But you can't trust a Texan as far as you can spit. Those eyes of his, they make me nervous."

"Does he drink? Gamble?"

Mrs. Burkett shook her head. "I don't have all day to stand around chatting, miss. See if you can get a straight answer from him."

She herded us to the back door like wayward chickens. Our footsteps clattered on the porch steps as we made our way toward the small stable. Kate grabbed my elbow.

"Maybe this is a mistake, Lily."

"Let's hope not."

I marched toward the weathered building. A man with a pipe between his teeth slathered whitewash over the boards, his back to us. Ducking under a low hanging tree branch, we crept through the stable's open doorway. I had to stifle a sneeze at the musty scent of hay and dust. Sunlight streamed into the stalls where several horses nickered. In an empty one, we found Ace Diamond sleeping on his stomach. When I prodded him with my foot, he rolled over with a loud pig's grunt and squinted up at us both. A glass bottle lay in the dirty hay.

"Uh, wh-what time is it? Who the devil—ouch," he said and touched the crusty stitches on his forehead. "Dagnabbit. My head feels like a squished melon."

"Do you remember our meeting yesterday, Mr.

Diamond?" I asked. Kate peered over my shoulder. "I see you found a doctor as well as some whiskey."

"Needed it to cut the pain." Ace sat up and scratched his soiled shirt. "Thought you was headin' to California."

"I am leaving in a few hours, yes. This is Miss Kimball, she's also traveling on the Union Pacific." I brushed sawdust off my split skirt and jacket. "I spoke to Mrs. Burkett, your landlady, who sounded quite unhappy with you."

"That dried-up prune?" Scrambling to his feet, he weaved sideways until grabbing the half wall. A horse nuzzled his arm. "Never satisfied, no matter what I do."

"Not if you're prone to drink."

Ace rubbed his eyes with the back of one hand. "I don't suppose this is a social call, miss. Or that you'd lend me two bits. I got a powerful headache."

I eyed him from head to foot. A beggar would look more presentable. "You wished to go to California. Miss Kimball and I need protection on the Union Pacific. Perhaps we can come to an agreement, Mr. Diamond. Is that your real name?"

He dodged the question. "What are your terms, miss? Sorry, I forgot your name."

"Miss Granville. I'll provide you with a ticket now and twenty dollars when we arrive safe in Sacramento. Provided no harm comes to us, that is."

He stared with bleary eyes. "Why would two pretty fillies need me to ride shotgun? It's a far sight safer on a train than travelin' by stagecoach."

"I'm tracking a murderer—"

"Whoa," Ace cut in, fully alert now. "Who was

murdered?"

Letting out a deep breath, I folded my hands together over the pocketbook's strap. "My father was shot on Saturday in Evanston, north of Chicago. I believe someone's following me, too. Perhaps the killer or his colleague."

I sketched out a brief timeline of events, leaving out the missing deed, Aunt Sylvia and Sir Vaughn altogether. The Texan listened without interruption. He scratched his jaw stubble when I finished my story.

"So you need to track this man Todaro—why'd he kill your pa?" Ace cocked his head, as if sensing my hesitation. "He must've had a reason to do it."

"He stole something valuable. The police believe he left Evanston, and I assumed he'd taken the train to California. It's possible he stopped here in Omaha, and is following me now."

Kate patted a curious horse's nose. "It's half past seven, Lily. The train departs at nine or nine thirty, and we can't be late."

"You realize we'll be stuck on a train for near five days," Ace said. "With nowhere to run if there is trouble."

"'Man is born unto trouble as the sparks fly upward,'" I quoted but he rubbed his mismatched eyes. I retrieved the Pullman ticket from my pocketbook. "Are we agreed on the terms? My uncle may reward you extra when we arrive in California."

"Is that right." Ace Diamond lurched toward the doorway and then staggered outside. At the trough, he dunked his head and came up spluttering, tossing water droplets everywhere. He coughed and then slapped his hat into place. "How about this? Fifty dollars now, and a hundred when we get there. Plus meals on the train and the ticket."

"Twenty now, plus meals and the ticket."

"Thirty-five."

"Twenty-five, take it or leave it."

"Thirty. You don't have a choice," Ace said, grinning again, "unless that preacher man you were with last night has a wicked left hook."

"Charles has not graduated from the seminary yet."

"Ha. I knew he was a lily-livered type."

Ignoring that, I rummaged for a slip of paper and a pencil from my pocketbook, plus extracted the coins from my money belt. Thirty dollars—it reminded me of the thirty pieces of silver paid to Judas. Indeed I had no choice, and wrote out a receipt with the agreed amount.

"You must buy a clean shirt and necktie. Sign this paper, please."

Ace balked. "I'm good as my word, miss. Don't need to sign anything."

"I insist." I waited with the pencil outstretched. He grabbed it with a scowl and scrawled an X using his left hand. "You have less than two hours before the train leaves, Mr. Diamond. With your help, I'll make certain that Mr. Todaro hangs for my father's murder."

"I bet you'll get a receipt for the body, too, after he's dead. Well, ladies, keep a spur handy." Whistling a carefree tune, the Texan strutted back inside the stable.

Kate led the way to the street. "Are you sure he won't sell that ticket, Lily? He reminds me of the village drunk back home. If anyone gave him a nickel, he'd run to the nearest saloon."

"Let's hope not." I glanced up and down the busy

street. No one had followed us or skulked in any doorways. "Maybe I am crazy, but if Aunt Sylvia and Sir Vaughn do follow me out to California, they won't want to keep us company with Ace along."

With a sigh, Kate followed me back to the Herndon to fetch Charles and our valises.

****

Once I helped Kate convert her first class ticket to a berth, I bought the last available Pullman seat. Charles joined us in line waiting to board the luxurious Palace car. A swarm of other passengers and porters streamed around us, lugging trunks and wooden crates. The engine's bulbous smokestack belched a plume of white steam into the clear azure sky. A large family paraded by, the mother holding firm to her younger children, while the father carried a stack of strapped cardboard cases on one shoulder. The paneled siding and brass trim, the Union Pacific's gold insignia all implied money and privilege.

Kate tugged my sleeve. "Oh, look!"

I stole a glance backward. Aunt Sylvia and Sir Vaughn joined the Pullman line, although Charles broad shoulders soon blocked my view. "Remember, Kate, let's keep Ace Diamond a secret," I said. "I'd rather not tip off Aunt Sylvia—"

"What about Ace Diamond?" Charles asked when he joined us. Jealousy narrowed his eyes, and his fists clenched. "I hope you didn't run into him again."

Kate clapped a hand over her mouth and surged forward where a porter helped her up the car's iron steps. I followed. At the top, I scanned the Union Pacific platform and the dusty streets for any sign of the Texan. Only ten minutes before our departure. What if Kate was right? Ace might have sold that ticket and spent all the money on God only knows what vices beyond whiskey, women and song. Kate found a seat halfway down the aisle. Charles sat across from us and brushed stray cinders from his sleeves.

"Robert said we'll be living in a boardinghouse," Kate said. "Last year Cheyenne had tents and no buildings. I wish I could see California one day."

"I wish you could to. I'll be bored without your company."

"It's so elegant in here." She bounced up and down on the thick padded seat cushion. "Carved arms like in that theater in Chicago Aunt Zoe told me about."

I viewed the Palace car's interior with fresh eyes. Had I always taken such luxuries for granted? With rich velvet upholstery, oiled mahogany wood and brass trim, the wide settees did offer ultimate comfort. The double window panes were supposed to keep out the sparks and smoke that had been a bane between Chicago and Omaha. I was grateful for that small blessing.

"Where are the berths?" Kate asked.

Charles pointed to the sloped ceiling. "The uppers fold down from there. The porter will bring extra cushions to make these seats into beds."

I noticed several new holes in my split skirt. Quickly I retrieved the new sewing kit from my valise, glad that Kate had left the needle threaded and ready after repairing my jacket. I focused on the task, half-listening to Charles and Kate discussing the weather in Wyoming.

My aunt's booming tone rang over my head, startling me. I pulled the needle's sharp tip from my thumb and pressed a clean handkerchief to the crimson bead.

"—that porter! Incompetent, like all the rest. I thought my touring days were over," Aunt Sylvia said with a groan, settling in a seat across the aisle. "Back and forth across this country, living out of a trunk for half a year, playing a different city every week. I'm exhausted just remembering all those trips."

Sir Vaughn hushed her, one hand resting on his silver-headed cane, the other tucked inside his suit pocket. "No need to bring that up, dearest. It's all in the past."

My aunt glared at me. "This trip is a waste of time, Lily. Anyone could slit our throats at night here on the train. There's such a thin drapery between the berths."

"You must have traveled between cities on tour without a drapery," I said without raising my eyes from my mending. "But· if you're worried, you could return to Chicago."

"And let you wander the country alone? Harrison would never forgive me."

I bit back a sharp retort. My uncle would no doubt have something to say about Aunt Sylvia unexpected arrival in Sacramento.

Sir Vaughn cleared his throat. "American railways are so primitive compared to the one in the British Isles," he said, his accent and limp restored in full force. "Individual compartments are far superior in terms of privacy and comfort. And one avoids lower class undesirables."

Kate flushed crimson to the roots of her hair. "The theater offers far more chances to mingle with lower class undesirables," I said coolly. "Actors are society outcasts."

"That is changing, Miss Granville. Perhaps you are unaware that Miss Fanny Kemble married a wealthy Southern gentleman." Sir Vaughn's smile hid a glint of satisfaction.

"And she divorced him."

Sir Vaughn eyed the ceiling above, as if counting to ten before replying. "I'm surprised you'd insult your aunt's profession so openly."

"She told me she left the stage and her career."

"Lady Sylvia did agree to that when she married me."

I gave up and resumed my mending. What good would it do to let either of them know of my suspicions? If 'Sir Vaughn' was an imposter, they would have to deal with Uncle Harrison. Let them waste their money on a trip out to Sacramento.

Kate nudged me. "Is it true someone might slit our throats at night?"

"No, of course not. There's no danger whatsoever—"

"Once again, Miss Granville, you are sadly mistaken." Sir Vaughn settled his monocle into place and eyed Kate's ample bosom. "Since the recent massacre in Colorado Territory, red-skinned savages have been attacking settlers. Trains with passengers will be next. You must have read about the numerous attacks while surveyors and workers built the track."

"I never saw any stories like that," Kate said and shivered.

"I'm sure the Union Pacific suppressed such stories. Their business would suffer if people knew the danger is real," Charles said, glancing up from his newspaper.

"It can't be true." My aunt brought out a bottle of smelling salts. "Indians and murderers! We should have stayed in Chicago."

"I will inquire about purchasing an insurance policy, Lady Sylvia," Sir Vaughn said. "That may ease your mind."

He strolled down the aisle, cane in hand. "Are you sure Ace Diamond is coming?" Kate asked me, and then clapped a hand over her mouth in horror.

"Ace Diamond? That ruffian who crashed through the window last night?" Aunt Sylvia's demanding voice had returned. "Why would he be coming?"

Raising my chin, I met her direct gaze. "I hired Mr. Diamond to protect us on the journey to California." Charles dropped his newspaper, his mouth open in shock. "Someone searched my pocketbook and my valise yesterday. It could have been the man who killed my father."

"But I'm here to protect you, Lily," Charles said. I caught wounded pride behind his spectacles while he folded his newspaper. "You don't trust me?"

"Of course I do, but—well, two men are better than one," I said lamely.

Aunt Sylvia shook a finger at me. "The last thing I expected of you, Lily Granville, was being a shameless flirt. First Charles Mason, and now a Texas hooligan who brawled in the street and ruined your dinner. By his name alone, he must gamble at cards."

"I admit Mr. Diamond may have an unusual name," I said, "but you cannot assume that he's a gambler."

Charles frowned. "I think your aunt may be right—"

"It's Lady Sylvia to you, Mr. Mason," she said. "And of course I'm right."

I refused to defend Charles or challenge Aunt Sylvia. Kate studied her gloved hands, fidgeting beside me, while I packed my sewing kit away. My stomach churned. If Diamond failed to arrive, I knew I'd strangle my aunt and

'Sir Vaughn' within an hour of leaving Kate in Cheyenne. Gritting my teeth, I took out my sketchbook. The train's final warning whistle sounded a few minutes later but I fumed in silence.

Sir Vaughn arrived with good news. "Quite a reasonable rate for a policy, my dear, given the fifteen hundred miles to California." He dropped a packet tied with red ribbon in his wife's lap. "San Francisco's harbor will be a welcome sight after the dreary prairie. That fair city in California has a unique charm."

"I long to see the hills and the fog rolling into the bay," she said, hands clasped in a dramatic pose. "We'll walk among the towering redwoods north of the—oh!"

A hard jolt sent my pencil skittering beneath the opposite seat. The train started slow and then built up speed, skirting the river until the tracks curved west. Kate nudged my elbow and leaned close to whisper.

"I guess he did take the money and run."

"If I had a spur handy, I wouldn't think twice about using it," I murmured. She squelched a giggle. "We'll have to rely on Charles, I suppose."

"What's that?" He peered over the newspaper's top, eyebrows raised.

"I said my pencil rolled under your seat."

I knelt to grope for the slender length of wood on the scrolled Persian carpet, irritated by his childish pout and how he hadn't offered to fetch it. Charles could be stubborn and blow up a slight beyond proportion. I caught the gleam in the eyes of an old man, who held out my pencil with a smile and then rose to sit behind Charles. I scrambled from my knees as the receding smudge of Omaha with its courthouse spire vanished behind the hills. No doubt Ace

Diamond was enjoying his easy money in a saloon. He must have laughed at his good fortune when Kate and I left the Burkett stables. What a low-down scoundrel!

Numb, I buried my raw anger. Since Father's murder, my life resembled a freefall into total chaos. A scripture verse from Isaiah came unbidden to my mind.

The Lord avenge me of mine enemies.

My determination to find Emil Todaro had not changed. No matter what the danger, no matter how much hardship I had to endure, no matter what the consequences. No matter who accompanied me, Charles or Uncle Harrison, I knew in the long run I would have to use my own wits to recover that missing deed to the Early Bird mine. It wouldn't be easy.

Golden grain fields and scattered farms passed by outside, with stands of wispy cottonwood trees as windbreaks. But no lovely scenery could soothe my irritation. I'd been too trusting. Ace Diamond had stolen my money and an expensive ticket. Someone on this train may have bought it from him, in fact, for more than its value. I inhaled deep and tried to forgive him. I wouldn't forget, but I doubted I'd ever meet him again. I couldn't help recalling those odd eyes, that lopsided grin, the stubble on his jaw and devil-may-care manner. Something about Ace had drawn me to him. Perhaps I'd misinterpreted that as an answer to prayer.

The train soon reached its maximum speed of thirty miles an hour. I inhaled a deep breath to relax, opened my sketchbook once more and focused on the page.

"Excuse me, miss."

I almost dropped my pencil again when a man claimed the seat beside Charles. If not for that mischievous grin, I wouldn't have recognized Ace Diamond. He wore a clean white shirt and string tie, and a buckskin coat fringed at the sleeves and hem. He looked so different clean-shaven. A thin white scar started beneath his lower lip and stopped at his jaw. His hat was as misshapen as ever, though, and dusty. Dried blood crusted between an uneven row of stitches above his one blue eye. He winked at Kate, who blushed prettily.

"Bet Miss Granville thought I'd cut loose," Ace said. "I seen that prissy look on her face when I walked up the aisle. Am I right?"

Kate hid a smile. "We both wondered if you'd run off for a bender."

My voice cracked. "You can't blame us, Mr. Diamond. You <u>are</u> a perfect stranger, after all. And wild given your behavior last night."

He leaned back, eyeing us both, while Charles withdrew into the corner. "Sure am lucky, headin' west with such pretty ladies. I don't expect we'll meet up with much trouble beyond a sore backside—er, beg pardon. I ain't used to such fine company."

"I'm sure that's true," Charles said wryly, "given your reputation."

I aimed a discreet kick in his shin, appalled by his lack of Christian compassion, and ignored his glare in response. Kate leaned forward.

"What kind of reputation do you have, Mr. Diamond?"

"I dunno. Ask him," Ace said and hooked his thumb at Charles.

"I heard a few things last night. Nothing I would repeat to these ladies."

He raised his newspaper as if that ended the matter. I considered it cowardly. And one more black mark against my accepting his marriage proposal.

"I guess it depends on who you were talkin' to, mister."

Charles lowered the paper. "The name's Mason. I talked to several people at the hotel."

"You'd have done better talkin' to the horses at the livery."

I hid a smile at Ace's sarcasm. "Don't mind Charles, Mr. Diamond. He's in a sour mood today for some reason."

"Call me Ace, ladies," he said and tipped his hat. The Texan didn't remove it, though.

"Is that your real name—Ace Diamond?" Kate asked.

"My friends started that because my luck's never run out. At cards, at least." Ace rested one dusty booted ankle on his knee, oblivious to the passengers strolling the aisle who had to turn sideways to avoid him. "So when do we eat?"

I dug in my pocketbook and produced the two green apples. Kate and I both watched in fascination as the Texan devoured them both, core and all, leaving the stems. He flicked them with his thumb and forefinger, clearly aware of our interest. One soared over and landed on Aunt Sylvia's shoulder. She didn't notice. The stem matched her nut brown traveling suit. Sir Vaughn leaned forward, dark eyes narrowed, and plucked the offending bit from his wife's suit with stern disapproval. Within minutes, they'd exchanged seats further away with two gentlemen in wrinkled suits and derbies, who resumed their conversation about peddling wares.

That was worth the extra ten dollars I'd paid for protection.

'They also that seek after my life lay snares for me...' Psalm 38:12

Chapter Seven

Long after midday, the train stopped at a station house in Fremont. I stood, weary and stiff despite walking the aisle several times. Grateful for a chance to get some fresh air, I followed the line of passengers to the door and out to the open viewing platform. Fine dust in the wind made me sneeze. The bright sun hurt my eyes but I welcomed it. I smelled grass, the scents of food and the inevitable horse dung. I'd missed those familiar scents.

The town spread beyond the depot and roundhouse. Church spires rose above shops and white frame homes with painted shutters. Children played near a school house. The busy Courthouse had a crowd of wagon teams and single horses tied at the rail out front. Residents ignored us, going about their business, although a few enterprising young boys held up newspapers to sell to passengers. Charles bought several and claimed my elbow to escort me to the eating house near the Union Pacific depot.

Ace shielded Kate from the passengers jostling to enter the building. We found seats together at the end of one long common table. Red-checked cloths covered the trestles. The hard chairs were a welcome respite, and flies buzzed over the screens that covered large china bowls of white butter. Kate and Ace both dove for the heaping baskets of fresh crusty bread and slathered several pieces each. Charles held the basket out to me before taking a piece.

"It's not sourdough," Kate said, examining the fluffy white slice. "There's white sugar for coffee too! We always had molasses or brown sugar at home."

I chewed my buttered bread with care, grateful I couldn't reply. Cook had always baked white bread and sprinkled fine sugar over cookies and fruit pies. Due to my father's sweet tooth, she concocted huge filled and iced cakes, tiny tarts or meringues. I'd taken such simple pleasures for granted all my life. I sent a guilty prayer of thanksgiving heavenward.

An apron-clad woman brought platters of corned beef and cabbage, another basket of spongy white bread and a pot of coffee. Conversation ceased while we ate, since everyone acted ravenous. I paid for three meals, although Kate protested.

"My treat, please. Save your money for Cheyenne. You might need something you didn't bring from home," I said, "or you can buy white sugar and flour for your pantry."

She laughed. "Thank you, I will. Anytime you're passing through Cheyenne, you're welcome to stay with us for as long as you like. You too, Mr. Diamond."

He tipped his hat. "Much obliged, miss. You ladies

are the best thing that happened to me all month, and I'm grateful."

Charles grasped my elbow. "There's the whistle, Miss Granville."

He escorted me back to the train, followed by the others. I sensed Charles' jealousy had festered given his tight grip. Earlier he'd stared at Ace while polishing his spectacles or reading brief excerpts aloud from the newspapers. Showing off his literacy, no doubt, although the Texan listened with interest and asked questions about certain stories. Kate brought out knitting while I shifted in my seat, restless.

"The Cincinnati Red Stockings remain undefeated, with Harry Wright pitching and his brother George at shortstop. I saw them play against the Knickerbockers. Have you seen a baseball game, Diamond?" Charles asked.

"Can't say that I have, Mason."

"It takes skill and daring."

"So does workin' a rodeo. Ever seen one?"

Charles shrugged. "In Chicago. I found it tedious."

"Is that right." He pulled out a pack of cards and began shuffling them, back and forth, their edges snapping. Ace stopped once to crack his knuckles but resumed cutting and folding the deck. "You play cards, Mason?"

"No."

"Too bad. A bit of poker might help pass the time."

I knew Charles objected to cards due to his strict religious beliefs. "Did you serve in the Confederate army?" I asked.

"Yep. Second Texas cavalry," Ace said with pride. Charles rustled his newspaper, diving for cover since his father had paid to release him from conscription.

Kate's eyes widened. "You don't seem old enough to have served. Robert said he was too young to enlist, although he came of age the year the War ended."

"Fifteen when I joined in sixty-four, under Colonel Rip Ford."

"Rip? Is that his real name?"

"Rest in peace, that's what it stood for, since he killed so many Yanks. We routed 'em at Palmito Ranch back in May of sixty-five. That was something to see."

"But General Lee surrendered in April," I said. "He signed the papers with General Grant at Appomattox Courthouse, a week before President Lincoln was shot."

Ace hitched his boot across one knee again. "Most of the boys wanted to keep fightin' even after Kirby Smith surrendered in June. News travels slow in Texas, miss. At least we got to keep our horses and weapons."

"Some people thought you didn't deserve to be pardoned," Charles said, his voice stiff.

"Yanks started the war—"

"South Carolina did when they seceded from the Union!"

He snorted. "All I know is Texas has every right to be independent. We fought our way free of Mexico. We don't need no Yankee government tellin' us what to do!"

"Gentlemen, please," I said, holding up my hands. "The war's long over."

Ace folded his arms across his chest, glowering now. Charles rose from his seat and stalked off down the aisle without excuse or apology. Kate resumed her knitting with a shake of her head, as if in silent agreement about such animosity.

"What did you do after the War, Mr. Diamond?" she

asked.

"Did some rodeo work, bronco-busting here and there. Then my brother Layne and me signed on to hunt mossy horns in the Piney Woods." He laughed at my puzzled expression. "East Texas, near where we was born and raised. Mesquite was so thick we had to use a hook to get 'em free. They was madder than all get out. Thorns tore our britches to pieces, every day."

"A mossy horn?" Kate asked. "Is that a special animal local to Texas?"

"Cattle. Their horns grow so long and curved, as wicked as Satan's pitchfork. Sliced one man's belly clean open. Couldn't do a thing for him with his innards spilling out, but we stuffed it all back in and wrapped him in cowhide."

"Did he survive?"

Ace snapped the cards between his fingers. "No idea. We didn't get paid to doctor. Had to keep rounding up or we'd be cut loose. Plenty of other ex-soldiers to take our place."

His natural storytelling ability intrigued me. "Where is your brother now?" I asked.

"He's a civilian scout for the Army. Third Cavalry. Makes extra money feeding the crews out working on the Kansas Pacific line down yonder. Buffalo, prairie chickens, snakes."

"Snakes?" Kate wrinkled her nose. "I'd rather eat squirrels or possum."

"Gophers is the closest thing to a squirrel here," he said and scratched his scarred chin. "They're pretty tender, if you can catch 'em. Ain't nothin' better than a buffalo steak, though. Layne brought down a bison a few months ago. We took the best parts and left the rest."

"You wasted all that meat, then. Such a pity."

"Saw a few Injuns headin' our way. We didn't wait to find out if they'd take it all and leave us to rot with the bones."

"Do you think the Indians are dangerous, no matter where they are?"

Ace settled in the corner against the window and stretched his lower limbs. "Depends if they're on the warpath." He shrugged. "You leave 'em alone, and they'll leave you alone. Unless they're out for scalps."

"Scalps?" Kate had to recount a few stitches, her needles askew. "Sir Vaughn said Indians attacked the train's building crew several times. He bought an insurance policy."

"No piece of paper's gonna stop an Injun arrow. You can bet they're hunting for winter up a ways north of here. Or south." With a yawn, Diamond tipped his hat over his face and slouched down. "After last night I need some shut-eye."

Inspired, I opened my sketchbook and tried to catch a rough likeness of the Texan's hat, jaw line, broad shoulders and torso. His slumped position made the task difficult while I added tones and values. Frustrated at the result, I flipped to a fresh page. Abandoned items from wagon trains littered a rutted trail running parallel to the track. I did several quick studies to develop later—rusty iron stoves and their pipes, broken wheels, barrels or crates, weed-choked pieces of wood with carved initials or words marking a hasty grave. The trail soon disappeared.

Hand-painted signs on water towers announced a procession of small stations as the train swept along the single track: Richland, Columbus, Jackson, Silver Creek, Clark's and Lone Tree. The latter stood forlorn and tiny, swallowed by the windswept ocean of grass. The Platte River's pale surface shone in the fading afternoon sunlight. Cottonwood and locust trees grew close on its banks. Constant rattling from the train's wheels soon lulled me into closing my eyes.

I woke, startled and unnerved. Ace Diamond stretched upward, yawning like a sleek cat after a quick nap. He straightened his hat and flexed his shoulders, then stalked toward the Men's washroom. I half rose from my seat, distracted by a distant shadow on the prairie.

"What is that? Do you see that dark spot out there?"

Kate stopped knitting. "I hope it's not a prairie fire!"

Several men bolted from their seats. "Buffalo," several shouted and raced out of the Palace, pushing and shoving each other and brandishing pistols.

One gunshot echoed along with their yells of excitement. The women all crowded at the windows to glimpse the boiling brown mass running pell-mell toward the line of cars. The train raced against the herd. At last the engineer must have realized they had no intention of halting their stampede over the prairie. We slowed instead, chugging to a complete stop moments before the animals split to flow around each end. I made a quick sketch of their massive heads and shoulders, awed by how their thin legs supported such bulk.

But they did, with an unbelievable majestic grace as the herd surged past. Other men shot their guns at the mass, futile at best. None of the animals fell. They sped up or ran in wild circles, bellowing and grunting, swerving and thundering past the window.

"I'm going out to the platform."

Kate protested but I hurried to fight my way down the aisle. The minute I stepped out of the half-open door, a cloud of dust kicked up by the herd swirled around me. Sneezing, I groped for my handkerchief. Most of the men had descended to the ground and stood in front of the train with a few standing on the bottom steps by the rail.

"Stay back from them bison," warned a crewman as he checked the coupling between cars. "You might be trampled to death if you get too close."

The men ignored him. The crewman swung up to the smoking car's platform, followed by a few others. I pressed against the railing, breathless with excitement, sketching fast. Three or four large animals raced beside the Pullman. Their shaggy manes and curved horns fascinated me, and their eyes rolled wild in their heads. Soon I closed my book when the train started heading west again. A few animals bellowed and raced beside the train, kicking up dust.

I dropped my pencil when someone shoved me from behind.

The railing cut into my middle. I gripped the iron's top bar when a knot of people surged against me, increasing the pressure. Fearing I'd flip over and be crushed beneath the buffalo's pounding hooves, I hung on for dear life until I could straighten again. Gasping deep, knees wobbling, I uncurled my fingers from the railing. I'd managed to save my sketchbook from falling to the prairie. My hand shook when I reached for the car's door handle. Once inside the Pullman's interior, I felt safe again. The idea of being trampled by buffalo or squashed like jelly under the train's merciless wheels frightened me more than the realization that someone had searched my pocketbook at Porter's store.

Everyone would have considered it an unfortunate accident. I blotted my damp neck and face and limped back to my seat in a daze. Who shoved me? And why?

It wasn't my imagination this time.

****

Aunt Sylvia's voice boomed over the excited passengers. "I don't understand men at all, wanting to see such beasts up close."

"My dear wife, there was no real danger," Sir Vaughn said as he passed by in the aisle. "We ought to have had a competent crewman shoot one of the slower creatures. Then we would feast on marrow and tongue. The choicest parts. Quite right."

I for one was glad not to have witnessed any of the magnificent animals slaughtered. By the time Ace and Charles returned, I knew I had to confront the issue of my safety. They would have to take turns keeping watch. I'd decided that was the best solution, and hoped it wouldn't be difficult convincing them. But Charles scoffed at my story.

"I saw you on the platform, Lily. Nobody shoved you."

"Hold on a minute, Mason," Ace said. "She oughter know the difference between a hard push to topple her over the rail and a bump."

"It was a hard push," I said, grateful for his support, and glared at Charles. "Did you see who was on the platform behind me?"

"I didn't notice."

"All those men, and you couldn't tell who pushed me?"

"No." Charles poked up his spectacles and frowned. "They all wore suits and hats. I can't recall any of them standing out in my mind. When I realized the train was moving, I jumped up the steps. But if it will make you feel better, one of us will stay by you wherever you go. All three of us. I wish you'd just agree to marry me—"

"I already gave you my answer, Charles. Please don't bring it up again."

He stood, his mouth curved in displeasure. "I promised to help you reach California, Lily, and I'll stand by my promise. I don't need payment like some people."

Ace squinted at him. "That bargain's between me and Miss Granville."

"She didn't ask my advice, that's true." Charles straightened his tie. "I'll go check the smoking car and see if I recognize the men. But I have my doubts."

Once he stalked down the aisle, Kate patted my hand and resumed knitting. "If the man who killed your father is on this train, he must be sitting in a different car. You'd have seen him here, Lily. Even if he was in disguise, don't you think?"

"Yes, probably." I studied my rough sketch of the running buffalo. "I'm glad you believe me, Mr. Diamond."

"Call me Ace," he said, and stretched out his lower limbs into the aisle. "So Mason asked you to marry him?"

"Yes." I shunted aside my uneasiness and changed the subject. "How did you manage to end up in Omaha? You said you wanted to go to California."

"Lost my cutter." His voice tightened. "Had to find some way to live. Ended up working for room and board for that—Mrs. Burkett."

Kate straightened up, one hand covering a yawn.

Ace bent to retrieve the ball of yarn that had rolled under the seat. "What's a cutter?"

"My horse. Used to smell out cattle in the dark, he was so skilled on the trail," Ace said. "I was workin' in a rainstorm and he caught his leg in a hole. Had to put him down. Worked my way to Omaha. Been stuck most of the summer. Should've gone to Abilene instead of visiting Layne, I guess. Something wrong, Miss Kimball?"

"Your eyes—" Kate blushed and apologized. "I'm sorry, but I wondered why they're not the same color."

Ace shrugged. "Never noticed a difference till my oldest brother punched me in the eye, real bad. Royce felt terrible about it. I can see fine."

The Texan sat up with interest when a train butcher passed in the aisle. The boy wore a uniform similar to the conductor, with brass buttons on his coat and a small cap. Kate and I were unimpressed by his mesh bags of sweets or peanuts, slim packages of chewing gum and assorted newspapers from Chicago and St. Louis. Ace sank back against the seat, as if disappointed when I didn't buy anything.

"You can't be hungry," I said. "I'm sure we'll stop for supper before long."

"Another hour," Charles said from above. I glanced up to see him scowling at Ace. Kate jumped to her feet and placed her knitting bag on the spot beside him.

"Take my seat, Mr. Mason. We ought to switch back and forth to get a different view. Excuse me." She hurried down the aisle toward the Ladies' washroom.

I slid over to the window before Charles planted himself beside me with a feral smile. In the distance, the prairie was as flat as the horizon. Up close, however, swells

85

and grassy dips showed the land's deceit. Anyone could get lost and die without a horse, without water, without knowing how to find the nearest settlement. I opened my sketchbook, but my pencil had worn down to a flat nub. I rummaged in my pocketbook, found the others that were in worse shape, and let out a deep sigh.

"Here, let me."

Ace pulled a huge gleaming knife from beneath his coat and held out his hand, waiting. Once I handed him my pencils, he whittled the points with care, oblivious to the shavings that dropped on the carpeted aisle. I stared at the wicked double-edged blade and shivered.

"What kind of knife is that?" Kate slid past me to sit once more, so fascinated she leaned over his arm. "I've never seen anything like it."

"Same kind Jim Bowie used at the Alamo."

Charles guffawed. "Too bad the Mexican army won that battle."

"Texans got 'em back, though, and chased 'em out." Ace brought forth a Colt revolver and held it up. "Had it converted this summer. Fires cartridges instead of balls and caps, all because of this rotating cylinder. Shoots six bullets now before reloading."

I wondered if anyone else noticed the Texan's weapons. "Is it loaded now?"

"Sure is. Ready to use, or it wouldn't be no good to me." He pointed to the hammer. "It ain't cocked. My brother prefers using a Remington rifle, though."

"The porter might throw you off the train, Mr. Diamond, if he sees you waving that revolver. I am grateful you're armed to the teeth, though. I feel much safer."

He slid the weapon under his coat and finished

sharpening the pencils. "You're safer than a baby in its cradle, Miss Granville."

That eased my worries indeed.

'…with their tongues they have used deceit…' Romans 3:13

Chapter Eight

Supper at the eating house proved no different, from the fare to the price and the crowded tables. We gulped our meal in the half hour allotted and trooped back to our seats. The beef and cabbage formed a lump in my stomach after rushing so fast before the train's whistle. I opened my book but the words blurred together.

Ace scratched his jaw. "I need a smoke. 'Scuse me, ladies."

He ambled toward the back of the car. Thinking fast, I jumped up and followed him to the platform outside. The refreshing breeze sent curly wisps into my eyes. I brushed them aside, deafened by the rattling wheels, and snagged his arm.

"I didn't get a chance to tell you what happened yesterday."

"Besides me tellin' you about Sir Vaughn?" Ace

hooked an arm around an iron post as if to steady himself, then dug paper and tobacco out of his pocket and fashioned a cigarette. "What's on your mind, Miss Lily?"

"It's Miss Granville." I waited until he struck a phosphorous match, the fringe of his coat swinging with a hypnotic motion. Blinking hard, I explained the incident at Porter's store. "It may have been the same man who tried to push me off the train."

"Maybe." He blew smoke over my hat. "Maybe it was Mason."

"Charles? You can't be serious—" I stopped, realizing that he'd disappeared in Omaha. Had he searched my valise in the hotel room? "I don't think that's possible."

"Well, you never told me who you think killed your pa."

"Emil Todaro. He's a lawyer, heavyset and balding."

"A lawyer who might want to play some poker." Ace finished his cigarette and ground the burning tip beneath his boot heel. "I'll scout for you, don't worry."

" Todaro may be using an alias."

"I figgered that out already."

Diamond jumped the gap to the next railed platform with ease and disappeared inside the smoking car. I lingered for a moment, since no one else was out here. The wide expanse of prairie to either side of the speeding train held a sharper tang in the air. The duskier reeds, the chill air, the large number of birds flying overhead all heralded the coming autumn and winter. During the last several hours all I'd seen was an occasional sod farm in the empty land. The sun dipped toward the horizon, and nothing blocked the pink-tinged clouds streaked with blood-orange and purple. Forests had no place here. The prairie possessed a luminous glory all its own, mesmerizing and free, unashamed of its naked grassland.

The wind threatened to tear my hat free. Shivering, I ducked back inside the Palace car. What a shame that Father wasn't here. He would have enjoyed this trip. So much had happened since Saturday's casual shopping spree, it didn't seem real. Like a toy I once had, with a horse painted on both sides of a wooden disk. When I spun the disk by its long string, the standing horse and cantering horse blended together in motion.

A clever illusion.

Was Emil Todaro sitting on the train or skulking about? Had he stolen the Early Bird deed, or had he failed to find it in Father's safe? I had no proof of anything except a ripped jacket and my Father's missing Army revolver and ammunition. I didn't even know if Uncle Harrison was safe, or lying dead and unable to answer my telegrams. That thought sent me scurrying past Aunt Sylvia and Sir Vaughn, who conversed with another couple, and into my seat. Charles patted my hand but I pulled away. He scowled in disappointment.

Father's murder had shocked me into a headlong rush into madness. I didn't want to be pampered or coddled. I could face the truth. Revenge was a dangerous game to play, and I had little experience dealing with evil.

Thank God I'd hired Ace Diamond as protection. Charles had never even hunted for sport. His world was of the city, books and the law, not street brawls, Colt revolvers and Bowie knives. I couldn't picture Charles in a brawl, much less drinking or gambling at poker. Was it possible he had ransacked my baggage? Why? Perhaps he wanted to control me, foster my dependence on him during this trip.

I spent an hour finishing the rough sketches I had, keeping boredom at bay, and tried my hand at drawing Lucretia. Without my pet sitting on a rock, however, I couldn't remember her exact shape.

At that moment I glanced up and spied Ace Diamond enter the car. He ambled around the porter and then tipped his hat to my aunt. She ignored him. Charles headed down the aisle, as if he didn't want to remain in the Texan's company. Kate moved to sit beside me and Ace sprawled out opposite from us. His string tie lay loose around his shirt's soft collar, and he folded his hands over his chest. He smelled of beer and tobacco. I waited, hoping he'd inform me of any progress. Several minutes passed before I spoke.

"Were you successful, Mr. Diamond?"

"Won a few hands, as usual."

"I meant finding Mr. Todaro," I said. He raised an eyebrow at my harsh tone, but I didn't soften it. "You've been gone over an hour, playing cards and drinking—"

"Did you expect him to mosey up and introduce himself?" Ace snorted. "I found a few gents from Chicago. One said he recognized Sir Vaughn, same as me, on stage."

Charles arrived and forced Ace to scoot over beside the window. "In St. Louis?" I asked. "Which theater?"

"He couldn't remember. Drummers get around the country, you know."

I knew that salesmen always exchanged news with servants while displaying their wares. Disappointed, I sat back and watched Kate knit several rows. Perhaps my expectations had been too high. Charles lowered his newspaper.

"Lily, I've seen Emil Todaro before. If I notice him in

disguise, I shall tell you."

"Thank you. But Ace has a point. Who is Sir Vaughn? Is he an imposter?"

"I don't think it matters," Charles said.

"I suppose you're right," I said. "What name did Sir Vaughn use on the program in that St. Louis theater, Mr. Diamond?"

"I never saw no program," he said and tipped his hat over his face.

"They always hand them out—"

I stopped. He'd made a crude mark on the receipt instead of signing his name. Ace probably couldn't read or write. Perhaps he never attended school. I knew nothing of Texas except its location between Indian Territory and Mexico. The thought of being unable to read was incomprehensible.

The train slowed to a stop. Three crewmen jumped down to load wood from an unmarked station, while others refilled the boiler from the water tower. Hundreds of golden-brown animals, the size of squirrels but with thin stubby tails, scampered between holes in the sloping prairie. They would vanish and then reappear a yard away from the tracks, while others sat on their haunches, oblivious of the train. They acted so carefree.

I wanted to feel that way again.

On the other side of the train, campfires and conical teepees marked an Indian settlement not fifty yards from the track. Kate followed me to the back platform. We watched bronzed, dark-haired children chase and tease each other, their shrieks and yells mingling with the noises from the train and busy crewmen.

"They act like the schoolchildren playing back

home."

"I suppose so." Kate stretched and yawned. "Robert said I'd better get used to seeing Indians but they frighten me."

"They look so peaceful now."

The Indian women squatted before their cooking fires in the growing dusk. Long braids dangled over their fringed tunics and faded calico skirts. Young girls lugged baskets of buffalo chips from the prairie, and barefoot boys ran back and forth near the train daring each other to touch the steaming engine. Dogs trotted through the small camp with bones in their mouths, or barked at the working crewmen.

"See them scalps, miss?"

We both whirled around at the gruff voice speaking behind us. A man with a reddish-brown goatee squinted into the sun, pipe in hand. He lifted it to his mouth and drew deep before he sent smoke curling into the sky.

"Where?" Kate asked. "I don't see anything."

"Them strips hanging on the poles, right by the tents."

I stared at the curled bits he pointed out, attached to feathers and beads. "They don't look like much. Are you certain?"

"Well, they been dried in the sun. Warriors show off trophies to prove their courage." His smile showed tobacco-stained teeth. "Pawnee back in Elkhorn milked the emigrants on the Oregon trail. Scalped those who wouldn't pay a hefty toll to pass through in peace."

"I never read about that in the newspapers."

"They wouldn't, since people made money to outfit them people moving out west. Was a big business, till the train came through. Now the railroad's gettin' all the money."

"How could they do such things, and then hang scalps by their doors?" Kate asked. "If you call a tent any place civilized to live."

"You got that right, little lady."

I took an instant dislike to the man. His presence made me uneasy. "They're not all savages. I've read about many tribes who prefer peace."

"I wouldn't trust an Injun if you paid me. You seen the brakeman who was scalped and left for dead?" He flashed a predatory smile. "Gruesome Gus, they call him. Gus was lucky to survive at all. You two young ladies take care now."

The man's goatee bobbed as he rammed his pipe between his teeth. Several pierced coins jangled from the watch chain across his suit coat when he sauntered back inside. An altogether unpleasant man. Kate shooed me inside when the shrill whistle blew, and the train soon rolled west again. While Sir Vaughn read a newspaper, Aunt Sylvia sang popular songs with two other couples. Soon the drummers joined in, using spoons as makeshift instruments.

The porter finished lighting the lamps overhead. I saw Charles sitting with two gentlemen, talking politics. Ace had stretched out once more, hat over his face, and didn't flinch when Kate and I crabbed sideways to reclaim our seats. I opened my Jane Austen book while she unraveled half her knitted scarf, concentrating this time on counting stitches. Darkness hid the prairie outside by the time Ace sat up straight. He folded his lower limbs out of our way.

"Still trying to catch up on my sleep."

"You ought to keep those stitches clean, Mr.

Diamond," I said. "You might end up with another scar if you don't."

"Don't bother me how many I get. I got more you'll never see."

I ignored his quick wink. "Is it true the Pawnee Indians killed travelers on the Oregon Trail if they refused to pay a toll?" Kate asked him.

Resting one booted foot over his knee, clearly a favored position, he settled back against the cushion. "First I heard such a thing. Pawnee kill the Sioux quick enough, they been enemies forever. Not that the Pawnee ain't ready to turn a profit like anyone else. Heard when the railroad was near finished, the bigwigs came out—"

"Bigwigs?" I cut in. "Do you mean Mr. Durant of the Union Pacific? I read that he and several other railroad officials inspected the work."

"They did. From what I heard tell, they wanted entertainment. The Pawnee charged 'em plenty for riding around on their ponies, all painted up, whooping and hollering like they was on the warpath. And they threatened to make it real if they didn't get paid."

Kate's needles hesitated. "That sounds like a tall tale to me, Mr. Diamond."

He shrugged. "Maybe. Now Sioux, they're the worst of the lot. Layne says they'd kill anyone come hell or high water. Beg pardon, miss."

"Has he ever met George Armstrong Custer? I saw him back in Michigan once," I said with a fond memory of that day's excitement. "He charmed all the ladies with his impeccable manners. They were so impressed by his long hair and moustache."

Ace shook his head. "That's all for show. Layne says

Custer shot two deserters after marching his men all day in the hot sun. Treats his hounds better."

"He sat his horse beautifully," I said. "He looked as regal as a prince."

"Big difference between sittin' a horse and working with one."

"And you're an expert?"

"You'll have to see for yourself one day."

"Why aren't you an Army scout with your brother?" Kate asked, her needles slack.

"Don't like taking orders." Ace took out a small pocketknife and a piece of wood and started whittling one side into a rounded curve. "I got my fill of drills and watch duty in the Texas cavalry. I'd rather do as I please and go where I choose."

He reminded me of a stone kicked loose from the ground, rolling and changing direction. I closed my sketchbook and placed it inside my pocketbook with my pencils.

"You said you met several gentlemen from Chicago. Who were they?"

Ace leaned forward, his voice low. "I got to know four of 'em, Cooper, Gentry, Hayes and Young. It won't take long to figger out if one of 'em is following you."

"Does anyone have a goatee?"

I described the man who spoke with us earlier about the Pawnee. Ace verified him as Tom Gentry. Dan Hayes was a whip-lean gentleman, and Randle Young white-haired with a thick beard. His description of Seth Cooper came closest to Emil Todaro, portly with a thick beard. Gentry and Hayes had seats in the Palace car, while the other two sat in first class. Too bad women weren't allowed in the smoking car.

Ace would have to be my eyes and ears there.

"Tell me about where you lived in Indiana," I asked Kate. She laughed.

"There's not much to tell. I grew up on a farm three miles from the village, so I jumped at the chance to go visit Aunt Zoe. I didn't want to get stuck marrying a hayseed."

"There weren't any men besides farmers in the village?"

Kate shook her head. "You don't know Turkey Run. I'm happy enough with Robert, Lily. One of my friends answered a newspaper advertisement for a wife in Minnesota. She was fifteen then and wrote me once, she's that busy on their farm. I know that life. It's back-breaking, and she has four stepchildren to care for and three of her own already."

I didn't doubt Kate. Once again, I had to thank God for being born to a wealthy man who insisted I delay any decision about marriage.

"One thing's certain—"

"Ladies and gentlemen," a Negro porter interrupted, "allow me to introduce you to Gus. Mr. Gentry, if you would please step aside."

The drummer obeyed, revealing the crewman in uniform behind him. Gus doffed his cap, looking sheepish, to show a mass of hideous scar tissue crowning his bare skull. Kate gasped in shock, and nausea gripped me. The raised ridges in his flesh glinted in the lantern's soft light.

Gentry slapped his thigh. "Ain't that a sight? Tell 'em what happened, Gus. A humdinger of a story, all right, and chills you to the bone."

The crewman shrugged in apology. "Three of us

was repairing the telegraph line last summer," Gus said in a soft voice. "Band of Sioux jumped us without warning. Stuck us with arrows like pincushions. I pretended to be dead, but a few Injuns dismounted to take scalps."

"You were alive when—they—" Kate sagged against me. I kept my gaze fixed on his warm brown eyes and weather-beaten face. "How horrible!"

"Felt like my whole head was taken off, miss." He shuffled his feet, as if reliving the experience pained him as much as our shock. "Once the Sioux left, I was lucky to find my hair on the ground—the Injun must've dropped it. I guess they was so excited to kill us. I crawled for miles till I came to the nearest station house. Them Injuns do love taking scalps."

"Plenty of whites scalped the Injuns right back in revenge," Ace said. "Soldiers and mountain men both."

"True enough, sir." Gus dipped his head lower and pointed at it. "I ain't condoning the practice, that's for sure. Only telling people how I managed to survive it."

"Whoa." The Texan poked at a few scars. "Glory be, that's a fine mess. You're lucky you didn't bleed to death."

"Wish they coulda stitched my scalp back on. The cold bothers my poor head more'n anything else, I gotta line my cap with wolf fur, summer and winter. If you'll excuse me, ladies and gents. I gotta get back to work."

"Sure thing, Gus," Gentry said. "Hope you sleep well tonight, missies."

His sly grin disgusted me. He knew Kate was frightened half to death now, and yet sauntered down the aisle to the smoking car without remorse.

"Excuse me."

Kate scurried to the washroom, one hand clamped

over her mouth. I followed, worried sick. No doubt she might be reconsidering her choice to marry and raise a family in Wyoming, where Indians remained a danger. She'd been so happy when we first met, so excited and so proud that she would be starting a new life. Once she emerged, still shaky, I walked her back down the aisle with an arm around her waist and then sat beside her.

"Oh, Lily. I wish I could go back home," Kate said, her voice a whisper. Her huge blue eyes swam with tears, showing fear and deep doubt. "It's too late. My aunt won't take me back, and my father and stepmother—they'd never understand."

"I do." Although I hated myself for saying it, I stuck to the truth. "Make the best of it, that's all you can do. It might not be so bad in Cheyenne. You'll be in town, not out alone on a ranch. Since Father died, I'm in the same boat. I have to find his killer or die trying."

"I'm sorry! I never even thought how much worse it is for you." Kate swiped at her tears with a handkerchief. "I'll be married to a wonderful man and safe enough. I hope."

My misgivings increased. While I wished Kate all the happiness she deserved with a husband and family, I wondered how she could blindly trust a man she'd just met in June. I was no better, however, since I'd agreed to consider Charles' proposal and serving in China as missionaries. Did I know him all that well? No. And I'd been wrong to ask him to escort me out west, similar to dangling a carrot in front of a horse. I was certain he expected to marry in California, once we—or I—saw Emil Todaro hanged for murder.

I studied Charles when he came back to sit down.

His fair hair, pale plump cheeks without any sign of stubble and soft brown eyes gave him the look of a puppy dog. So different from Ace Diamond, with his dark hair and strange eyes—the two men were night and day. Ace's past hinted at darkness and danger. He'd served in the war, unlike Charles who stayed in school. Ace experienced hardships during and after the War. Charles was fearful of change and breaking the rules of propriety. He'd been reluctant to leave Evanston. He hadn't defended me against Aunt Sylvia either, and I had my doubts about Charles if any real danger threatened us.

As for Kate, I wondered what her fiancé was like. She admitted they had not courted long. Robert, a placid bank clerk, must be looking forward to meeting his young bride at the Cheyenne depot. Who was I to judge them?

I knew I could never adjust to living with a near stranger after a wedding, much less sharing intimacy.

The train reached maximum speed once more, as if trying to make up for lost time. Kate poked me with a furtive whisper. "You're right. I could be living there—look."

A glowing station house grew larger as the train approached. The telegraph operator stood in the open doorway, silent and dour, arms crossed over his chest. He didn't move an inch despite the noise and gush of steam as we passed. He resembled a ship's captain on the prairie's dark-green swells. Darkness swallowed both man and wooden shack in less than two minutes flat. I sank back against the seat cushion.

"Robert considered a job at a station house like that one, somewhere west of Rawlins," Kate said. "I'm glad he turned that down."

Lost in thought, I headed for the washroom and bumped into Sir Vaughn. He blocked the door and didn't budge when I waited for him to move aside.

"I expect that crewman who was scalped opened your eyes to the dangers out west," he said, looking down at me through his monocle.

"A threat of Indians will not stop me from finding my father's killer."

"Lady Sylvia is worried about your stubborn resolve, Miss Granville. She believes this is a wild goose chase. If I didn't have business in San Francisco, I wouldn't have suggested following you on the train."

"There's no need to follow me at all." I grasped the washroom's door knob, which gave him the hint. "If you'll excuse me."

"Not until you reconsider associating with undesirables." He sighed, as if I was a child incapable of understanding him. "Mr. Diamond is a scoundrel, plain and simple. He's unworthy of your money or your avid attention."

I bit back a sharp retort. "That is my business. Not yours."

"Perhaps you're unaware that this Texan mercenary bragged about his plans to open a floating gambling parlor in San Francisco's harbor. Similar to one in St. Louis, a converted paddleboat steamer." Sir Vaughn shifted his stance. "You may also be unaware that Ace Diamond is wanted for murder in Texas. Ask him if you don't believe me."

He walked away down the aisle. I stared after him, my mouth open, doubts swirling in my head. For all his faults, Ace didn't seem capable of cold-blooded murder.

Emil Todaro hadn't either though, until I found my father's body.

'Be not far from me, for trouble is near; for there is none to help.'
Psalm 22:11

Chapter Nine

I had much to think about and paced the aisle several times for exercise. Sir Vaughn's steady gaze haunted me while I passed by the porter, who lowered an upper berth and smoothed the linens. Aunt Sylvia stood waiting with two other women, her garish blue suit sporting black velvet collar and cuffs, and her veiled hat a full peacock plume. How dare she chide me about not observing proper mourning etiquette! Her booming voice followed my progress.

"I was famous for my death scenes, you know. Edwin Booth opened his own theater in New York earlier this year. He complimented me on my technique...."

I tuned her out and sat down again. Kate stopped her knitting. "Where have you been? I thought one of us was supposed to follow you."

"Maybe that isn't necessary—"

"I was watchin' her," Ace said, tipping his hat back down. "Hope that 'Sir Vaughn' didn't bother you, miss."

"No."

The porter arrived then to convert our seats into berths. "Thank goodness, I've been half asleep for almost an hour." Kate packed away her knitting with a huge yawn. "How in the world will we manage to change into night clothes?"

Within the hour, she'd succeeded behind the curtained alcove of our lower berth. Shocked by my short hair, Kate listened to my brief explanation but fell asleep before I could finish. I lay down, although the rattling wheels under my head and smell of oil and smoke proved distracting. Despite clean crisp sheets over the cushions, and the clever wooden support that bridged the makeshift berth, I tossed and turned. Ace had insisted on taking the upper berth above us, leaving Charles to accept the one opposite. My habit of reading late into the night at home, hearing chirping crickets and an owl's hoot, was another thing I'd taken for granted.

After sleeping for a few hours, I woke at dawn to silence. The enclosed alcove was stuffy and hot. "Where are we? Have we stopped again?"

Kate groaned. "I have no idea. I've been awake long before we stopped," she said and sat up to peer out the window. "It's not Cheyenne. There's only one street from what I can tell."

"Time for breakfast, ladies," Charles said from outside the curtain. "You'd better hurry and get dressed. The porter said we have boiler problems. There's a restaurant here, and they're taking passengers in shifts.

We're somewhere in western Nebraska."

Yawning, I rummaged in my valise for my toothbrush, hairbrush and clean underclothes, then gathered up my skirt, shirtwaist and jacket. With my shawl acting as a semi-robe, I dashed toward the washroom—and waited in line. Four other ladies kept their eyes down, avoiding the sight of men who struggled into their own clothing behind curtains or in the aisle. Most people respected the lack of privacy and kept their gazes averted.

Before long, I walked with Kate, Charles and Ace to the small restaurant. The settlement had one street, dusty and rutted, with a few shops, a blacksmith, several houses and the telegraph office. Canvas covered a few half-finished buildings. Inside, I smelled grease and burnt bacon. We had a dismal meal of tough steak, doughy biscuits, lumpy gravy and coffee thick as mud. Kate rubbed her eyes and yawned in exhaustion.

"If I ever get the chance to take a Pullman again, I hope I sleep better."

"You slept well at first," I said and eyed the cream pitcher. Empty. "How was the upper berth, Mr. Diamond?"

He shrugged. "Better than a thin bedroll on the ground. I've slept in the saddle, in a tree, on a rock ledge— don't much matter. Here, breakfast is my treat." Ace slapped a coin on the table. "Lady Luck is back on my side. I won at poker yesterday in the smoking car."

"My treat," Charles said wryly. "I lost."

"Perhaps we ought to call this Miss Kimball's wedding breakfast. Have another cup of coffee," I said and was glad to see her worry vanish.

"Thank you," Kate said with a smile. "I'm so nervous. I couldn't choke down more than a bite of

105

anything, though."

"No reason to be scared. He's one lucky bank clerk." Ace sopped the gravy with two more biscuits. "Cheyenne's a lot tamer now than it used to be, from what I hear."

I poked at the tough slab of meat, not recognizing its color and texture. "Is this chicken? It doesn't taste like salted pork."

"Or beef," Charles said and cut off a piece. "Not even chicken."

"Might be prairie dog," Ace said with a wink. I dropped my spoon, horrified. "But I don't think so. Tastes more like shoe leather."

"I'll miss you all so much," Kate said, misty-eyed. "I wish Robert could meet you, but I'm not sure how long the train will stop in Cheyenne."

"We shall all miss you, too," I said. She sounded so forlorn. I thought hard to change the topic of conversation while buttering my tough biscuit. "Are your other brothers living in Texas, Mr. Diamond? Or somewhere else?"

Ace cleared his throat. "All three of my older brothers died at Shiloh. In the Hornet's Nest, so they called it."

"I read about that battle," Charles said and sipped his coffee. "Wasn't Colonel Granville wounded there, Lily?"

Ace stabbed a finger at him. "My brothers' best friend came home without a leg and told us what happened. Me and Layne joined up soon as we could earn money for our horses. We wanted revenge on the Yanks."

Had Father or Uncle Harrison commanded the men who'd killed his brothers? I wished I'd never brought the subject up now. My face hot, I glanced at Kate who didn't say anything. Her gaze remained fixed out the window. I gulped coffee and then choked hard. Alarmed, Kate pounded on my back until I caught my breath, which ended that topic of conversation.

"My stomach hurts. Are we in Wyoming Territory yet?"

"Here, have a peppermint." I handed her the sweet I'd taken from my pocketbook and searched for a second one. "We'll be in Cheyenne by noon, I hope."

I popped the peppermint in my mouth to soothe my aching throat. The sun climb higher in the cloudless expanse of blue. We walked back to the train, eyeing the rust-hued sand hills and rocky buttes. Spindly trees sculpted by gale winds grew in clumps on the plateaus. A thin column of rock stabbed skyward in the distance with rugged, smoky blue peaks to the north and west.

"Chimney Rock," Ace Diamond said, pointing at the arresting formation.

"Have you been through here before, Mr. Diamond?"

"Nope. My brother Layne came out this way before he ended up in Kansas."

Sir Vaughn and Aunt Sylvia stood on the platform near the front of the Pullman car, their heads close together, their voices low. I wished I could eavesdrop on their heated exchange. What were they up to now? I hadn't forgotten what Sir Vaughn had told me about Ace, although I'd considered the source. Tom Gentry tipped his hat to us with a wink and mounted the steps of the smoking car before he disappeared inside. I tugged at Ace's sleeve.

"Did you learn anything about that man who walked past us?"

"Who, Gentry? He's a drummer," Ace said and

dusted his hands on his trousers. He squinted at the sun, eyeing two hawks that soared high. "Sells everything from hatpins to shoes. Told me he's headin' to the mining camps out in California."

"The boiler's fixed, from what I overheard the porter say," Charles said and shooed us into the Palace car. "We should be in Cheyenne before noon."

"Goodness, my hair's a mess. Excuse me," Kate said and darted into the washroom.

I followed Charles to our seats and didn't object when he claimed the spot beside me. Besides my aunt, there were eight other women on the train—two widowed, one elderly, the rest married. I'd miss Kate's company. Ace sat down and brought out his deck of cards. His deft fingers stacked, cut and then riffled the worn pasteboards, caressing them. Taking a deep breath, I settled back against the seat. It was now or never.

"Mr. Diamond, is it true you're wanted for murder?"

Half the deck fluttered in the air. I smiled in triumph, watching him drop to the floor and gather the cards. Charles muttered something, which brought a loud thump and a hissed curse from the seat's underside. Ace snatched his hat from being trampled by a passenger walking past. He scrambled to his feet and set his hat back into place.

"I hope you're going to explain," Charles said when Ace plopped down on the seat.

"I take it the answer is yes," I said, "or you wouldn't have been so surprised."

"No." He sounded annoyed, slapping the cards together while counting them. "Who the devil told you that bald-faced lie?"

"There must be something to the story. You said yourself you haven't returned to Texas since the War. Did the carpetbaggers scare you away?" I crossed my arms and stared until he met my gaze. "I'm waiting for the truth, Mr. Diamond."

"I'll be happy to toss him off at the next station," Charles said. "He ought to be thankful he got this far after misleading you."

Leaning back in his seat, Ace flashed a sour look. He held the whole deck between thumb and forefinger, pausing to think for several minutes. I must have struck a nerve with my question. Charles hadn't helped with his comments either.

"My cousin's wanted for murder, not me. I was with him that night. Couldn't talk a lick of sense into that boy, even at fifteen years old. Heard he's killed a few more since, too." Ace pointed a thumb and forefinger at Charles. "I never misled anyone. No reason to go back to Texas, since there ain't no kin left. Now, miss, who told you I was wanted for murder?"

"Sir Vaughn."

"And you believed that no-good liar?"

"I never said I believed him."

"I think there might be something to the story," Charles said, glaring at the Texan. "Why not turn him over to the sheriff in Cheyenne?"

"You may have book learnin', Mason, but you don't know jack about common sense. You'd be dead on the floor right now if I was a killer."

Ace rose and stalked off toward the smoking car, dodging a few men in the aisle. He bumped into Kate but didn't seem to notice. She stared after him, a hurt expression in her eyes and slid into .the empty seat.

"What's wrong with him?" she asked, pouting. "He nearly bowled me over."

"Sour grapes," Charles said.

I repressed a laugh, aware of his simmering jealousy again. Kate stood and smoothed her skirt. "Sit down, please. You'll be more nervous by pacing back and forth."

"I need to re-pin my hat—"

"You look fine," I said and caught her arm. "You'll ruin the bluebird if you keep fussing with it. Your hat is perfect with your suit, too."

"Thank you." Smiling, Kate settled down. "I do hope Robert's arranged everything with the minister for the wedding ceremony. Do you think my trunk's safe? It did get into the baggage car, didn't it?"

She fretted until the train steamed into Cheyenne, half an hour short of noon. A dozen people climbed into a dusty Denver stagecoach waiting near the train tracks. The depot's rough construction mirrored the rest of the buildings in town, along with the Union Pacific's hotel. A Pullman porter, armed with dinner orders from the passengers, hurried toward its long porch past a crowd of men. The windmill creaked beside storage sheds strewn with lumber.

"Why are there so many men in town?" I asked, descending the Palace car steps. "It's Thursday, isn't it? You'd think they'd be here on a Saturday instead."

"Election, from what I heard," Charles said and stretched his arms back and forth.

"I don't see Robert," Kate said, shading her eyes. "He promised to meet me right here on the platform. I haven't heard from him in three weeks, though."

"Which bank does he work for?" I eyed the group of surly men who lounged near a saloon. Another tied his horse at a wooden railing and joined them. "Did he mention the name or what street it's on, Kate?"

"Eddy Street, past Thompson's Boots and Shoes. I'll find him, Lily. You go on to dinner or you'll miss your chance."

I shook my head. Coarse men spitting tobacco and cracking crude jokes filled a freight wagon with goods from the train. Five others with teams of oxen or mules waited, and more men had joined those in town for the election. I picked my way around a pile of fresh dung on the rutted street. I'd never abandon Kate to walk alone on a street here.

"Charles, will you escort us?" I snagged Ace's coat before when he walked past. "Come along with us, Mr. Diamond. We may need your help."

"I was fixin' to get me a beer—"

"I paid you for protection, remember. You can drink later."

The Texan gazed with longing at the first saloon we passed. Several passengers entered Dyer's Hotel on Eddy Street, which we entered to ask for directions. The clerk's thick Irish brogue was difficult to understand, but Kate caught on and led out back outside. We paused under the pretentious portico, getting our bearings, before searching for a path or alley to Third Street. I didn't envy Kate living in such a rough town.

Tin warehouses hunkered behind the rows of shops with false fronts. Other buildings had been built with lumber scraps, canvas and broken furniture. A thorny tumbleweed blew past. I wiped gritty dust from my face and mouth, wishing I could spit like the men. Ace lagged behind and stopped to chat with a livery stable hand. We saw few women in Cheyenne. One tired-looking girl in calico hung sheets behind a sad wooden shanty. A baby hung over one hip inside a dirty muslin sling.

"I didn't expect it to be so—so rustic," Kate said in a timid voice. "Omaha had more trees. And far more houses."

"I've seen two newspaper offices, and a church," I said, trying to cheer her. "I'm sure there's a sheriff in town, too."

"Yes, we ought to visit the sheriff's office," Charles said, his hand gripping my elbow. "You won't regret it, Lily. We'd at least know the truth about Diamond by the wanted ads posted there. His name must be an alias for a horse thief, if not a murderer."

Kate tugged my arm before I could reply. "You don't think something's happened to Robert, do you? Oh, what would I do then?"

"Don't worry." I squeezed her elbow. "I'm sure he had no idea the train was delayed. That must be why he didn't meet you. We'll find him."

She said nothing, biting her lip and glancing around in fear. Above a saloon with a sign that creaked, men played billiards to tinny piano music. Two mangy dogs bared their teeth when we passed another narrow alley. I led the way inside the dim bank, blinking to see. Behind a wooden counter, a pimpled clerk glanced up in surprise.

"May I help you, miss?"

Kate spoke up. "Yes, I'm looking for Mr. Robert Rayburn."

"Rayburn?" The boy stared at us, glassy eyed, a little perplexed. "Try next door at the saloon. He's there every day."

My suspicions high, I marched Kate to the street. "So he isn't a bank clerk."

"Why would he tell me that, Lily? There must be a mistake—"

Three men in soiled shirts and denims appeared, jaws working at tobacco plugs. They eyed Charles, who came out of the bank behind us. He straightened his tie and tugged his derby hat into place. I sensed his nervousness was greater than Kate's.

"Miss Kimball? Mr. McDaniel's waitin' to meet you."

"Mr. McDaniel?" she asked, her chin high. "I don't know a McDaniel."

"You will, soon enough."

Kate shrank back. I stared at the tallest man in the eye, unflinching. "We're looking for Mr. Robert Rayburn, a bank clerk. Please step aside, gentlemen."

"McDaniel knows him," the other man said with a smirk, "so follow us."

Charles stepped forward. "These ladies cannot enter a saloon. Tell McDaniel to come out here and speak to them about Mr. Rayburn's whereabouts."

The two men eyed him from head to foot, grinning wide. The taller one waved him off. "Keep outta this, boy. Miss Kimball's coming with us, so mind yer own business."

"Mr. McDaniel can send Rayburn to the Union Pacific depot—"

He reeled backward from a vicious punch. The ruffian cracked his knuckles. Horrified, I drew Kate behind me with indignation. How dare these men impede us?

"Charles! Are you all right?"

He didn't move from his spread-eagled position in

the dirt. Blood streamed from his nose and mouth. His hat lay upturned behind him. When the two men closed in on us, fists clenched, Kate and I gripped each other and glanced around in desperation.

Ace Diamond was nowhere in sight.

'Who can find a virtuous woman? For her price is far above rubies.' Proverbs 31:10

Chapter Ten

I swung my pocketbook at the taller man, who laughed and wrestled me inside the saloon. Kate bit and scratched, earning a howl from her captor. Inside, the smell of stale beer stung my nose and our shoes crunched on scattered peanut shells underfoot. The ruffian took pleasure in bumping me against scarred tables and chairs in the grimy room. He let go and pushed me toward the long polished wooden counter. Kate clung to me, sobbing.

"I hope you realize this is kidnapping," I snapped. "Let us go or we'll have the sheriff arrest you for assault!"

The men laughed and slapped their thighs. I wanted to kick Ace Diamond to kingdom come. Signs on the walls proclaimed 'No Markers Put Up' and 'Faro Game Limit $12.50.' Bottles lined the wall behind the bar and a portrait of a reclining woman, half-naked, hung above it. Ace would have known how to deal with these types. I'd asked him to protect us and he disappeared. Along with the money I'd paid him for his services.

"Unless you wanna work here too, miss, you'd better clear off," the tall man said. "Katie owes the boss a lot of money. She ain't going anywhere."

His foul breath fanned my face when we tugged Kate between us. "She doesn't owe your boss anything! She's going back with me to the train—"

"What's the trouble here?" A handsome, debonair man in a well-tailored gray pinstripe suit hurried down the stairs and slicked his dark hair back. "Johnson, let go of Miss Kimball."

"Robert!" Kate sounded relieved. "Thank goodness you're here! You told me worked at the bank. The clerk said you'd be here, but I didn't believe him."

"I work here now, my love."

I saw why Kate had been swayed by such a man. His blue silk ascot matched his eyes, and he carried himself with confidence. His voice sounded as smooth as a preacher's but his courteous smile didn't fool me.

"Why did this man attack my friend and leave him out in the street?" I asked, one hand on my hip. "It's not the kind of welcome we expected."

Rayburn—if that was his name—eyed me coolly. "Who's your friend, Kate?"

She stepped forward. "I brought Miss Granville to meet you. Who is Mr. McDaniel?"

"Johnson, see to this lady's friend outside." Robert crossed the room, adjusting his cuffs, while the tall man brushed past me. "So you used the ticket I bought," he said to Kate. "A wise choice. How do you like my place? You can see customers trying to buck the tiger."

Kate stared at him in confusion. "You own this saloon?"

"Much less tedious than a bank position. And more profitable." He focused his smoky gaze on me. "Davis, escort Miss Granville back to the train depot."

I narrowed my eyes. "I understand your little game, Mr. McDaniel, from what your men said. You bought Miss Kimball her train ticket, and you expect her to pay you back for the expense. Am I right? You don't intend to marry her at all."

"A first-class ticket and twenty dollars for a new dress is a wise investment. She'll marry whomever she wants, once she works off the debt. You'd better hurry along, Miss Granville, or you'll miss the train."

"But Robert—I brought my mother's wedding dress." Kate's voice faltered at the quick change in his expression, from self-satisfaction to cunning. "You-you said you wanted to start a family. That we'd grow old together here in Wyoming."

"She's not staying," I said and pulled her toward the door. The squat man blocked us, cracking his knuckles. "Please move aside."

McDaniel's tone turned to steel. "Katie said she wanted to come out west. I didn't force her to use that ticket. But she's here, and she'll stay."

David brushed a hand over my waist. "A money belt, boss."

"How interesting." McDaniel walked over and flipped up my jacket's hem. He avoided my attempt to slap his hand. "It seems we have a bonus—"

"'Fraid you don't." Ace Diamond's slow drawl came

from the doorway where he stood, Colt in hand. Metal whirred as he cocked it. "Walk this way, ladies."

"Come now, sir, there's no need for weapons," McDaniel said, the well-mannered smile back on his face. "We have French postcards and stereoscopes for your perusal. Although we don't open till four o'clock, I'll make an exception in your case. Or perhaps you'd like to try one of these new girls. Fresh from the East."

"I'll take both." Ace drew his Bowie knife for good measure. "Walk this way, slow. Come on, Lily. Kate."

Davis backed off when I pushed Kate toward the door. McDaniel's eyes smoldered in contempt and rage. He stepped forward.

"I invested good money in Miss Kimball. Everyone knows I treat my girls well. They belong to me."

"Wrong!" I whirled around once we reached Ace's side. "By your own words you've admitted to slavery. I ought to bring charges against you in court—"

"Quit jawing." Ace motioned us outside. "Mason's waiting outside. Let's go."

Arms around each other's waists, Kate and I fled to the street.

****

Stragglers hurried down the weathered steps of the Union Pacific hotel while the train's final whistle blew. Charles, his suit damp and holding a soggy crimson handkerchief against his face, urged us to run the last ten yards. Ace drew up the rear with a backward glance. He'd put his knife away, but held his Colt at the ready.

I sent a thankful prayer skyward. If not for him, I'd have been trapped with Kate.

Breathing hard, I raced up the Palace car's steps. Kate stumbled when the train jolted forward, but Charles boosted her up to safety. Ace leaped for the railing and caught it. He swung himself onto the lowest step as the train picked up its pace, and then hid his revolver inside his jacket. I noticed his skinned and bleeding knuckles and handed him a handkerchief. Nodding his thanks, he wrapped his hand with the linen.

"I take it you met Johnson outside the saloon?"

"Yep. He'd stolen this," Ace said and handed me a leather wallet. "I bet Mason would rather you gave it back to him than me."

"I thought you were right behind us when we found the bank."

"Always scout ahead. The men at the livery knew about McDaniel going east twice a year for new girls. Figgered you'd been ambushed when you two disappeared. Mason was out cold, but I dunked him in the horse trough till he came around."

Laughter bubbled up inside me and I couldn't hold it back. I held my stomach, imagining poor Charles being baptized that way, until tears rolled down my cheeks.

"I'm sorry—it's just—funny."

Ace flashed his lopsided grin. "Doubt if Mason would agree."

I leaned back against the Palace car's exterior, watching Cheyenne's dusty buildings, the distant reddish buttes and the track leading east recede in the distance. This adventure west had surprised me. What would Aunt Sylvia think about my escapade? I'd been kidnapped, threatened and offered to a man for entertainment purposes. Worst of all, I'd missed dinner.

Ace shook his wrapped hand. "You're lucky I rescued you."

"I'm lucky you showed up," I said lightly. "But thank you."

"I earned twice that hundred dollar bonus," he countered and opened the car's door. Ace beckoned me inside. "After you, Miss Granville."

I noted his emphasis on the last two words before I surged past him. "That's right, Mr. Diamond. Don't get too big for your britches."

Sir Vaughn and Aunt Sylvia blocked the aisle, as if they'd been waiting for me. "Where have you been, Lily? Your friends wouldn't answer our questions—"

"They don't have to answer to you. And neither do I."

"Such an ungrateful child," she said and cocked her head. "People are already gossiping about you and that ruffian."

I pushed past them both, ignoring the disapproval on Sir Vaughn's face. Curled up near the window, Kate had hidden her face in her hands and rocked back and forth. I slid into the seat beside her. Charles poked up his spectacles, his brown eyes full of compassion, as if unsure of what to say or do. His split swollen lip had traces of dried blood, with more beside each nostril. When I held out his wallet, he accepted it and then shifted over to allow Ace room.

"She won't listen to me," Charles said. "I told her it wasn't her fault."

"McDaniel tricked other women in the same way," I said and touched Kate's shoulder. She shuddered under my hand. "Blame him, not yourself."

"I was so blind. So stupid."

Her voice shook harder. Kate huddled in the seat's corner, still weeping, so we remained silent. Perhaps our presence alone would help. She bolted upright.

"Oh, no, my trunk! I saw it on the platform—my mother's wedding gown!"

Inconsolable, she rushed toward the Ladies' washroom. I sent Charles to find the conductor and explain the situation and see what could be done. Ace tipped his hat over his eyes, hands folded over his stomach, which I'd heard grumbling along with my own. I didn't have the energy to read or sketch. Hunger gnawed me, and closing my eyes to rest didn't work. I sat up when Charles returned with a Negro porter, who held a thin envelope in his hand.

"You're Miss Granville?" He handed me the telegram. "I been lookin' all over for you since we got this. Your aunt sent me over with it."

I dug in my pocketbook for a tip. The envelope's seal had been broken, but a lump rose in my throat when I saw my uncle's name at the telegram's end. Excitement and relief flooded me and I read the words twice.

Returned from business in Reno, stop. Received sad news, stop. Trust no one, stop. Will meet CP Sacramento depot. Harrison Granville.

I didn't care that Aunt Sylvia had intercepted and read the message. I knew now that Uncle Harrison was safe, and that I'd see him soon. Thank God for that blessing. I smiled at Charles and Ace and blinked back tears.

"My uncle will meet me in Sacramento. It won't be long now, only a few more days to get through. I hope we won't meet any further trouble."

"We might." Ace pulled a worn leather handle from his boot. "This will come in handy if you do. Whenever I ain't around, that is."

The thin pointed blade resembled the ice pick Father kept on the library's sideboard with his Scotch. With a flick of his wrist, Ace hid it once more in his boot. The next thing I knew, the blade flashed in his upraised hand. Ace feinted several times and before I could follow, the knife vanished for the second time. He leaned back in the seat.

"Your turn. See if you can reach down and get it without anyone noticing."

Charles coughed. "I don't think Miss Granville needs a weapon—"

"I disagree," I cut in. "Whoever searched my things in Omaha stole my father's Army revolver and ammunition. I hope they hurt themselves, because it has a bad kickback."

While I spoke, I'd stretched my hand downward— but Ace plucked the stiletto out of his boot before I could touch the handle.

"Too slow." He held it out so I could grip the handle, showed me the proper way to grasp it before he replaced it in his boot. "Try again."

"Lily, this is absurd. You might end up slicing your hand open," Charles said, his posture as stiff as his tone. "You did cut yourself after all."

I examined the tiny nick on my fingertip. "I'll survive, it's not bleeding. Much."

"Here, I have an extra handkerchief."

He held it out to me. I leaned across the aisle, my fingertip in my mouth, aware that both men watched in fascination. They stared at me like men stranded in the desert without a canteen or a creek in sight.

"Is something wrong, gentlemen?"

"Uh—no," Charles said and unfolded his newspaper

with a scowl at Ace.

The Texan surveyed me with an odd smile, half mischievous, half sly. "You keep that handy then. If I had a derringer, I'd give you that instead."

"This is fine." I took care to slide the stiletto inside my pocketbook between my book and the silk lining. "Thank you, Mr. Diamond. I do feel safer now."

"Don't drop it on your foot."

Kate trudged down the aisle, forlorn and lost. The train slowed again. I halted beside the porter who was counting muslin sheets and blankets in the cupboards.

"Excuse me. It seems we will never get to California if we stop so often."

"We need extra horsepower, miss, to make it up the mountain. Sherman's at the top, you'll see. After that, it ain't so bad," he said with a bright smile, "till you get to the Sierras anyhow. Now them be peaks, higher than any I seen."

"Thank you—Kate, where are you going?" I hurried to overtake her, since she carried her pocketbook and valise. "You can't leave the train. There's no depot."

"I'll wait at the station house, then. Or walk back to Cheyenne," she said and pushed past me. "I don't have a ticket, and I won't take charity. Please, Lily. Let me be."

I realized she'd gone through a trauma but didn't expect such stubbornness. "Kate, stop. You're disappointed, I understand that. But you'll throw your life away if you go back."

"I'll find other work there."

"You saw what it was like," I said. "There aren't many women yet. Come to California. I'll help you find work there."

"I'll wait tables at that hotel in Cheyenne." She dodged out of reach and then ran smack into Charles, who'd stepped through the door from the platform. "Oh! I'm sorry, Mr. Mason—"

"Here, take this." He handed Kate a stub. "I already bought it, so you can't return it. Lily's right. You'll have a better chance of finding work out in California."

Kate stared at the ticket, eyebrows drawn together, and closed her eyes. "I-I don't know what to say. Except thank you."

"You're welcome. Take my arm, Miss Kimball."

She allowed him to escort her back through the Palace car. I followed, aware of the passengers who stared at Kate and whispered together. Didn't they have a shred of compassion? Aunt Sylvia sniffed in contempt when we walked past. I knew she lacked any true sympathy and manners, since she'd feigned plenty at Father's funeral. A credit to her days on stage. Sir Vaughn ignored us. I sat beside Kate and squeezed her hand. Her mouth trembled and she looked close to tears again, but squeezed back. She finally relaxed. After she rewarded Charles with a shy smile, she took out her knitting needles and yarn.

"I received word from my uncle," I told her and explained the telegram. "He'd been in Reno. Mining business, since the Comstock Lode is somewhere near there."

"He has a share in that?" Ace asked, sitting up straight.

"I doubt it, but there are other mines in the area."

That wasn't a lie. I'd never understood half of what Father told me about my uncle's feud with George Hearst, or their claim on the Early Bird. I hoped Uncle Harrison didn't

expect me to produce the deed in California.
If so, he was in for a rude surprise.

'God hath delivered me… into the hands of the wicked.' Job 16:11

Chapter Eleven

Two seats away, Ace Diamond held a wooden board across his knees supported by three other men. Tom Gentry was one, but I didn't know the other two's names. Silver coins and one gold eagle lay in the board's middle with the discarded pasteboards. Gentry laid down his hand with a satisfied smile and tugged his coin-encrusted watch chain.

"Aces and jacks! What have you got, Morris?"

"Nothin', that's what."

The third man threw his cards down in disgust, which brought a hoot from the others. I knelt on the seat and peered over the elderly couple and a sleeping gentleman who blocked my view. Gentry reached for the pot but the Texan laid his cards on the coins.

"Not so fast. Three kings. Maybe next time you'll get luckier."

"How the devil did you pull that off?"

Gentry stood up so fast the board, cards and coins toppled sideways into the aisle. "Hey," Morris protested. "Tex beat me too, you know."

"If I could prove he cheated, he'd be dead."

"I don't cheat." Lithe as a cat, Ace rose to stare the man down. "Go on, take your money back. I don't play poker with sore losers."

"Only losers, so it seems," Gentry muttered.

"I've had my share of losing hands."

"I bet you have."

The drummer stalked out of the car in the opposite direction. I sensed he might be the perfect candidate for being Emil Todaro's colleague. Why else would he pay attention to me? And scare us half to death, too. Ace Diamond gathered his cards in silence and pocketed the money he'd won. Once he returned the board to the porter, he stretched in that same cat-like manner and reclaimed the seats across from me. The Texan pulled a harmonica from his coat pocket. He examined the holes and smoothed the metal covering.

"You seem to be a man of many talents, Mr. Diamond."

"Huh?"

Clearly I'd interrupted his train of thought. Kate stopped knitting. "Play something, could you please? I'm so tired of sitting here."

Ace shrugged. "Sure thing, miss."

Eyes on the passing scenery, he produced a low, wheezing, plaintive tune that matched the train's progress upward. His rough hands cupped the metal and wood instrument with a lover's caress. Unsettled by that thought and such melancholy music, I interrupted.

"Something a bit more uplifting, perhaps?"

"I can't play 'Dixie' among so many Yanks," he said. Ace pocketed his harmonica and stood up. "Think I need a smoke."

He strolled down the aisle, no doubt bored. Perhaps the confrontation with Gentry and then Robert McDaniel had whetted his appetite for danger. I needed some kind of distraction. As the train climbed higher, I shifted away to avoid the view. The uneven ridges, stacked like a child's blocks on either side of the track, drew my gaze like a siren's song. Dry creek beds cut into their sides at times, and I shuddered.

Our speed soon decreased. Sheep with long, twisting horns chewed bits of grass or fronds of purple and yellow wildflowers near a patch of rocks. The bracing scent of pine trees washed over everyone when Sir Vaughn entered the Palace car.

"Is that snow?" I asked Kate. "All that white powder in the gully over there."

"Alkali, worse than prairie dust," a woman passing in the aisle said. She stooped to check the view. "Wait till we get to Utah. There's ten times more due to the Great Salt Lake."

Soon the train stopped at Sherman Station, treeless and windswept. I walked the aisle, rubbing my arms and trying to warm up in the chilly Palace car, while Kate huddled in her seat. The crewmen refilled the boilers and unhitched the second engine. Most of the men had gone out to survey a scattering of wooden shacks near the rickety windmill on the track's south side. Low stone walls, with yellow moss trailing across their pocked surface, marched up and over a desolate bare ridge in the distance.

Without trees, the wind moaned and whistled with an eerie presence. I shivered harder. The distant frosted peaks and steep valleys, from what little I could see beyond the window, were indeed breathtaking.

"Who in their right mind would choose to live here. Besides a mountain goat," Kate said. "I feel bad for the station crew."

A flash of light caught my eye but it proved to be the sun reflecting off Sir Vaughn's monocle. Ace Diamond jumped from the top step of the smoking car and walked past my aunt's husband with a nod. Hat shadowing his face, he joined Gentry and several other men standing near the fresh rack of antlers nailed to a shack's wall. Blood stained the ground and smoke wafted from the shack's crooked pipe. I guessed the makeshift smokehouse cured meat.

Aunt Sylvia rose from her seat down the aisle. She raised her chin, her dark eyes stormy and her mouth a thin line. "I hope you're satisfied, Lily," she said and brushed dust from her suit's sleeve, "although I can see you don't care one whit—"

"Excuse me?"

"Here we are, up in these Godforsaken mountains, and you seem oblivious to the inconvenience you've caused us."

Teeth clenched, I met her gaze without flinching. "I thought your husband has business in San Francisco," I said. "You could have returned to Chicago or St. Louis."

"I decided to visit my brother. Not that Harrison will appreciate that, I suppose, or welcome me. He has yet to reply to any of my telegrams. Still, I hope to reconcile with him before it's too late like with John."

Her haughty tone spoke volumes. She knew I'd

received word from California and resentment flickered in her eyes' dark pools. Before I could think of a reply, an older woman in black with a white collar and cuffs joined us while she pulled a shawl closer around her.

"Lady Sylvia, come and recite a few passages for us. Please?"

I witnessed the instant change in my aunt, from bitterness to a full-blown smile that would light up a stage's gas lamps before the curtain rose. "I'd be delighted, Mrs. Pierce," she said, and tucked her gloved hand under the woman's arm. "What an honor it's been to help entertain the passengers on this boring trip! I was telling my niece how wonderful it's been to travel on this new line. So much more exciting than back east..."

I choked back a laugh at such a bold-faced lie. Her ego soothed, Aunt Sylvia joined the knot of people at the front of the Palace car with Mrs. Pierce in tow. The train lurched a warning of its departure. Ace, Charles and the other men trooped in from the cold and the wind, laughing and joking, a few aiming tobacco juice toward the spittoon before they sat down. We left Sherman Station behind and rolled west once again.

"Well, ladies, it won't be long till we switch trains to the Central Pacific," Ace said and tipped his hat over his eyes. "I'm gettin' used to traveling in this kind of luxury."

"Don't get too used to it," Charles said grumpily. He poked his spectacles up and folded his arms over his chest. "Or the free ride either."

"I'm getting paid for services rendered," the Texan shot back. "Like haulin' you up from the dirt in Cheyenne after that roughneck kicked you in the gut."

"Johnson? He kicked you?" I asked. "What a

coward!"

Charles shrugged. "Thanks for helping me, Diamond, but he'd finished his abuse."

"Not with that knife in his hand, he wasn't." Ace lifted the brim of his hat and squinted. "You're lucky you didn't get your throat cut from ear to ear."

"Did he try to hurt you, Mr. Diamond?" Kate asked.

"Nope, my knife's bigger. Cowards always cut and run."

The memory of Emil Todaro and his friend rushing away from the house in Evanston sprang into mind. My doubts of seeing him hang for murder crowded in next. He was a coward, true enough. He deserved justice. First I had to find him, though. Perhaps I could search the second class cars at some point. Glum, I breathed in deep and prayed for patience. It wouldn't do to show my frustration after such a close call in Cheyenne. I had to cheer up Kate.

Her eyes no longer looked puffy and red, but she twisted the ends of her shawl with nervous fingers. "I hope my trunk won't be stolen," she said. "It's all I have left."

"I'm sure it's fine. It's freezing in here," I said with a shiver. The wind whistled and cold air invaded each time someone opened the door. "Why not finish that scarf for yourself?"

"I threw it down the commode. It made me sick looking at it."

Ace and I both laughed. Even Charles smiled. "Good for you," I said. "I hope you kept the needles, though. They might be useful as a weapon."

If Kate had recovered a sense of outrage, then she was on her way to forgetting Robert and nearly ending up in a brothel. I pulled out my necklace to check the time and flexed my cold, stiff fingers. My sketchbook was half-filled now with drawings in various stages, most hasty renderings of prairie dogs, antelope, buffalo, the train's interior, an eagle in flight. I surveyed a profile portrait of the older woman Aunt Sylvia had befriended, her black gown and bonnet quite detailed. I'd finished the sketch while they'd been close in conversation. Now I flipped to Ace's portrait and added more tonal values to his wide-brimmed hat.

"Where did you learn to draw like that?" Kate asked. "In school?"

"I had a tutor who was a gifted artist." I kept working on the sketch. Not that I minded her questions but her odd mood bothered me. "Before that I attended a private school."

"What's it like, being rich?"

Her wistful question surprised me. "Father called us 'comfortably well off' because the real rich are the Vanderbilts and Astors of New York," I said and changed the subject. "You must have attended school, Kate. What was it like?"

"I had to quit at fifteen to help on the farm. But the teacher had forty or more children, some of them as young as three. We had a few older boys during the winter, too. Miss Bass had her hands full. Some of us girls helped out with the younger children."

"I would have enjoyed that."

"Yes, I thought of being a teacher myself. I do love children."

I twirled my pencil, thinking fast. "You could teach, you know. In California—I could loan you the money to attend a good Normal school and earn your certificate."

She gazed out the window. "I do appreciate your

offer, Lily. You're so generous, but I'm already in your debt. I need to pay my own way. Whether it's school or in a job somewhere to save up my money. You understand, don't you?"

"Yes," I said. "You know, I'd give all my money to have my parents back."

Kate squeezed my hand, her eyes glistening, and faced the window. I closed my sketchbook, since I'd lost interest. The train descended a long slope. The brakes hissed every so often as they released steam. My ears popped. The wind rushed past with a shriek now and again, although the chill faded a little. I straightened when we jolted to a stop. The cars snaked around the bend behind us. Most of the Palace car passengers craned their necks, puzzled by another delay. A skeletal wooden trestle bridge crossed a rocky ravine about a quarter of a mile down the track and around a curve.

I stood, peering over the heads of other passengers, eyeing the crew and engineer when they headed toward the rickety structure. Was it damaged in some way?

"Looks like a bunch of matchsticks that wouldn't hold a goat," the woman behind me said. "You oughter draw that bridge, miss, before the wind takes it."

It did indeed sway with each strong gust, despite thin wires stretching from the top level of the railroad bed to wooden posts on both sides of the ravine. The conductor hurried to join the crewmen, holding his pocket watch and shaking his head, and argued for another five minutes. Even the porter acted worried. He muttered to himself while he fussed with a whisk broom, then polished the carved arms of the empty upholstered seats.

"I'll go find out what the delay's about," Charles

said.

Another five minutes passed. Kate and I woke Ace when we both rose to go outside. "What?" He yawned wide and stretched before getting to his feet. "More trouble?"

"I don't know yet, but I'm going to find out."

Uneasy, I followed Kate down the aisle with Ace trailing us toward the crowd of buzzing passengers on the platform. With a wave, I caught Charles' eye. He slipped through the crowd and joined us near the washroom door.

"Why aren't we crossing?"

"They're sending the train over the bridge without passengers. The wind's too strong, or so the engineer says."

"What if the bridge doesn't hold?"

"Reckon we'll hoof it to California, miss," Ace said.

I didn't appreciate his attempt at humor or that lopsided grin. "The train can't be put in reverse, can it, Mr. Diamond? The engine, perhaps, but not with the cars."

"Yep. Either way we gotta walk over the bridge."

"You can't be serious," Kate said with a gasp. "It must be over fifty or eighty feet high from that ravine's bottom—"

The conductor's loud announcement drowned her words. "Ladies and gentlemen, please listen," he said. "Leave any extra baggage on the train. It won't take more than an hour for the passengers to cross over, but first the train." Shouts from several men blew away in the gusty wind, but he held up both hands. "I don't like it any better than you. We're already running late on the timetable."

"We didn't pay to walk," one woman grumbled.

"It don't make sense to send the train over without the weight of the passengers to keep it from blowing over," a man said. "Don't make sense at all."

"We lost several freight cars last month," the conductor said. "Wind's bad through this area, and they were loaded full. I'm not risking anyone's lives today except the engineer. He has no choice. Please, line up by twos or in single file."

"I heard that bridge was built in less than thirty days," another man said. "You should've built an iron replacement by now. It's been six months since the Golden Spike ceremony. You knew back then it didn't meet standards."

"I can't answer that, sir." The conductor checked his pocket watch again. "We ought to be in Weber canyon by now. I'm sorry, but this can't be helped."

"I will not walk over that bridge!"

I whirled at my aunt's booming voice. Sir Vaughn dragged Aunt Sylvia to her feet. "You will, my dear. I will not allow you to lose your footing."

"I can't do it—I want to stay on the train."

He half carried her past us to the door. "It will soon be over."

Charles grasped my elbow. "I hope neither of you ladies are afraid of heights," he said. "The bridge is six hundred and fifty feet long and over a hundred feet high. We have to be careful and watch where we step."

"I hate tunnels worse," I said. My skin crawled at the thought of walls pressing in on all sides. "We'd better get this over with then."

Kate's face paled when she grabbed Ace's arm. "The sooner, the better indeed."

"Wait—"

I hurried back to retrieve my pocketbook and made sure my sketchbook and pencils were tucked inside. Then I returned to Charles, who slid an arm around my waist and escorted me to the open platform. The cold wind took my breath away. We descended to the rough ground and lined up according to the conductor's directions. The thought of crossing a bridge over such a dizzying height made me nauseous, but I had to reach California. No matter what the inconvenience, no matter what the danger. With sweaty palms and a parched throat, I followed the crowd to line up beside the track's stony slope. My skirt flapped so hard in the stiff wind, I stumbled several times.

Kate's bluebird twisted free of her hat and flew away, too quick for Ace to snatch it in time. My stomach fluttered as I neared the bluff's crumbling edge. Everyone watched the train slowly steam over the flimsy bridge. I held my breath when it reached the halfway point. The engine and cars, strung like a delicate necklace, danced over the shaky stilts. The bridge shuddered in a gust of wind after the cars reached safety. A few men threw their hats in the air and the crowd cheered.

"Lord have mercy," my aunt whimpered. "Let's go back, forget all this."

Sir Vaughn shook Aunt Sylvia like a rag doll. "Bear up, madam."

She sagged against him, her face alabaster. The first group of passengers stepped out onto the first span of the wooden railroad ties, Aunt Sylvia and Sir Vaughn included.

"Step carefully! Take your time," the conductor called out, standing aside as the next group walked toward the bridge. "Don't look down and don't crowd each other. One beam and then the next. Get a rhythm going, count the ties on the way if it helps.

I glanced at the creek bed full of boulders below.

Debris from the freight cars that had fallen off the bridge lay scattered at the bottom. A trickle of water meandered its way among the rocks there. Despite the wind that whipped and tugged at passengers' hats or capes, I focused on the plumes billowing from the engines' smokestacks. My knees shook but my stomach finally settled. Kate hung back.

"You go first, Lily. I-I'm too scared, I need more time."

Ace nodded. "We'll wait till the next group then. I ain't afraid of heights but I don't fancy 'em. Be careful, Mason."

Charles nodded and adjusted his spectacles. "Are you ready, Lily?"

"Yes."

He gripped my waist tight and grasped the guideline rope. I placed my foot on the first wooden beam and I froze. The dizzying drop made my head spin. I closed my eyes for a minute and then prayed for strength. In less than five minutes, we'd be across.

"Keep your chin up. Your feet will find the ties," Charles said. "You can do it."

I summoned a final shred of courage and started walking. In two or three days, I would meet Uncle Harrison in Sacramento. I couldn't falter now, crossing a silly bridge. My feet did find the ties when I started counting them.

"This isn't so bad once you get used to it," I said.

"Could be worse."

"You mean it could be raining? That would be bad."

"Thank God for summer." Charles grunted when another wicked gust pushed him into me. His grip on my waist slipped, so I grabbed his hand instead.

"I read that storms race across the prairie with

lightning speed."

"Nothing to block their way, I suppose." He squeezed my hand. "Halfway across, Lily. You're doing fine. Keep walking—"

Something hard crashed into me. I fell forward, past the iron railroad ties. Before I realized how, I found myself dangling from the edge.

A horrible yell echoed in the ravine below, but terror had struck me dumb.

'O spare me, that I may recover strength...' Psalm 39:13

Chapter Twelve

Images flashed before my eyes: Father sprawled across his desk, the bullet hole in his temple. My mother lying cold and gray in her casket. The horrible accident in Chicago when I'd been a child, seeing a horse bloody and dying on an icy street, and the driver's legs crushed beneath the wagon. Screams echoed through the ravine. The iron rail was inches from my fingers. I dared not reach for it, knowing my grip on the wooden tie needed both hands.

My arms grew numb and my shoulder felt on fire. I couldn't think straight. It seemed like hours since I ended up hanging here. All my senses dulled to the burning pain and terror.

No one can help me. I have to save myself.

My feet scrabbled for a foothold on the bridge's scaffold, but my efforts loosened my grip. Fear choked me. I heard a hoarse voice below.

139

"I got you, Lily."

"Ace!" My lower limbs no longer dangled in space but rested on something solid. "Where are you?"

"Crawl upward, and I'll give you a boost."

"I'm not sure I can." My body shook and the pain seared every nerve. The wind whistled in my face. "My hands, my arms—I can't feel them anymore."

"Don't push down, Lily," he panted, somewhere below, "or we'll both fall."

"I need a minute—"

"Move, woman!"

I obeyed without thinking. Somehow I managed to hook an elbow over the railroad tie. Ace shoved me harder, and someone grabbed me from above. Now that I wasn't in danger of falling, I glanced down to see a huddled figure below in the creek bed. Pain shot through each part of my body when the uniformed crewman lifted me over the edge. I knelt on the bridge and gasped for breath. I looked up when a second man reached down to haul Ace onto the bridge with a grunt. The crewman helped me stand.

"Where is Charles? Did he fall?"

"Are you all right, miss?"

"Yes, but who fell? Was it Charles—"

"Mason's all right, Lily," Ace said. "He made it to the other side."

Dazed, I glanced around and saw Kate with Charles, watching a crewman wrap his arm in a sling. The two men walked me across the bridge until I stood on firm ground again. My eyes closed in relief, mixed with joy and pain. I fought a heaviness overcoming me but lost to total darkness. A strong burning odor brought me back into awareness. Sunshine seared my vision and the woman with a vial of smelling salts drew away. The pain had dulled to a steady throb in my shoulder, arms, hands and one hip.

"Oh, Lily! Are you all right?" Kate asked, helping me to sit up. "You fainted and we need to know if you broke any bones. Can you move your hands and feet?"

"Yes. Yes, I think so." I wiggled toes and fingers. "Nothing broken."

"Are you sure, Lily?" Charles stood over me. A nasty cut on his cheek trickled blood, and he dabbed it with a handkerchief. "I couldn't grab you in time, I'm sorry—"

Kate helped me to my feet. "What happened?" I asked, still groggy.

"We're not sure, but we think someone tripped and fell forward," the conductor said. He addressed a crewman standing near. "Send some men down the ravine to bring up that man up, whether or not he's dead. We can't leave him to the wild animals."

"That fella didn't trip," Ace said. "He shoved Miss Granville toward the edge. I saw what happened, I was six or seven people behind. That bast—he passed us all to get to her."

"Why would he do such a thing?" Charles asked. "He fell himself, right off the edge."

The conductor glanced at me. "What do you remember, miss?"

"I—oh." Taking a breath was agony. I shook my head. "It's all a blur. I'm sorry."

"I know what I saw." Ace plucked large splinters from his palms and thumb. "I hope he's alive so I can strangle him."

My own hands had been scraped raw. My whole body ached and throbbed and I touched my side gingerly.

"How did you—end up below me?"

"He climbed down to save you," Kate said, her eyes shining with admiration. "We both saw what happened, and he swung down to the scaffolding and climbed over to you. I've never seen anything so brave in my life."

"More luck than bravery." Ace rubbed one shoulder. "Mason was about ready to go over, but someone had already grabbed his feet and—"

"Lily, darling Lily! You might have been killed!"

I should have recognized that booming voice as a warning sign. Aunt Sylvia caught me in a tight embrace. I gasped aloud at the stabbing pain in my ribs.

"No, please." I pushed her away, fighting for breath. "It hurts. So much."

"Bet you cracked a rib." Ace flexed his arms and shoulders. "If I feel like I got throwed from a snake-eyed bronc, then you must be hurtin' pretty bad."

Sir Vaughn walked over to join us. "I hope we can resume our journey soon. Everyone has crossed now," he said and adjusted his monocle. His temple and eye socket bulged over the rim. "If the east-bound train meets us at some point, we could crash."

"They won't leave till we arrive in Ogden," the conductor said. "They'll bring that man up soon. We'll know if he's alive or dead."

Two porters had somehow climbed down the ravine, perhaps along a snaking path I'd noticed before. Now they appeared over the edge with a makeshift stretcher between them. The conductor hurried over to speak to them.

Ace shook dust from his dark hair. "Guess my hat's somewhere in the creek."

"My pocketbook!" I wrung my hands, frantic. "I

must have dropped it. My money's in it, and your knife—oh no, my sketchbook! I can't lose that."

"Hold your horses, Lily. Maybe the porters found it."

Ace stalked over to the group around the stretcher. Aunt Sylvia caught my elbow. "How can you allow that ruffian such familiarity, using your first name?"

"A ruffian who saved my life."

"Like that matters," she scoffed. "I can see you'll never take my advice—"

I had no patience for her usual rant, so I stumbled toward the knot of people beside the stretcher. Charles blocked my way. "You'd better not look, Lily. Someone said he's dead from the fall. The skull's all smashed in. It looks bad."

"My pocketbook fell to the creek bed. Did anyone find it?"

"Yes, miss," a porter said, "and I was lucky to snatch it before the creek done took it. Sure am sorry it's a mite wet. Found this hat, too."

"Thank you," I said. "I'm so grateful, more than you can imagine."

"Here you go," Charles said and handed the porter a coin. "We appreciate your efforts."

The porter nodded and handed Ace his hat before he herded passengers to board the train. I caught sight of the body on the stretcher and gasped. It wasn't the blood matting the misshapen skull, the graying face, the patched and wrinkled suit that stretched tight or the thick goatee that drew my eyes. Not even curiosity would have drawn me forward. Sheer instinct sent me tottering over to stare at the dead man's face. That proved more frightening than my near fall from the bridge.

"My Lord, it can't be true."

"What is it, Lily?" Charles tugged me backwards but I fought his grip. "There's nothing to be done for him. Come away, darling."

I clutched my pocketbook to my stomach and struggled to swallow the gorge in my throat. "It wasn't an accident after all."

Ace whacked his damp hat against his thigh. "What do you mean? You know him?"

Still in shock, I nodded. "That's the man who killed my father. Emil Todaro."

****

Back on the Palace car, I surveyed my pocketbook's scarred leather exterior. Thank goodness the clasp had held tight. The contents inside had jumbled together—my novel, the sketchbook, pencils, even the stiletto Ace had lent me. The silk lining had a rip, so I slid the weapon beneath it to prevent further damage to anything else. I'd suffered worse. No matter how I moved or what position I sat in, a wash of pain gave me pause.

"I think Ace is right about a cracked rib. What can I do? I can hardly breathe without a stabbing pain in my side. I'm aching all over."

Charles glanced at Kate. "I'll see what I can find, Lily."

He walked down the aisle to consult the porter. I clutched at my mother's necklace that had caught on a button, the silver clasp torn away. Thank goodness it could be fixed with a new one, but the tiny watch that Charles gave me had smashed glass and a missing minute hand. I

144

didn't hear any ticking, but tucked it away. Before long, Charles returned with a shot glass and a snifter in hand.

"This should help."

I thanked him, although my hands still shook when I sipped the brandy. It took the edge off the pain and spread a fiery warmth through me. Ace tossed back the shot of whiskey and squinted hard. He hailed a porter and handed over the small glass.

"Now that's good whiskey."

"The best Kentucky bourbon, sir."

Ace leaned back against the seat with a comfortable sigh. "We can relax now, Lily —"

"Miss Granville to you," Charles snapped. "We can visit with your uncle as long as you wish before we leave for China. We'll be there for several years."

I couldn't reply. Kate appeared with an armful of clean linen. I clung to each seat back while we made our way to the Ladies' washroom. Aunt Sylvia and Sir Vaughn ignored me, intent on playing whist with another couple. Kate bumped my shoulder when the door shut.

"Oh — I'm sorry!"

"Don't apologize. I couldn't do this alone," I said and allowed her to pull my jacket away. "Ow! I feel like I've been trampled by a team of horses."

"Hush, don't talk. That might be best." Kate peeled my shirtwaist and muslin corset cover downward and then frowned. "I thought so. A whalebone is poking into your skin. Hold still and I'll pull it loose. You're chafed raw on this side."

Within five minutes, she'd wrapped me, re-laced my corset so I could breathe and move easier, and then helped me dress. I flexed my arms and shoulders, which eased the stiffness. Kate brushed out my unkempt hair once I'd washed my face. She insisted on twisting my hair up for me, using her own pins to tidy the stray curls.

"Are you going to marry Charles?" she asked, her eyes wide.

"He seems to think so," I said wryly, "but I never said yes."

"I don't ever want to travel again. Wherever I end up, I'm staying there for good," Kate said with a laugh. "No more bridges, or saloons, or strange men. I'll find someone who's well known and court for at least a year before I marry."

"I don't blame you. It seems both of our plans have changed. I must see my uncle, but I'm not sure what I want to do after that."

That was the truth. I had trouble believing that my father's killer was dead. I'd seen the proof, though, in Emil Todaro's battered body. His goatee and shabby suit had fooled me after all. I might have seen him at one of the way stations, although I hadn't given him more than a passing glance. If he'd been walking, would I have spotted him by his frog-like gait? I wasn't certain. He must have followed me to Porter's store in Omaha, searched my pocketbook and then my valise at the Herndon Hotel. His reasons for doing so were another puzzle.

To see if I had a copy of the Early Bird's deed? Maybe he assumed I'd be taking it to my uncle. Todaro knew Father's penchant for hiding things in a safe place. I'd searched the bedrooms back home before leaving Evanston, and didn't find anything of value except the gold pocket watch.

"Is that better?" Kate asked, taking my arm.

"Yes, thank you." I took a deep breath. "My head still hurts, but not as bad."

We walked back to our seat. Both Charles and Ace must have gone to the smoking car with most of the other gentlemen. The ladies' loud chatter didn't help my headache. The train slowed, passing several stations, and stopped at Rawlins. The crewmen filled the water tanks while we ate a supper of fried mountain trout, sizzling steak and potatoes. Charles and Kate stood by the track to watch the fiery sunset afterward, but I had to sit down. My knees remained wobbly, and I couldn't think straight. I stared at the sky when the train headed west again, my mind blank, and watched the glowing ball of orange vanish. A hazy purple smudge and scarlet ribbons streaked the horizon. Twilight deepened into full night.

I jumped whenever someone strolled down the aisle in close proximity. No matter what, it was difficult repressing the terror of that hard shove and the memory of dangling from the bridge over Dale Creek. The train's swaying motion and the rattling wheels intensified my irritability.

"I hope we both sleep better tonight," Kate said. "You're out of danger, now that your father's murderer is dead."

"Are you still in pain, Lily?" Aunt Sylvia stood and held up a brown bottle. "I have more than enough of Mrs. Pinkham's Elixir. It might help you sleep easier."

"Thank you, but no," I said. "I'll manage."

"It works wonders, you know. Take a few spoonfuls."

I shook my head at the familiar label. Mother had dosed me once when I was ten, and tried for hours to wake me the next morning. Frightened, she poured the bottle's contents into a pile of dead leaves. I'd been sluggish and weepy for three days, or so she told me. I had no memory of the incident at all. No wonder I preferred clear glass bottles and avoided any others. How odd. I'd never realized that before. I held my sketchbook and pencil while the wilder scenery and scraggly pine trees passed by the window.

Aunt Sylvia studied Kate, as if noticing her for the first time. "I thought you were supposed to be married in Cheyenne."

"My plans changed." Her face flooded with color.

"Lily, who is Dudley?" my aunt asked. "I saw that inscription on that page."

"I'd rather not say." I sensed that answer did not satisfy her curiosity.

"Perhaps your private tutor?" Kate smiled in a conspiratorial way.

Luckily I didn't have to reply since Charles returned to claim his seat. My aunt moved on to join another group of ladies at the front of the car. My heart leaped into my throat when the train approached a bridge, the stones piled in haphazard fashion, with little or no mortar between. I clutched my sketchbook but we crossed without any trouble.

Again I shivered without control when the train later crossed a flimsy wooden span that held the rails a few feet from the river bed. Kate dozed across from me, and Charles read his newspaper without noticing. A higher trestle than Dale Creek's appeared ahead, and I swallowed the saliva that filled my mouth. I sat frozen in place, unable to move, silent in horror with my eyes closed, until the nausea receded.

This was ridiculous. I had to regain control or I'd

never make it to Sacramento.

Kate woke up and yawned. "There's no water at all in that creek," she pointed out. The train track ran parallel to a rock-strewn bed. "They must not get much rain here."

"Sure don't," Ace said and sank down across from us. He pulled out his cards and shuffled them. "Too dry this summer. A whole street burned in Omaha last month."

They discussed the weather until I posed a question. "Did you happen to play cards with Emil Todaro yesterday, Mr. Diamond?"

He squinted at me with those odd mismatched eyes. "Yeah. Stayed pretty quiet."

"Did you ask for his name?"

Ace shrugged. "He didn't fit the description you gave me."

I glanced at Charles, my anger rising. "You told me you'd recognize Emil Todaro."

"I met him once, Lily," he said and adjusted his spectacles. "That goatee changed his face so much. Along with those heavy sideburns."

Frustration gnawed my stomach. "Did he talk to anyone in particular? Two men left the house right before I found my father's body."

They shrugged. I wished ladies were allowed inside the smoking car! It didn't seem fair. Not that I cared for tobacco, although I had sneaked a cigarette once behind the stables. If I'd seen him up close, I might have recognized Emil Todaro alive and well, disguise or not. They both had failed me.

"It seems odd you didn't recognize his voice, Charles."

"He's dead, Lily. Why are you so upset? You ought

149

to be glad of it."

I sat back against the cushion, hating the condescension in his tone, hating myself for sounding like a shrew. My hands trembled when I searched for my pencil on the floor. Kate held it out to me, her eyes full of compassion. Close to tears, I put my my sketchbook and pencil away and stared out the window again. What was wrong with me?

Ace held up his deck. "Interested in a friendly hand, Mason?"

He shook his head. "Gambling leads to the devil's playground."

Ace hooted with laughter. "Tell that to the minister who beat me this morning."

Charles grunted in disgust. "You must have coerced him into a game."

"Nope. His idea. The good reverend had a streak of luck goin', too."

I should have known better than ask them about Emil Todaro. They'd wiped the slate clean, but I remained haunted by his gray face and bloody skull. Kate helped me stand when the porter arrived to arrange our berths. We prepared for the night and soon pulled our curtain closed, too exhausted to talk. The rattle of the wheels beneath my aching head lulled me to sleep this time. I woke at some point from a bad dream of being locked in a dark room with no doors or windows. Perspiration trickled down my face and neck. I groaned. My soreness increased full force, and I had trouble rolling onto my side.

Something niggled at the back of my mind. I'd seen a group of men at Sherman Station, clustered around the shack. I closed my eyes and tried to picture the rough building. Boards with wide cracks, the door hanging crooked, the huge antlers taken from deer or caribou—I had no idea which. Ace had joined them, running his hands over the points while another man measured the width. Gentry stood on the group's other side, talking to someone. I sat up and bumped my head on the upper berth. That man had worn a thick goatee and sideburns.

He must have been Emil Todaro. Gentry might not be tall and thin, but had Todaro shared his plans to arrange an accident? If so, Kate was dead wrong.

I wasn't out of danger after all.

'For where envying and strife is, there is confusion and every evil work.' James 3:16

Chapter Thirteen

After a quick breakfast at Green River, I gulped a third cup of strong coffee before we boarded the train. I'd lain awake after that bad dream, restless and disturbed by the noise and the stuffiness of the berth. I ached all over. Flexing my arms, shoulder and hips did not help.

Charles had bought another newspaper. His swollen lip had faded from the altercation in Cheyenne, and he'd abandoned the sling. Kate read my Jane Austen book. Ace had tipped his hat over his eyes, looking none the worse for wear after yesterday's incidents. I watched the scenery outside. At least the pillars, spires and towering castle formations kept my interest. Beige and brown ruled, with swaths of green on occasion, but the vivid robin's egg blue sky overwhelmed everything. I paced the aisle to ease my stiffness.

Thank goodness for that.

The train snaked onto a narrow winding shelf that hugged a mountain. Panic sent me back to my seat, and I gazed at the ceiling to avoid seeing the sheer drop. Ace withdrew his lower limbs from the aisle when a lady passenger prodded his boots on her way past.

"There's the Thousand Mile Tree," Charles said. He pointed to a large pine towering into the sky. "I read about it while the UP built their track."

Ace glanced up from cleaning his fingernails with a small pocketknife. "It's a pine like any other. Ain't too many in these parts, that's all."

"It marks the point where the Union Pacific reached one thousand miles—"

"Save it, Mason. I already figgered that out."

Charles scowled and left for the smoking car. Ace folded his knife and pocketed it, then strolled off toward the Men's washroom. Bored, I rubbed my sore arm. I didn't feel like reading or sketching, so I put both books away. Kate yawned. An unusual rock formation caught my eye. Two long gray humps ran up the side of a mountain, with a narrow gap between.

"What in the world—"

"That's the Devil's Slide, miss."

I jumped. Tom Gentry stood in the aisle beside our seat and ducked his head to glance outside. He stabbed a finger at the window. "Limestone, so I been told. People try climbing up that thing and have a devil of a time. That's why they call it that."

I snapped my pocketbook shut. I'd noticed his eyes shifting downward, as if he'd wanted to see the interior. "Yes, I imagine it would be difficult."

"Can't say I ever tried, but a friend told me how it near killed him."

Gentry plopped himself down in the empty seat across from us. My stomach clenched and I scanned the car to see where Charles and Ace had gone. How could they leave us alone? My uneasiness worsened when the drummer asked Kate a string of personal questions. He glanced at me, as if hoping I'd offer information, but I focused on controlling my fear. Kate seemed to enjoy the man's attention, laughing at his jokes and listening to his rambling stories. She must have forgotten his past attempt to scare her about Indian scalping practices.

"So you're lookin' for a job out in California?" He winked at Kate. "Pretty young lady like you ought to be married. You spoken for?"

"No." Her cheeks flushed darker pink. "I mean I was, but not any longer."

"And what about you, miss?" Gentry asked me.

I swallowed hard. "My business is my own, sir."

"No harm askin', is there?"

I didn't reply. Gentry rubbed his face, as if hoping I'd say something to fill the heavy silence. "Heard your father was killed," he said. "Poker player you sit with mentioned it."

"He told you that?"

"Last night. Said the killer was the same man who tried to push you off the bridge."

Flustered, I stared at Gentry. "He had no right to say anything."

"Lots of talk been goin' around about you, miss. Thought you'd want to know," Gentry said. "Folks are curious. Is it true you're rich because you're gonna inherit a gold mine out in California?"

"Did he—"

"Like I said, miss. Rumors spread fast."

I straightened my shoulders, fury overwhelming me. "Like I said, Mr. Gentry, my business is my own."

"Your business is mighty interesting to the wrong kind of folks. Keep that in mind."

He stood, grinning wide, and walked back to his seat. Charles and Ace both arrived at that moment and nodded to the drummer when he passed. Anger boiled inside me. I imagined the satisfaction of slapping the Texan in private. I'd trusted him and he betrayed me by talking freely to a man like Gentry. The drummer might be Emil Todaro's colleague, for all I knew. Kate patted my hand as if she sensed my nasty mood.

"Are you all right, Lily?"

"I will be."

Once I confronted Ace and received an answer, that is. He seemed oblivious to my frustration, tipping his hat over his eyes and stretching out. What did Gentry mean by the wrong kind of folks? Himself, or other men? I stared out the window when the train swept into a broad valley. Beautiful mountains ringed the meadows, filled with tiny yellow flowers and dotted with farms and villages. Several rivers meandered like shiny satin ribbons through rich grain fields. Despite the bright sunshine, my mind remained dark in a shadow world of betrayal.

The train stopped at Ogden Station for passengers to disembark. Weary of sitting so long, Charles, Kate and I left the Palace car to stroll on the platform with other passengers. After days of enduring stuffy air and sweat-soaked clothing, I inhaled the fresh clean air despite the dusty grit that accompanied it. Ace headed for a knot of men further off, so I started in his direction. Aunt Sylvia and Sir Vaughn blocked my way.

"Since Mr. Todaro is dead," my aunt said, "are you sure you want to continue on? We could wire Harrison to meet us in Reno and then return home."

I shook off her grip on my upper arm. "I'm going to Sacramento."

She shook her head. "A young woman your age cannot be too careful to guard her reputation. Harrison would want me to keep an eye on you."

Sir Vaughn stepped forward. "You came close to being killed at Dale Creek, Miss Granville. You must realize we have your best interests in mind."

"I am aware of that—"

"Mr. Diamond may fail to protect you if there is a next time," my aunt interrupted. She glanced at Sir Vaughn, who cleared his throat. "My husband tells me that Texas ruffian has been bragging about you in the smoking car."

"Yes, I know," I said and gritted my teeth.

"What's this about giving him a bonus once you reach California?"

Stunned, I glanced at Ace who had joined Kate and Charles at the platform's end. So Gentry's warning was true. If Ace had been bragging about the Early Bird gold mine, that could cause more trouble than I'd experienced with Emil Todaro. I tapped my foot on the wooden boards. Should I fire Ace? His ticket was good all the way to Sacramento, however. He'd stick like a pesky burr to a blanket.

"I'll talk to Mr. Diamond, Aunt Sylvia."

"The damage has been done, I'm afraid." She took

her husband's arm. "Come along, Sir Vaughn. It's no use talking to her."

Together they returned to the Palace car. I hurried toward Kate, Ace and Charles, who gestured to a white-bearded gentleman. He met two younger women, close to my age with squalling infants in their arms, and an older woman standing near a small paint-worn stagecoach. They all embraced warmly. I assumed the older man was the younger women's father, but Charles smirked.

"Mormons," he said in a low voice. "Some have over a dozen wives. The government's tried to outlaw the practice for years."

"Do you think he married all three women?" Kate asked and shook dust from her striped skirt. "I can't imagine living like that."

Charles nodded. "I heard Brigham Young, their leader, has at least fifty."

"Is that right. He's a mighty busy man then," Ace said with a mischievous grin. "If we don't have time for a beer at the saloon, then I'll see you ladies later."

"Just a minute, Mr. Diamond," I said and marched after his retreating figure. I slapped a fly away from my hat brim. "I hear you've been talking about how rich I am, and the bonus I'm supposed to give you when we reach California."

"So?"

He signaled to one of the barefoot children who walked back and forth on the platform with shiny tin pails or napkin-lined baskets. A red-cheeked girl wearing a snowy pinafore over her yellow and white gingham dress sold him an apple and a chunk of cheese between slices of brown bread. Ace pocketed the fruit and took a huge bite of the sandwich. My anger fueling me, I tracked the Texan to the smoking car.

"Mr. Diamond, you must realize the danger has not passed. Emil Todaro may be dead, but his accomplice could be on this train."

His boots clattered up the iron steps before he turned to face me. "Maybe, but I kept my end of the bargain at Dale Creek. I earned twice that thirty dollars, in fact, climbing down that scaffold. You kicked me so hard, I'm lucky I didn't fall myself."

"It's not that I don't appreciate your efforts—"

"Good. I'll be lookin' forward to that bonus then."

"Wait! I'm not finished," I said and caught his coat's suede fringe. "Have you been telling people about my father's murder? And the Early Bird mine?"

"Don't know what you're talkin' about, Lily."

Ace headed inside the door before I could protest. The train lurched, signaling its departure from Ogden. Furious, I climbed the steps and then pushed my way past the portly gentleman in the doorway. The smoky interior smelled awful. Spittoons in every corner had spatters of brown tobacco stains on the floor surrounding them. Men glanced up from their newspapers, pipes and cigarettes, their shock laughable. The majority of them stood when I walked down the aisle. I sensed their displeasure at my invasion and heard muttered complaints behind my back.

I intended to get a truthful answer from Ace, though.

He stood at the polished wooden bar, one foot on the brass rail. Behind the counter, the porter's eyes grew huge and beer from the tap foamed over the glass he held in his hand. He shut the spigot, wiped the excess with a damp towel and clanked the drink in front of the Texan. The porter's tone dripped politeness when he addressed me.

"I sure am sorry, miss. Ladies ain't allowed in this here car."

"I am aware of that. Mr. Diamond, I must speak to you. Now."

Ace took a sip of his beer and then eyed the other men in the car before he swiveled his head. "Go ahead. I'm among friends," he said with a wink.

"Outside—please."

Without waiting for his reply, I retraced my steps. Most of the gentlemen scrambled to stand once more when I passed their seats. They were welcome to the car's plush armchairs, fringed lamps and grimy windows. I had no desire to linger. Outside on the open platform, I gulped fresh air. The car's hard rattling threw me backwards. Ace caught me, his strong hands around my waist, but didn't let go when I twisted around to face him. I grabbed the iron post. He held me against it, his mouth near my ear, arms surrounding me.

"Must be in a frisky mood if you dragged me out here."

"I'm not—"

The warmth of his body and roving hands sent delicious shivers through me. I flinched from the roughness of his jaw against my earlobe, but his breath danced along the sensitive skin there. It gave me visions of what I'd never experienced with Charles or any other man—a hint of reckless passion and stolen kisses. I couldn't move when his lips nuzzled downward along my bare neck. When I breathed deeper, my bosom pressed against his hard chest. I placed both gloved hands there but could not budge him.

159

"Mr. Diamond, this is not why I asked you out here."

Ace pulled his head back. "You sure, Lily?"

"It's Miss Granville," I said sternly and shoved harder. A bad idea, since the train jolted me off balance. I had to grab his arm and the post. "I want a straight answer about what you've been telling people about my inheritance and the Early Bird mine."

"What mine? You never told me anything about a mine."

I stared at his puzzled expression and one green eye with its cornea's jagged pattern. Had I ever mentioned it to him? I did tell him about Uncle Harrison's business in Reno. Charles knew about the deed, and so did Kate—but not Ace. I'd kept him in the dark about that.

"I-I heard rumors."

"From who?" He cupped my face with one rough hand. "That Sir Van again?"

I dodged away from his touch. "I don't know who."

"I seen Sir Van talking to Mason while I was playing poker," Ace said. "Now what's this about an Early Bird mine? Or ain't you gonna tell me?"

"I'm not sure I should."

"Because you don't trust me, is that it?"

"I never said that, Mr. Diamond." I noted the worry crease between his eyes. "It's not a matter of trust. The less people know about it, the better."

"Seems the cat's outta the bag already." Ace rubbed the dark stubble on his jaw. "Let me guess then. You told me Todaro stole something valuable. Must be this deed, right?"

I nodded. "Yes. If he'd succeeded in pushing me off the bridge, then Uncle Harrison would have a harder fight in

160

court to claim the Early Bird," I said and bit my lip. "Todaro must have thought I had a copy of the deed. He searched my things in Omaha."

"Hm." Ace snagged a stray blonde curl between his fingers. "So how rich are you, Lily? Maybe that bonus ought to be tripled."

I looked up the moment his mouth descended on mine. The shock, the musky scent of Ace and the unfamiliar taste of him collided with the excitement of that heady kiss. His tongue snaked over my bottom lip, which sent another shock wave from my head to my toes.

"Lily Rose Granville!" Aunt Sylvia's booming voice shook me out of my frozen state.

Ace drew away, his eyes hooded, his breathing shallow. She slammed the door of the Palace car. Ace slipped inside the smoking car without a word to me or Aunt Sylvia.

Leaving me alone to face her wrath.

'… whoso putteth his trust in the Lord shall be safe.' Proverbs
29:25

Chapter Fourteen

"What game are you playing, Lily?" Aunt Sylvia's
horror emphasized the crow's feet near her eyes and the
pinched shaped of her mouth. "How could you allow that
man to ruin your reputation and honor?"

"My honor and reputation are intact—"

"We warned you of the rumors circulating about
your behavior, but you seem determined to defy any
common sense. Have you no shame?"

I faced her, my cheeks hot, with matching anger.
"What right have you to judge me? Father told me you ran
away from home at fifteen to go on stage. And that's why
the family disowned you."

"You dare throw that in my face?" Her eyes blazed
and a fleck of spittle formed at the corner of her mouth. "I
married that actor. I didn't throw myself at men without any

breeding or manners. Three ladies saw you out here, kissing that ruffian in public! What would your Father say? He'd horsewhip any ex-Rebel soldier who dared to lay a hand on you."

"Leave my father out of this."

"Not even a week in his grave—"

I pushed past her and crossed to the other platform. The door yanked out of my grip and Charles stood there, his eyes reflecting hurt and bewilderment. I swept past him as well. Without a doubt he'd heard about the kiss by now. Charles must have discussed the gold mine with Sir Vaughn, which started the rumors. I plopped down next to Kate, my fury increasing, and shook my head when she whispered under her breath.

"Oh, Lily! Are you—I hope you're all right."

I shook my head. Tears burned my eyes, but I raised my chin in defiance. One thing my aunt said hit home. I ought to be mourning Father, not forgetting him. Confusion had blurred everything. The ordeal of Cheyenne, coupled with my near death at Dale Creek, and then seeing Emil Todaro's smashed-in skull, had taken its toll on my fragile emotions. I couldn't blame Ace. I was to blame for letting down my guard.

I fled toward the Ladies' washroom. Several pairs of eyes followed me, reflecting the condemnation at my behavior. I locked myself inside and sat on the commode's wooden seat, inhaled deep breaths and tried to think. Words and images jumbled together, and I patted my damp face and neck with a clean handkerchief. I pulled out the sketchbook Father had given me and opened it to the inscription. Splotches marked the vellum where I'd wept over his beloved handwriting. Closing the leather book, I hugged it to my chest and wept.

My stomach muscles knotted and I leaned my aching head against the wall. I'd betrayed Father. I'd also betrayed Charles, as surely as he'd betrayed me.

Did it matter, though?

Had I ever been serious about accompanying him to China? Father had not approved of the idea. I doubted if Uncle Harrison would either. I hadn't seen him since Mother's funeral. What would my uncle think about Ace Diamond? What did I think of him? I relived that moment when he'd kissed me, remembering the gentle touch on my cheek, the playful look in his odd eyes, the pressure of his hard body against mine.

His words haunted me. *So how rich are you, Lily?*

I'd failed to consider his underlying meaning. Ace played poker after all. Was he no better than Charles, who wanted to use my fortune to get to China? I straightened up, regained my composure and dried my tears. Once I washed my face, I felt better. I glanced in the wavy mirror. My hair was unkempt, the short wisps curling around my ears. I spent time combing the tangled tresses and gathered it in a soft knot.

"I have to get to Sacramento."

The train's rattling wheels drowned out my shaky words. Now my focus would be narrowed to three things. Not Charles, not Kate or even Ace Diamond. Not Aunt Sylvia or her husband, and their stubborn determination to follow me from Evanston to California as so-called chaperones. Three things only.

Sacramento. Uncle Harrison. The Early Bird gold mine deed.

****

We passed Corinne, the second to last station on the Union Pacific line, which proved to be a cluster of weathered shacks and sheds, alkali dust and few people. I'd read about its terrible reputation in the newspaper last year, and even Father had remarked about the lawless town where the weary railroad workers had gambled, fought over soiled doves and drank themselves into early graves. I stared out the window to avoid Charles and the lingering accusation in his eyes. Ace, slumped in the opposite seat, had tipped his hat over his eyes.

"Ouch! Did they build this track on shifting sand?" Kate asked and rubbed her elbow. "It's never been this rough—oh!"

No one said anything for the next half hour. Kate and I both jumped, though, when the train shifted hard as if it might tip off the track. Broken tools, soil piles and bent spikes had been left abandoned here and there beside the sloping grade. Rising halfway from my seat, I peered at a cluster of buildings half a mile ahead.

"Promontory Station," the conductor sang out. "The Central Pacific depot can verify your transfers to the Silver Palace car."

Within minutes, passengers clogged the aisle in a hurry to disembark. I folded my shawl and stuffed it inside my valise. Kate scrabbled for her baggage claim ticket in her bag. I did the same, my heart in my throat, and emptied the entire contents of my pocketbook in my lap. Kate found hers snagged in the lining's bottom seam. I came up empty.

"I know I put it—oh, no."

"Wait, Lily. Maybe it's in your book," Kate said. The train slowed while we searched for the third time. "There's a line already at the ticket window. Take your time."

"But we have to make sure our tickets transfer."

"Here, I'll go stand in line while you check for your baggage," Charles said. "Diamond, do you still have your train ticket? Or did you lose it at poker?"

"I got it right here," Ace said and dug it from his pocket.

"Too bad."

Charles plucked mine and Kate's as well and then hurried to line up in the aisle and disembark. How could I have not noticed it was missing? Ace, Kate and I searched each item, flipped through the pages of my novel and sketchbook, and then gave up at last. I realized then that Emil Todaro must have stolen the claim ticket in Omaha.

"I'd better check out my trunk," I said. "You don't have to tag along—"

"Oh yes, we do," Kate said and stuffed everything back into my pocketbook. "Mr. Diamond will escort us. We can't take any chances, Lily."

I trailed Kate out of the empty Palace car, followed by Ace. Despite being upset, I remained acutely aware of the Texan's presence behind me. My nerves tingled when he touched the small of my back, a gentle warning to avoid a porter who struggled with a heavy trunk on his shoulder. The hot sunshine beat down on my head, and I coughed on the choking acrid alkali dust raised by the crowd and the wagons lumbering past. The bitter taste parched my throat. I had no peppermints left to mask that taste either.

People crowded around the baggage car with claim tickets in hand. The porters unloaded trunks, valises and cartons as fast as possible, sweat pouring down their dark faces, oblivious to the noise and chatter surrounding them.

Once I described my small trunk, Ace shouldered his way past several rough men and hauled himself up into the baggage car. He disappeared inside while I waited, one gloved hand over my mouth. Kate waved a handkerchief in front of her face in vain. The alkali dust coated the rough buildings and roofs, the wooden walkways, the train platform and everyone's clothing.

Chaos reigned. Several men bumped into me or Kate, apologized and then ended up being shoved along with us into the baggage car's siding. I lost my footing and fell, my straw hat knocked askew over one eye, but someone set me upright. Tom Gentry, the drummer—who flashed his stained smile and tipped his hat.

"My pleasure, miss. You waiting for someone?"

"Yes. Over here, Mr. Diamond!"

Relief swept me when Ace jumped to the ground, one hand on my trunk's leather strap. He hefted it onto his shoulder and carried it toward an open shed. One porter followed, dodging us and other travelers, shaking his head and frowning.

"You can't take that, not without a claim ticket. I gotta stick to the rules, sir."

"I told you, the lady lost her ticket."

"My job's to see all unclaimed baggage goes to the right office. You be gettin' me in trouble if you take something without a claim ticket."

"That's my trunk," I said. "I wanted to make sure it hadn't been stolen."

"Well, it ain't. But you can't keep it, miss. No siree. Not without a ticket."

"Then please take it to the Central Pacific baggage car."

"Can't do that without a claim ticket."

Ace knelt down to examine the lock. "Lily, you better take a look at this. Someone jimmied it open. Lots of marks on the brass here, from a knife or tool."

Once he unstrapped it, the trunk's contents tumbled to the ground. "Someone twisted the frame of my parents' picture and broke the glass," I said in dismay.

Kate stooped to recover the photograph before it blew away in the wind. "How awful. Here I thought the railroad kept our baggage safe."

The porter looked confused. "Only way to get anything from that car is with a claim ticket, miss. Iffen you done lost it, then you can't blame the Union Pacific."

"Is the baggage car locked?" Ace asked, but the porter shook his head. "So anyone could have walked in there."

"Not without a claim ticket, they couldn't. Lots of people come in to fetch what they need during the trip, but they gotta show a claim ticket."

I picked shards of glass out of my spare clothing. Kate helped to fold and repack my things, although they'd picked up a fine sheen of white powder. That couldn't be avoided. Ace had disappeared while we worked and came back with a length of twine. He tied the trunk, length and width-wise and knotted the twine with expertise. He rose from his haunches with a dissatisfied expression.

"Anyone with a knife can cut that, but chances are they took what they wanted."

"Or didn't find it," I muttered. "We'd better check to see if Charles—"

I coughed into my handkerchief, my throat so dry it hurt. "I'm thirsty too, Lily," Kate said. "There must be some restaurant with water."

"Charles first."

My words sounded like a frog's croak. We circled back and found Charles stood in the line's middle, far from the ticket window. I brushed alkali dust from his suit coat. He agreed to find us later. Many crude wooden storefronts had canvas tents behind them. Signs proclaimed 'Red Cloud,' 'Meals All Hours' or 'Keno, Faro, Monte' among others. Aunt Sylvia and Sir Vaughn stood in line at the Echo Bakery and Restaurant adjacent to the Pacific Hotel. People snaked around the building, speaking in low voices and complaining about the bitter dust.

Few trees offered shade from the blazing sun. I could hardly swallow, and talking was out of the question. Kate, Ace and I searched the street for anyone selling even a dipperful of water. We did find a small shop with horehound candy, but that proved to give little relief. I had to force myself not to rub my itchy eyes. Ace left us beneath a stoop with a sliver of shade and returned in a few minutes with a glass of warm beer.

I sipped it. I hated the yeasty taste but was grateful for its wetness. Kate gulped twice. Ace finished the beer and wiped his mouth.

"Nothin' better for a thirsty man."

"How much time until we leave, Lily?" Kate asked. I drew out Father's pocket watch and opened the case. "That must be solid gold. Is it?"

"Yes, it was my father's. We have less than an hour before departure," I said. "I'd like to find a few newspapers for Charles."

Ace snorted. "Can't he get his own?"

"He's been standing in the hot sun, Mr. Diamond, so

I'm returning the favor."

"I'm still thirsty. How about you, Miss Kimball?"

"Oh, no." She shot a guilty look at Ace. "I'm sorry I didn't save more for you."

"Don't you worry none. I'll be back in a minute. I think they were selling ginger beer, Lily—Miss Granville. I'll fetch you both some."

Tipping his hat, Ace ducked inside the saloon again. Kate and I headed to the nearest butcher with his burlap bag. The boy showed me a variety of newspaper editions, old and new. I chose the small *Utah Magazine*, since Charles had shown interest in the Mormons, plus the *St. Louis Globe* and the *San Francisco Tribune*. Inside the latter, I scanned the top mines' production forecasts. I also noticed an advertisement for shares in a quicksilver mine near Walnut Creek, owned by John William Parker and Rupert Chester, along with a report of hydraulic mining improvements. Father had mentioned something about hydraulic mining. I couldn't recall the details.

"I'll have to ask Uncle Harrison about this," I said aloud, but waved a hand when Kate glanced at me. "It's not important. Oh my—but this article is. George Hearst is being sued in California over a boundary dispute."

I scanned the story about Hearst and a neighboring rancher in San Simeon. So others beside my uncle had court battles scheduled against the businessman. Ace appeared at my elbow, holding a glass of paler liquid. I accepted with a smile. Unfortunately, the taste proved no different.

"What's wrong? I paid extra for that ginger beer," he said, a hand on one hip.

"They swindled you, Mr. Diamond. This is the same warm beer, and even the same glass we used before." I surveyed the mass of fingerprints and the flecks of dirt and scum inside the rim. "Perhaps Charles might be interested."

Ace snatched the glass back and gulped half of it. We followed him back to the line. Charles stood close to the window, and drank the beer with a grateful nod.

"I thought we'd be able to visit the spot where the two railroads met," he said, his voice tinged with disappointment. "I know they didn't leave the Golden Spike, but they ought to have a marker of some kind."

"They'll do it," Ace said, "when enough people wanna pay to see it."

I smiled. "My uncle spent several months on a steamer when he first went to California. It's amazing that this trip is only taking a few days."

"Ladies, you'd better find some shade. This sun is brutal," Charles said.

Kate and I passed by the Silver Palace car waiting on the track ahead. Plainer in style than the Pullman version, it was narrower in width and smaller in length, and sported yellow paint without brass details or fancy carvings. The bakery no longer had a line. Inside I inhaled the delicious scent of cinnamon and yeasty bread. My mouth watered at the tempting sights of a crumb-topped pie and over half a dozen sugared doughnuts left in a tray behind the counter.

"I'm starving," Kate said. "There's your aunt, sitting at the back table. Was she really an actress on stage?"

"Yes. But let's not talk about her."

I paid for the remainder of the donuts along with soup, coffee and cream. The split pea broth had chunks of ham and tasted thick and rich. Aunt Sylvia hurried through the side door, skirts swishing, before Kate and I finished our coffee. I watched as she met Sir Vaughn on the street and disappeared out of my line of sight. Charles appeared at the bakery door and gave us a frantic wave. We left our coffee, although Kate stuffed her unfinished donut into her bag.

The first warning whistle sounded. Charles boosted me up the steps of the Silver Palace car and handed us our tickets. "I'm sorry, but I couldn't find seats together," he said. "The porter assured me we could switch when we arrive in Reno."

"We'll manage." I handed him the greasy paper bag of donuts. "These are for you, along with a few newspapers I picked up."

"Thank you—where's Diamond?" he asked Kate, who glanced behind her.

"I thought he was with you."

"Maybe we'll get lucky and he'll miss the train," Charles muttered, but I poked his arm.

"I owe him my life, remember."

"He's bothered you to no end since you took pity on him in Omaha."

"I will handle Mr. Diamond. Do you feel all right, after standing in line so long?"

Charles shrugged. "Don't worry about me. Maybe I could convince someone to switch seats, Lily, so we could discuss our trip to China."

"I'm not ready to discuss anything."

I took a ticket at random. Kate chose the seat at the far end of the car, closest to a group of ladies who sat with my aunt and her husband. "Maybe I'll hear all the latest gossip about you," she said, her eyes twinkling, "or start a few rumors myself."

"I'm sure they won't need any help," I said.

She laughed and checked my ticket. "You'll have

lots of time to sketch without anyone talking your ear off, unless someone snores like a sawmill blade."

I slipped into the empty seat near the front. The heavy-set gentleman across from me tipped his hat and resumed reading his paper. The past hour had shaken my nerves again. Todaro must have used the claim ticket between Omaha and Dale Creek bridge to search my trunk. Had he been looking for money? He could have taken the roll I'd hidden in my riding boots. Breaking the photograph's glass and twisting the frame suggested deep anger and resentment, or so it seemed. Yet Father had given Todaro steady employment, a good salary and loyalty since the War. He'd refused to fire the lawyer despite my frequent urging.

Two gentlemen claimed the seat behind me. I scanned the platform. Where was Ace? Had he heard the train's whistle for departure? I had no idea where he'd gone. He'd left right after I fussed over Charles's coat, although I hadn't paid attention to which direction. Perhaps the saloon where he'd bought the beers? He might even be sitting in the smoking car right now. Irritated, I perused the few seats open as our fellow passengers filed into the car. I shoved my pocketbook into Kate's hands.

"I'm going to find him."

"It's too late," Charles said. "He must be—"

The last warning screech drowned out his words. A crowd had gathered near the saloon, blocking my view, and then parted like a curtain when several men crashed into the open. One man tumbled into a stack of baggage, while another swung a vicious hook at his opponent. The train started inching away from the platform.

Heart in my throat, I peered through the grimy

window at the swaying fringe on the man's jacket. It couldn't be Ace, brawling in the street again! The track curved, and I lost sight of the men. Within a minute, the train picked up speed and covered Promontory Station in a cloud of white dust.

Astonished, sick at heart, I leaned against Charles in despair.

'...the wicked shall be put out. . .for he is cast into a net by his own feet.'
Job 18:5-8

Chapter Fifteen

Disbelief drowned out all other emotions, except irritation and then anger. How could Ace do this to me? I would be at the mercy of Emil Todaro's colleague with only Charles as a protector. I tugged on Charles' sleeve. Startled, he caught his spectacles before they hit the floor.

He rose to his feet.

"What's wrong?"

"Do you still have Ace's ticket?" I asked. "Check your pockets."

Charles searched and drew out two stubs. "I thought I gave it to him."

"Oh, for heaven's sakes. You said you hoped he'd miss the train, too."

"I didn't mean it, Lily."

"Both of you have acted so childish—"

175

"He must be in the smoking car," Charles said. "Why are you worried? Diamond's the type who can take care of himself."

"I saw him fighting near the saloon with two men," I said, one hand on my hip. "He missed the train, I'm sure of it. Now what are we going to do?"

"Same as we did before, Lily. We don't need him. There's no chance we'll have any more trouble."

"You don't know that for certain."

He squeezed my shoulders with a reassuring smile, his warm brown eyes reflecting care and affection. "Don't worry. Everything will work out."

I hoped he was right. Charles tucked my hand into the crook of my elbow and escorted me back to the front of the car, although I barely listened to his soothing words. I figured we had one night, perhaps two at the most, before arriving in Sacramento. I didn't feel safe without Ace here, but I did have the stiletto he'd given me. I could place it under my pillow. Maybe I could stitch the curtains together from the inside.

"—teach the children. It wouldn't be difficult, you'll love them. Did you hear me, Lily? Aren't you excited about doing missionary work?"

"I'm sorry, what?" I noted his disappointment but didn't apologize. "I cannot concentrate on anything now. I'm too worried."

"But it's over now that Todaro is dead. The Lord takes his vengeance on the wicked."

"I told you I saw two men the night my father was killed," I said. "It's not over until we reach Uncle Harrison."

"Do you really think he'll give you permission?" Charles grasped both of my hands between his own. "You ought to make your own decision."

"I can't marry you and go to China. I'm sorry."

His smile faded. "You promised to think about it."

"I have. I don't have the same zeal for mission work as you do."

"I'll give you time to change your mind—"

Loud voices wafted from the back of the car. I whirled to see two porters rushing toward the washroom. Several gentlemen hurried to help, Charles included. Kate slid against the window when one man sprawled in the aisle. I heard a familiar Texas drawl tinged with anger.

"You can't deny it, you lily-livered coward! You hired those men."

"I say, porter, you ought to throw this ruffian off the train."

"If you don't stop your threats, young man, I will have to do that," the porter said. Ace grunted in disgust when Sir Vaughn brushed dust from his coat and straightened his cuffs.

"You cannot enter this car, sir, without a valid ticket," the porter said to Ace and blocked him. "I'll have to inform the conductor if you refuse to cooperate."

I'd already pulled Charles toward the group of men. "We have his ticket. Mr. Diamond is with our party."

Charles handed over the stub. "Here it is."

The porter accepted it and checked the date. "All right, sir. My apologies."

"What happened?" Kate asked. "We thought you'd missed the train."

My aunt glared at me when the Texan pushed past Sir Vaughn. "Trouble, but nothin' big enough to stop me."

"Your hands are bleeding again," I said and handed

him my last handkerchief. "How did you manage to catch the train after all?"

"Grabbed the last car's railing," he said. Ace wrapped his red-stained knuckles. "Got dragged a bit before I could climb the dad-burned steps. Nearly lost my grip."

"How did you get into a fight?"

"Two men jumped me inside the saloon. Neither of 'em tall and thin, if that's what you mean. I had a devil of a time gettin' free of them."

"We're glad you did," Kate said loyally. "You lost your tie, though."

Ace glanced around the car. "Looks like a full house in here."

I examined his ticket. "It's all creased, I can't read it."

"He can have my seat," Charles said and held out the stub. "I'll take his."

Suspicious, I eyed the car from front to back. "It looks like there's an open seat close to mine, Mr. Diamond. Your ticket must correspond to it."

"Good. I can keep an eye on you in case there's more trouble."

Ace lumbered down the aisle and plopped down in the seat across the aisle and one ahead of mine. Charles turned away, but I caught the flash of guilt across his face. I plucked his coat sleeve and lowered my voice to a whisper.

"Were you behind this?"

"What are you talking about?" His eyes shifted along with his feet. Deep red blotches colored his cheeks, but not from sunburn. "I didn't hire those men to fight him. He's not worth that kind of money."

He wasn't a good liar. "Charles, I understand that

you don't like Ace. Perhaps the feeling is mutual," I whispered, "but you both have to work together."

"I promised to act as your escort, Lily. Not watch you make a—" He stopped and inhaled, as if fighting to control his temper. His voice dropped lower and I had to strain to hear his next words. "You will reach your uncle. I won't fail you in that."

"Thank you."

Charles stalked back to the car's opposite end, beet red from the top of his shirt collar to the roots of his fair hair. I followed slowly. He watched him adjust his spectacles and straighten his collar and tie. I knew what he'd wanted to say before stopping himself. Charles must have heard my aunt's claim that I'd ruined my reputation with Ace. I sat down in my seat and ignored everyone. My temples throbbed, but I couldn't relax. The train's constant jarring and shaking worsened my headache. The donut I'd eaten felt like a lump in my knotted stomach.

I'd hoped to catch a glimpse of the Great Salt Lake. A pale gray shimmer to the south suggested water, since the tracks skirted the northern side. I'd read the lake was many times saltier than the ocean and contained only brine shrimp and flies. I did see huge flocks of birds wheeling overhead, and a smaller number of gulls, ducks, swans and geese. So different from Lake Michigan's beauty, with its deep navy water brimming with fish, and sailboats skimming the surface.

I didn't bother sketching. The dull scenery didn't inspire me, with so much sagebrush sprouting on the rocky plain. I'd never realized that gray and brown had so many different shades, from light smoke to smudge, from beige to warm chocolate. A stronger homesickness washed over me. I pictured Etta and Cook in the hot kitchen back in Evanston, eating supper or chatting over cake and tea. I missed them, and Father too.

More than ever I longed for clean clothes, a feather mattress, a meal at home. The seat cushions proved thinner than in the Pullman car, the windows mere single panes which allowed more alkali dust inside. Their incessant rattling grated my nerves raw. While my rib's soreness had eased somewhat, my backside suffered worse. I walked the aisle with restless energy. Most of the passengers dozed or read newspapers.

I studied the back of Charles' head, the pattern of his slick blond-brown hair, the set of his hunched shoulders. Why was he so jealous? I'd never agreed to wed or accompany him for certain. He had to face that. I paced back and forth, thinking hard, ignoring Ace's flirtatious smiles or quirked eyebrows. Maybe Charles hadn't paid those men, but he may have encouraged them. Who else would want him out of the way?

Todaro's colleague… if he existed.

I rubbed my throbbing temples when I paused near the car's door, my eyes closed. So much had happened since the incident at Dale Creek. I tried to remember feeling that hard shove from behind. I hadn't seen Todaro fall. But I'd never forget the echoing yell. Charles had not reached down to help me, but I wondered if he really had hurt his shoulder and arm. He'd abandoned the muslin sling within hours of the incident.

"You all right, Lily?"

I glanced up to see Ace blocking my way. "Yes. I'm thinking."

"She doesn't need your help, Diamond," Charles

said from behind him and gestured to the Men's washroom. "If you'll excuse me."

"Sure thing." Ace's arm circled my waist and pulled me back against his chest. "Go right ahead. We'll be thinkin' together while you're busy."

Charles waited, as if expecting me to protest. When I remained silent, he stormed past and entered the tiny room. The door slammed. I twisted free of Ace's hold.

"Must you bait him, Mr. Diamond?"

"Who, Mason?" Ace flashed that mischievous grin. "He's just sore—"

"He's a good friend. I hope you'll remember that."

I sank down beside the window. My heart thumped in my ears. Deep heat flushed my cheeks, and I couldn't deny the thrill that had flooded my senses when Ace pulled me close. I'd reveled in a sense of security. His rock-hard arm did more than support and steady me.

He must have sensed a change in our relationship, given the way his palm splayed against my abdomen. One thumb had brushed the upward curve of my bosom. Ace knew he was no longer a mercenary. We were now equals after the ordeal at Dale Creek. Our shared close call with death forged a bond and stamped a claim on me. Still, I had no intention of allowing him further intimacy. That stolen kiss had been foolish on my part.

It would not happen again.

****

I walked past Aunt Sylvia, whose head rested on her husband's shoulder. Both dozed in their wide seat. With each throbbing snore, her chin trembled. Wisps of gray escaped the mass of elaborate braids pinned beneath her small velvet hat. She had a vulnerable air, nothing like the domineering woman who'd barged into my life for Father's funeral. On my way back, I studied Sir Vaughn from his gray leonine head to his shoe spats.

His gold-rimmed monocle hung across his rumpled waistcoat. The skin beneath his eyelids looked puffy and limp like his shirt collar, and his veined hand clasped Aunt Sylvia's. They resembled the perfect married couple.

"Excuse me, miss."

The porter dodged me and resumed lighting the lamps. The brilliant red, gold and orange sky had faded to thin streaks between dark blue and purple on the western horizon. Ace's fingertips brushed my skirt when I walked past toward the car's front seats. By the time I glanced back by the doorway, he'd put his pocketknife away and tilted his hat over his face. I noted the tiny smile at the corners of his mouth, however. Perhaps he expected me to signal him in return. I fought the temptation, since I'd encouraged him enough for one day.

The train passed by several tiny stations in Nevada. Their names sounded odd: Deeth, Halleck, Peko, Osino and Elko, where smudges of distant mountains rose up against the sky far away. The crew loaded water and coal at the rustic settlement, treeless and dusty, while the porters prepared the berths.

I glanced at Aunt Sylvia and Sir Vaughn, who fussed with the draperies and complained about the comfort of their thin cushions. Kate had chosen the narrow shelf above them. Charles had already vanished inside his own, somewhere in the car's middle, while Ace stretched out in his upper berth. He'd taken off his jacket but not his boots. Did he always sleep in his clothes? The man below him fought over control of the draperies. Ace unhooked one side at the top and tucked part of it under his thin cushion. That compromise apparently satisfied them.

"Hotter than blazes up here," he said. "But this way, I can keep an eye on anyone sneaking around in the middle of the night. Sleep well, Lily."

"Good night, Mr. Diamond."

I climbed into my own berth. The flimsy drapes billowed too often for comfort, gaping open at times, so I searched for my sewing kit. Several straight pins held the fabric together at a few strategic points. Relieved, I slipped out of my jacket, waist, skirt and shoes. I debated over donning my nightdress or not. Out of propriety, I slipped it over my head and retrieved the pins. Let the curtains gape if they would. I plumped the pillow, stretched out and closed my eyes.

Unfortunately, the memory of Ace's mouth covering my own haunted me. I squirmed and rolled over. The clattering wheels echoed his teasing words.

How rich are you...how rich are you...

I'd never thought of myself as rich. My maternal grandparents had been. Their Puritan roots extended far back into New York State's history. They'd lived in the Hudson River valley, owned a quarry, brick factories and ice warehouses, plus a substantial amount of land. From what Father told me, my mother never acted superior to others. She may have been born to a wealthy family, but they lived simply.

Father had grown up in eastern Ohio, the son of a carriage maker. He'd learned the trade and then invested Mother's dowry in Chicago businesses long before the War. Money brought comfort, so he always said, but he also cautioned to never become its servant. He hadn't been impressed by any of the young men who attended the parties among my set. Charles, with his earnest desire to help the Chinese convert to Christianity, seemed to have both—the third son of a good family, with ambition to help others and the world.

I'd admired his character, but never felt any spark from his touch.

Ace, on the other hand, was an enigma. I knew nothing about his family except for his brothers, living and dead. He wasn't educated. He'd never learned manners. Sir Vaughn claimed he'd killed a man. The Texan claimed otherwise. I didn't know which of them to trust. Had this wild adventure left me vulnerable to a man like Ace Diamond? Would I have allowed him to kiss me otherwise?

I didn't want to answer that.

Long after the lamps had been extinguished and cooler desert air invaded the Silver Palace car, I grew more restless. At last I threw off the muslin sheet. I'd never be able to sleep with all that racket beneath my head. I slipped between the draperies, grateful for the darkness, although my eyes adjusted to the shadowy curtains and empty aisle. I groped for Ace's boot. He grunted something, so I kept my voice to a whisper.

"Will you trade berths with me? I can't sleep, it's so noisy."

He poked his head out between the curtains. "No thanks, it's hot down there too. You're welcome to join me up here, though."

"Don't be absurd."

"What? You afraid of me?" His hand snaked behind my head, caressing the knot of my hair loose. "This sure feels like silk."

"If you won't trade with me—"

"Did you say you'd like to trade, miss?" Another head emerged from the berth above my own. The heavy-set gentleman's fists clutched the draperies tight, as if he feared rolling out. "I'm having trouble sleeping myself. I'd be happy to switch with you."

I sighed in relief. Ace had ducked back into his berth while I waited for the gentleman to climb down. His bare foot caught my sore shoulder, but I stifled a gasp. Once he straightened his nightshirt, he disappeared into my lower berth with a long sigh. I tossed my valise overhead, along with my pocketbook, and then placed one foot on the lower berth.

"Need help?"

"I'll be fine, Mr. Diamond."

I boosted myself up, but slipped and banged my knee. Pain shot through my bones. Gritting my teeth, I planted my foot farther in and swung my other knee as high as I could reach. A hand grabbed the back of my nightdress and tossed me upward like a rag doll.

"I hit my head on the ceiling, thanks to you."

He chuckled low. "Don't mention it."

Someone else spoke up. "Shh! People are trying to sleep over here."

Once I'd crawled the rest of the way into the berth, I drew the curtains behind me and let out a long breath. The cushion beneath me was thinner. I wished I'd brought my cleaner linens from the lower berth, too. The rattling wheels receded as I drifted off to sleep.

My pleasant dream of sitting with my parents at home on a Sunday afternoon changed in swift progression: I aimed a pistol at an animal, a snake that hunted the underbrush for Lucretia. Stairs appeared before my eyes, and I climbed them to search the wardrobes, under the beds, behind a washstand for something I'd lost. Then I stood in the library, and saw my father's pipe and the blood-spattered desk blotter. Screams brought me out of the darkness to a pale diffusion of light. The light of dawn, and the train's swaying movement.

But the screams didn't stop.

'For they intended evil against thee...' Psalm 21:10

Chapter Sixteen

"What is it? What happened?"

"Ladies, gentlemen, calm down now—"

The train's brakes hissed. I stuck my head between the curtains and saw several women with shawls over their nightdresses, weeping openly. The conductor herded everyone away and shouted over their questions. Aunt Sylvia joined the other women while Sir Vaughn poked his head out of their berth.

"What is all this ruckus?"

Closing the curtains, I hurried to get dressed. I had less room than in the lower berth, but managed to struggle into my skirt and button my shirtwaist. Shoeless, I slipped downward onto the carpet and stepped in a sticky wet puddle. Had it rained overnight?

I glanced at my white cotton stocking, which had turned crimson.

Blood also stained the sheets of the empty berth below mine. Clapping a hand over my mouth, I clawed open the curtains of the opposite upper berth but it was empty. Where was Ace? And what happened to the man who'd exchanged places with me? Confused, I stripped off both stockings and left them on the floor. Then I followed a trail of blood to the car's front and saw the conductor huddled with two porters. Ace stood behind them, hatless, his shirt open. His glistening bare chest with a thatch of dark hair proved a worse shock to my senses.

"I didn't kill Robinson," he said, and slipped on an over-the-shoulder holster with his Colt revolver. "I seen a few people go back and forth to the washroom through the night."

"Did any of them stop at the man's berth?" the conductor asked.

"I wasn't awake the whole night."

"And neither of you saw or heard anything?" The porters shook their heads. The conductor frowned. "Seems odd that the victim wouldn't cry out."

"With all that blood, he was dead in an instant," Ace said, "or near to it. Whoever killed him used a knife, real quick."

"I seen him with a huge knife, sir," one Negro porter said to the conductor. "Ain't nobody else I seen with one on this here train."

"What, this?" Ace unfolded his pocketknife. "Do you see any blood on it?"

"What's in that flap?" The conductor tapped the sheath on the Texan's belt. "You can't tell me that's a butter knife."

Ace pulled out his Bowie knife. "You better search

all the men on this here train, then, not just me. I'll bet a gold eagle they all carry knives of some sort."

"That could be. Once we get to Reno, we'll have a doctor examine the body. He might be able to tell what kind of knife was used." The conductor noticed me, his eyes narrower, and gestured. "Miss, please go back to your berth."

"I-I switched berths with Mr. Robinson," I said, shivering, "and now he's dead."

"Switched berths?"

"It's my fault—"

"It's not your fault," Ace said and pushed past the railroad men. He cupped his rough hands around my face. "It's not, Lily."

Weary, I tugged free and stumbled down the aisle. Passengers who'd stuck their heads out to watch ducked back behind the draperies. Numb, sick at heart from a heavy burden of guilt, this second death cut me deep. I was responsible, no matter what Ace said. I'd been the intended victim. Emil Todaro's partner wanted me dead. No one but Ace knew that we had switched berths. Poor Mr. Robinson, who wanted to sleep in comfort. Now he was dead.

I opened the washroom door, closed it behind me and stood there, alone. My head pounded. The blood staining the carpet and sheets should have been mine. I lifted the commode's lid. The railroad ties flashed past below the open hole. Dizzy, I closed my eyes and heaved up bitter bile. I fought for control when nothing was left in my stomach and leaned against the train's shaking wall.

Despite my desperate prayers, heavy guilt plagued me.

****

Ace sat across the aisle with a sour expression and narrowed eyes. He'd been grilled by the conductor over his knife and revolver for close to an hour. Kate and I both vouched for him, explaining how he'd saved my life at Dale Creek. At last the Central Pacific official was satisfied that Ace had not stabbed Robinson. He hadn't been happy when the Texan refused to surrender his weapons. The conductor had asked each man about knives, although most refused to produce the ones they carried for protection.

"Your aunt's hysterical," Kate whispered to me. "Remember she said how we'd be murdered in these berths, with only a curtain—"

"Yes, I remember." I glanced at the knot of ladies near the washroom.

"I hope we don't have to spend another night on this train. I'll never close my eyes without being scared. Did you hear anything, Mr. Mason?"

Charles shook his head at Kate. "No. I slept through it all."

"What do you mean, you slept through it all?" Ace asked. "Those banshees screamed loud enough to wake the dead."

He crossed his arms and stared at the Texan. "What do you want, an apology?"

"I slept through it, too," Kate said, "although I heard the screaming. I thought it was a bad dream. Didn't you, Lily?"

"This whole trip's been a bad dream." I'd grown numb to the traumatic events of the past few days. "I wonder why the conductor questioned you and not the other men on the train?"

Ace turned to Charles. "Did he ask you anything, Mason?"

"No. I told you twice already that I slept through it all."

I stared at Charles. His flushed skin and downcast eyes confused me, along with the excuse he kept repeating. He sounded as if he'd rehearsed it. But why would he lie? Had he seen something last night? Or someone? Charles had never been secretive before, but things between us had changed since we left Evanston.

As for Mr. Robinson, I prayed for any loved ones he'd left behind.

The train soon pulled into Reno for breakfast. The Lake House hotel, a wide three-story frame building with a covered porch, stood south of the river and bridge. Inside, I chose a table near a window. The morning sunlight flushed the distant mountains with a bluish haze, and brightened the hills and plain near the river. We could see the busy train yard where crewmen loaded and unloaded cars with lumber, rolls of tarpaper, crates and barrels of various goods, even cattle. Scaffolding covered some larger buildings in the midst of construction.

Shacks and shanties filled the spaces along the streets, although most were saloons and shops for groceries or supplies. Many passengers disembarked from the train. The hotel's dining room was less crowded, a welcome relief.

"One of the ladies saw Mr. Robinson's arm stretched out between the curtains," Kate said. "That's how they found out he'd been killed."

"And the blood on the carpet," Ace pointed out. "I hit my head when I first heard that scream. Thought I was out on a cattle drive with a pack of ki-yotes roamin'

191

around."

A waiter in a loose dark blue tunic and pants set a platter of steak, potatoes, gravy and biscuits on the table. A long black braid twisted behind him when he whisked away soiled dishes from an adjoining table. Another silent waiter with the same Oriental features and outfit refilled our coffee cups. Kate was fascinated by their quick movements.

"I've never seen a Chinaman before. Can you speak their language, Mr. Mason?"

"A little," Charles said stiffly. "It's difficult to learn."

Kate glanced at me. "You ought to eat something, Lily. You're too pale."

"I'm not that hungry."

"You'll feel better with a square meal," Ace said.

Charles banged a fist on the table and slopped coffee over my cup's rim. "Stop telling her what to do. She does as she pleases, even when it comes to honoring her promises."

Stunned by his outburst, I picked up my fork. "That's not fair, Charles—"

"Excuse me."

With a black look, he threw down his napkin and departed. I watched him stalk toward the back of the dining room. His irritability and strange behavior stung me. He'd never lost his temper before, that I could remember, but I realized that the stress of this journey had affected us all. He must be suffering a sense of loss, perhaps betrayal, or disillusionment. But Charles had always talked of China in vague terms, never specifics. Perhaps the closer we came to California, the more he felt pressured to formalize his plans or give them up for good.

I doubted if he'd tell me which he preferred.

Kate acted hurt and ate without her usual chatter.

Despite the clatter of dishes and flatware around us, I took a few bites of juicy, tender steak and potatoes and then pushed my plate away. I breathed in deep to relax. Ace eyed my breakfast.

"You gonna finish that?"

"Help yourself. My stomach's all in knots."

"Never know when the next meal's comin'," he said cheerfully. Within a few minutes my plate was wiped clean. "That's one thing I learned in the War. Eat while the gettin' is good."

"It seems I haven't learned enough on this trip," I said, watching Charles as he left the restaurant. Another odd twist, since he'd hovered over me like a mother hen. Until Dale Creek.

Ace swiped the steak juice with a fresh biscuit and waved it. "You'll survive, Lily. You're a fighter, and that's sayin' a lot from me."

My cheeks grew warm. "I wish—well, that my plans had worked out better."

"You gotta roll with the punches."

"That's fitting advice coming from you," Kate said. "You might want to purchase a razor, Mr. Diamond, while we have the chance."

"Why? Somethin' wrong with my face?"

"I'm not surprised the conductor focused on you," I said, eyeing his dark stubble. "You hail from Texas, you're an ex-Confederate, and you look as disreputable as any outlaw."

He wiped his mouth. "You ever seen an outlaw?"

"No, but I'm sure you'd make good company among them."

"I doubt that." Ace leaned over the table. "For one

thing, I turned my own cousin in when he shot that man. He escaped, of course, but that was none of my doing."

"But you were blamed along with him?" I asked.

"I told the sheriff what I seen, except he didn't believe me. The fella who got himself shot cheated us at cards. My cousin took that as a personal insult."

"This was in Texas."

"Yep, near San Antone. I ain't never stole a dime from any man, not at cards nor any other way. I'm as fair a man as they come."

"That includes being rewarded with an extra bonus, I suppose." I noticed Kate brooding over her coffee. "Is something bothering you, too?"

"Mr. Mason is not himself," she said with a pout. "He's worried about having enough funds for his trip. He said he might have to raise twice the amount he expected—"

"Dearest Lily, are you all right? Have you recovered from that nasty fall?"

Aunt Sylvia stood at my elbow, one hand on the back of my chair. Her concern sounded genuine. Sir Vaughn walked over to join us. His monocle glinted in the sunlight from the window, blinding me. I nodded.

"Yes, I have. Thank you for asking."

"To think that poor man was stabbed in the night! Such a tragedy."

"Quite right," Sir Vaughn said and removed his monocle. "I have never heard of any violence on British trains. The private compartments are far superior."

"But couldn't someone walk in and rob the people inside, without anyone knowing?" Kate interrupted. "Or kill them, even."

He snorted. "Impossible, my dear young lady."

"Mrs. Ellis discovered that poor man, did you know?" Aunt Sylvia shook a gloved finger. "What a shock. His bloody arm was dangling between the curtains, and she fainted right there. Didn't I tell you back in Omaha about the dangers, Lily?"

"Lady Sylvia, we have errands," Sir Vaughn murmured and nodded to me. "Miss Granville, Miss Kimball, good day to you both."

He ignored Ace. The Texan had tipped his chair back and squinted under his hat at the older man. I watched my aunt's husband escort her out of the dining room and toward the open doorway of the trading post. Another woman, quite buxom and blonde, wearing a pale pink and green silk walking costume with an elaborate bustle, hailed them both. She caught Sir Vaughn's arm before he introduced her to Aunt Sylvia.

"Here," I said to Ace and handed him some coins from my pocketbook. "Pay the bill and escort Kate to the train. I'm going to eavesdrop if I can."

I walked out of the restaurant, following the threesome at a discreet distance. They headed inside a trading post. I heard snatches of their conversation from an open window, something about St. Louis and McVicker's theater in Chicago. Aunt Sylvia's shrill voice rose above all the other noises.

"Sir Vaughn urged me to resume my career, Dolly. I'm not going to fail—"

"I never said you would, Sylvia," the other woman said, "but don't expect it to be easy. Character parts, that's what you'll get. Better brush up on your other skills, old gal."

"You seem to be working that angle."

"It's steady money. Don't expect any stage manager to keep you for long."

Dolly flounced out of the shop and pushed past me without an apology. I followed her down the street and watched her avoid a pile of fresh horse dung. She increased her speed before I could overtake her and then disappeared into an alley. I hesitated at the first shrill whistle of the train, but peeked around the corner. A swirl of pink silk vanished through a saloon's side door.

I'd missed my chance to learn more about Aunt Sylvia and her husband.

*'How fair and how pleasant art thou, O love...' Song of Solomon
7:6*

Chapter Seventeen

The morning hours passed while the train snaked its
way toward the Sierra mountains. Ace found a few
gentlemen interested in cards. Kate dozed while Charles hid
his boyish face behind fresh newspapers. I opened my
sketchbook. My heart wasn't in it, but I managed to capture
a few brief landscapes of the crags and rocks, the closer
peaks, the churning Truckee River and clusters of birch and
aspen trees.

The tracks curved through shadowed valleys
between steeper rock faces thick with pines, following the
river bed, and emerged into sunlight at various points. I saw
snow-capped peaks ahead. The train stopped at Truckee to
load coal and water before starting the long climb to Summit
station. I'd never seen rough country like this, with no signs
of civilization. The wind's chill fingers invaded the car even

at midday.

Nestled between massive posts of an intricate series of snow sheds, the Summit Hotel loomed against the higher mountains. Other shops and buildings huddled around the sheds as if afraid of the thousand foot elevation, the bitter, cold winds and endless snowfall. Ace caught my elbow. Together we joined the line of passengers for lunch at the hotel. Bright sunlight warmed my face. I tightened my shawl anyway, chilled by an icy breeze.

"Did you win at poker, Mr. Diamond?"

"Some, until someone else stole my luck," he said. "Sure am glad we don't have to fight that alkali dust up here."

"I smell something delicious. Maybe I'm just hungry." I sniffed. "Sage and onion, for certain, dill—I hope it's stew, with chicken. Real chicken like back home."

"Let's go find out then."

Ace led me inside the hotel to the dim dining room. A crowd of passengers had filled the long common table so we chose a smaller one. Charles and Kate sat at the far end, their heads together, as if sharing a secret. Two seats were left across from each other. I slipped into the closest one with a sigh and stretched my lower limbs.

"Coffee with cream and sugar," I said and ordered the stew. "Do you ever eat anything else besides steak, potatoes and biscuits?"

"Grits." Ace's smile widened. "I ain't used to fancy meals like you. I'm glad you're in a better mood, though. This morning you looked like you'd just come in from the trail."

"I take it that's not a compliment." I managed to smile at the young girl pouring our steaming coffee. "Bless you. I feel like I've been cooped up in a cattle car for a month. A long hot bath would be heavenly."

"We're close enough to heaven. Heard it might snow."

"What day is it? I've lost track of so much on this trip."

"Dunno, but it don't matter to me. One day's same as the next," Ace said and fell to the hearty meal. "My mother was raised in Natchez. She was a lady like you, raised well, with real manners. Died when I was six or seven."

"I'm sorry," I said and meant it. "Five boys but no girls in your family?"

"Nope. My pa practiced law, but he drank himself to death after my mother died."

"Didn't he teach you to read and write?"

"Never sober enough, I guess. I was pretty wild, did whatever I wanted. Till I worked at the Fanthorpe Inn near town. I was twelve. Stable boy."

I remembered that my own father started working at that age. "So your older brothers kept the family together, I take it."

"Till they joined the cavalry. Layne and me got their jobs at the inn after that." Ace leaned back in his chair and pushed his empty plate away. He sipped his coffee. "Saw plenty of ladies in their silk and satin dresses at a dance once. Such a pretty sight."

"Didn't you want to study law like your father?"

"Me?" He shrugged. "Royce planned to, only he joined up to fight instead. Most every man did around those parts. Got shot to—pieces. That didn't stop Layne and me, though. Too bored to stay out of it, but then we were too

199

bored with all the drills."

"My father mentioned that, too. What about after the war?"

"I lived day to day. Never thought much about learnin' a trade beyond horses."

I studied the scar on his jaw, nearly hidden now by dark bristles, and his mismatched eyes. Ace had crammed a lifetime of hard experience into his interrupted boyhood. I'd enjoyed family, friends and social events, but he'd been abandoned to work for meals and a bed.

"I'm curious, what's your Christian name?" I asked.

As if reluctant to share any further, he rose to his feet. "Oh, I'll answer to anything. Ace, Tex, even worse things. But I ain't a murderer, no matter Sir Van says."

"You were baptized, though."

"I don't recall."

I straightened my hat and gloves. "You must have been, if your mother was well-bred. Did you attend church services?"

"What, are you trying to convert me?"

"Do you need conversion?"

"You should've studied the law, miss. You sure can ask questions."

"Perhaps," I said with a laugh. "I confess I had grave doubts about your character the day we made our bargain, Mr. Diamond. And I did believe that you'd conned me out of thirty dollars until you showed up on the train."

Ace raised an eyebrow. "I figgered as much. I'm sorry I didn't take your story more serious from the start. Never expected you'd be in real danger."

Touched by the concern in his eyes, I slipped my gloved hand under his arm. We walked back to the train with five minutes to spare. I heard Kate's bubbly laughter and Charles joining in. That warmed my spirits. He greeted me with a nod but ignored Ace. Charles boosted Kate up the Silver Palace car's iron steps and followed her inside. Ace pulled me toward the open platform's railing and allowed other travelers past to enter the Pullman car.

"What is it?" I asked.

"Need a bit of privacy to talk," he said, his voice low. "We'll be gettin' in to Sacramento before dark, or so I heard. You sure your uncle's meeting you at the depot?"

"Of course. He'd send another telegram if not."

The train pulled away from the shadowed buildings. When Ace slid an arm around my waist, I backed away. "Something wrong?" he asked.

"I shouldn't be out here with you. Alone."

"Is that right." He scratched his stubbly chin. "I won't bite."

"I don't feel comfortable at this altitude." I twisted to face the view. No doubt he would try to kiss me again despite his boyish mask of innocence. "These sheds make me nervous. Did you say it might snow? I ought to get my oilcloth cape, I'm so cold."

"Here, this might help."

He draped his fringed buckskin coat around my shoulders and then gripped the rail on either side of my own, his warmth behind me. Ace didn't brush his rough jaw against my neck or press against me. I leaned back and realized he'd left space between us. Perhaps he was learning manners after all. We stood there for several minutes in companionable silence until the weathered boards came to an end.

"Oh!"

Breathless at the gorgeous view, I drank in the deep blue lake nestled between sloping shoulders of green. Thick pines marched along the shoreline. Gleaming snow frosted the high, rocky peaks on all sides. How strange that such a beautiful place could be so far away where few people would see, unless they traveled along this rail line. Ace leaned toward my ear.

"Donner Lake. Wagon train got stranded over winter twenty some years ago."

"I read about the trial of those who chose cannibalism in the newspaper, Mr. Diamond," I said. "Don't remind me now and spoil the view."

He laughed. "Can't say I'd ever be that desperate."

I jumped when the train plunged into a dark tunnel. Ace tightened one arm around my waist and I hung onto the railing, breathing hard, staring at the rock-hewn interior, until light flooded my eyes. I shivered.

"I'm sorry. I never did like tunnels."

"Better get used to 'em, Lily. Heard there's one five miles long ahead."

"Five miles?" I calculated in my head, my knees weak. "That's at least thirty minutes."

"It can't be that bad," he said. "There's a trestle bridge coming up, but sturdier than the one at Dale Creek."

I grabbed his arm, too uncomfortable to reply. My heart pounded in my throat when the train passed over the curving span. Ace escorted me inside to my seat but set aside his coat. Another brief tunnel shrouded us in darkness. I choked down my fear, wishing I could remember why the panic intensified with each subsequent tunnel. I never minded being sent to my room, day or night, because I would read to my heart's content. Even exploring the attic was an adventure, as long as daylight reigned. But the cellar...

I forced myself to watch Ace shuffle his cards. He'd set his hat aside and his thick dark hair had a glossy sheen. I didn't mind his scruffy beard, since it added to his exotic appeal. He sensed my gaze, although I tried to be subtle, and a hint of a smile creased the corners of his mouth. Chiding myself in silence, I focused my gaze beyond him.

Kate and Charles sat across from each other in conversation. Kate listened as much as she chatted, a surprise to me. I didn't begrudge them a budding friendship. Charles ought to give up his dream and devote himself to ministry at home in Evanston. Anywhere but China. In fact, Kate would be perfect for him. She wanted a family and would be a loyal and devoted wife.

"Look, Lily. Ain't seen anything like that before," Ace said and pocketed his cards. His fringe swayed when he pointed. "Nothin' so pretty as that, is there."

I peeked out the window to see the sheer drop falling away from the railroad bed. A wide ribbon of water snaked along the valley's floor over a thousand miles below. My stomach jittery, I realized the train had slowed to chug along the ledge. It stopped beneath a massive granite cliff. People crowded by the windows or peeked over each other's shoulders, Aunt Sylvia included. The men scrambled out of the car for a better view. Some walked to the edge and peered over, pointing at various trees that resembled tiny bushes below.

"Go on outside," I urged him but he shrugged.

"I can see fine from here."

Ace interlaced his fingers with mine, but our hands remained hidden between the wall and my skirt. My agony decreased when the train finally started moving again at a snail's pace. I breathed a sigh of relief.

"You all right now?"

"Yes. I don't know what's the matter with me."

"You had a bad scare at Dale Creek, Lily. May take you a while to get over that."

I nodded. His words rang true when the train crossed another bridge and headed toward a tunnel. The masonry arch, shaped like an inverted horseshoe, grew larger. Closing my eyes, I tightened my grip on Ace's hand when the light failed. The darkness didn't last long.

"It's silly to be afraid of a tunnel."

"Everyone's afraid of something."

"What about you?" I asked him.

"I'd have to think about it. Been knifed, snake-bit, beat up—even shot once, a nick right here." He showed me a short scar between his neck and shoulder under his shirt collar. "An inch closer and I'd have bled to death, or so the sawbones told me. Lucky it was a flesh wound."

"You're quite the adventurer, Ace."

"I'd say the same about you. No woman I ever met has the gumption you do. They'd have given up back at Promontory, or even in Omaha."

My face grew hot. "So you aren't afraid of anything? Nothing at all?"

Ace scratched his chin. "I'd never want to be shot in the back by a coward, I guess. I fight fair and square. Fists, knives or what have you. Face to face," he said and leaned forward. "I'm glad that coward who killed your father fell off that bridge. If he'd been hangin' on I wouldn't have climbed down to save his sorry hide. I might have pried his fingers loose."

"We should forgive those who wrong us, Mr. Diamond."

"Maybe, but I ain't about to forget."

His stark honesty held an underlying sourness, but I changed the subject. "Why are the signal posts so tall?" I asked.

Ace scratched his jaw. "So they won't get buried in snow drifts, probably."

A fine grit scoured the car's windows. I realized that it was ice pellets, not sand. I reached out and placed my palm against the cold glass, which left a clear hand print surrounded by a misty outline. Snowflakes soon began drifting down from the sky and iced the trees and ground in white. If traveling in early September proved cold, what would the middle of January be like? The railroad claimed the snow sheds would prevent stoppages, but I had my doubts.

"Ain't that a sight," Ace said. "Can't get prettier than snow in the mountains."

"Have you ever seen snow in the mountains before, Mr. Diamond?"

"Nope. Have you?"

I shook my head. The train swept between thick pines on either side. Mist obscured the heights above us, and I drew in a ragged breath when I saw a rock-rimmed black oval ahead. No pinprick of light signified its end.

"Here we are, Summit Tunnel," someone sang out. "Five miles long."

I fought cold terror before the train plunged into darkness. A heaviness pressed my chest like a solid iron anvil, and all rational thought left me. I panicked when strong arms pulled me to the edge of my seat, but heard

Ace's reassuring whisper and inhaled his musky scent. I saw a dim flash of light pass by, and counted the seconds until the next one came at twenty-five. That helped me relax my grip on his forearms.

"Is it safe to burn torches with the train giving off sparks?"

"No idea. It won't last too much longer."

I focused on each flash, although sometimes I had to count to fifty before seeing the next torch. Ace cushioned both my hands between his warm ones and rubbed them. It helped, but the lights failed completely a few minutes later. I lost count and fought deeper panic.

Suddenly I found myself in his arms. "You're safe, Lily. With me."

"I know."

His mouth pressed against my own with a softness that surprised me. One hand cupped my neck and his thumb circled my earlobe, slowly, that broke down any thought of resisting. Delicious yet wicked sensations filled me when Ace deepened the kiss. The taste of him, shocking and primal, at last forced reason into my head. I scrambled backward in the dark. He let me go, as if aware of my confusion, and then cleared his throat.

"Lily, I'm sorry. I didn't mean to scare you."

His whisper didn't ease the intense heat in my cheeks, my neck and my entire body. Suffocating guilt threatened to overwhelm me. Was Aunt Sylvia right? Had I lost all my sense of decorum and shame? Allowing a man like Ace such liberties, when I'd never even accepted a chaste peck on the cheek from Charles Mason! While this journey west may have turned my world upside down, I knew it was long past time to regain common sense. My hands cooled my burning cheeks while I willed embarrassment to subside.

I should have known he might take advantage of the darkness.

Within moments, sunlight filled the car again when the train emerged from Summit Tunnel. I squinted like a mole and glanced at Ace sideways. He gazed out the window, his face unreadable, his hands folded over knees. I kept my voice low.

"I-I accept your apology. Only because you are unmannered and no gentleman."

"Guilty as charged. That don't mean a wild mustang can't be tamed."

"I beg your pardon?"

Ace met my gaze. "Our bargain's still good. But the reins are in your hand."

Bewildered, I folded my arms beneath my bosom. "I don't understand—"

"Like Mason said, you do as you please in the end."

He tipped his hat over his eyes and slouched down. I closed my mouth, shocked by his words and resentful. A few other passengers glanced my way, as if they'd overheard our cryptic words. Perhaps they wondered what had transpired in the tunnel. I hated the flush of heat at the memory of that deep kiss, which started with gentle probing and then changed to an unleashed hunger. Was I afraid of such intimacy? Or afraid of losing my independence? And what right had either Ace or Charles to fault me for that? Besides, I had vowed to focus on three things.

I renewed my resolve and pushed every other issue aside.

Other small stations passed by: Dutch Flat, Gold

Run and Colfax. We stopped for ten minutes, far too short to leave the Silver Palace car, but no explanation came. Ace shuffled his cards, one eye flickering toward me on occasion, while I pretended to sketch. My pencil stub had worn down and I refused to ask him to sharpen the tip. Instead, I gritted my teeth and hung on to the seat's edge when the train whirled around a jutting spur of the mountains. 'Cape Horn,' as someone called it, frightened me more than that long tunnel but I resorted to prayer.

One rock face dropped at least two thousand feet. The train swooped around on a slender ledge, and people cringed at the speed and gripped their seats with nervous energy. A narrow trickle of water streamed down from a jagged break. The wet rock's mineral hues gleamed in the sunlight. At one point a tiny wooden shack appeared, tucked beneath overhanging pine tree boughs. Ace sat up, tipped his hat back and stretched.

"You're not worried, Mr. Diamond? What if the brakes fail?"

"If they do, then I'll worry."

The train continued its reckless descent to the valley. I jumped, unnerved, each time the steam-powered brakes shuddered. They didn't fail as we progressed through the lower ridges of the Sierras. I welcomed the sight of other trees besides the sturdy green pines.

A porter tapped my arm. "Miss Lily Granville? Done got this back at Truckee, miss," he said and thrust a telegram into my hands. "Sure am sorry for the delay."

I thanked him and tore the envelope open, overjoyed to see its seal intact. Aunt Sylvia had not read it first without my knowledge. Uncle Harrison's name jumped at me. I scanned the flimsy sheet twice and puzzled over the message.

Business in Vallejo, stop. Meet Parker House hotel, stop. William Harrison Granville.

"What is it? Bad news?" Ace asked.

I glanced up, surprised by his interest. "My uncle wants to meet me in Vallejo. It must be a town somewhere in California. I've no idea where it is."

"'Val-lay-ho,' not Vall-a-joe." Ace drawled. "We have plenty of Spanish names down in Texas. Know anybody with a map?"

"Charles had one back home. I wonder if he remembers that town."

I rose to my feet and started toward the car's far end. Kate sat with my aunt, chatting away, and that surprised me. Charles walked in from the outside platform. I thought I glimpsed Sir Vaughn behind him, but the door shut. I hurried forward with the telegram in hand and beckoned to him. Charles joined me halfway and listened to my explanation.

"I think there's a railroad heading southwest from Sacramento that goes to Vallejo." He adjusted the wire of his spectacles resting on one ear. "We'll have to ask at the depot. Once we get to Sacramento we won't need Diamond's help."

Charles stared over my shoulder. I glanced around to see Ace behind me. "I'll decide when our bargain has ended, Charles. I'd like to stop at my uncle's office first. He might have changed his plans at the last minute, or returned early."

"Where's that?" Ace asked.

"The corner of J Street and Fourth. I have no idea what kind of building is there, of course. Father never told me much, but Uncle Harrison does have a partner in business."

"What about Kate?" Charles asked and ducked his head closer. "She's made friends with your aunt, who's trying to talk her into going on stage."

I stifled a smile. He looked disappointed. "I doubt if Kate's serious."

Morose, he nodded and headed back. I jumped when Ace touched my elbow. "I'm sorry, I didn't expect that. Or this telegram," I said with a shaky laugh. "But I'm glad we'll arrive in Sacramento soon. It's much prettier here in the foothills."

I settled against the cushion, my shawl folded away in my valise, soaking in the warm sun and enjoying the lush green hues of the valley below us. Settlements clustered on the riverbanks, with fruit orchards and fields spread on either side. Green-crowned trees, alone or in dense numbers, showed a hint of autumn gold. I breathed deep and released it when the train approached the town of Sacramento and the Central Pacific's acres of timber sheds on the waterfront. Steamers, paddleboats and sailboats of all types dotted the river's rippling surface.

People crowded the platform and waved, while passengers rose to their feet before the train stopped. Huge painted letters on a building proclaimed the California Steam Navigation Company, with prices for cabin or deck. Men loaded a steamer, the *Chrysopolis*, with goods and baggage and people lined up by the dock to board. Beyond the brick and frame houses, the town spread out in cobblestoned streets full of shops, mills, factories and foundries. A large building with scaffolding had a gleaming white dome surrounded by iron pillars.

"It reminds me of Chicago," I said, unable to contain

my excitement. "Have you ever been there, Mr. Diamond?"

"Nope. Didn't like St. Louis." Ace peered out the window with apathy. "Too many people for my taste. You sure your uncle's not waiting here somewheres?"

"I plan to find that out before I take any other train."

The last thing I wanted was another trip. If Uncle Harrison had gone to Vallejo, however, then I'd follow his directions. I waited until most of the passengers disembarked before taking my pocketbook and valise. Ace followed me, fingertips on my elbow, and remained at my side when I scanned the crowd for my uncle's familiar face. Taller than Father, he'd always worn a beaver top hat and formal suit. I didn't see him among the few men wearing such clothing.

"At least Charles can catch up on the latest news," I said. "There'll be more than enough papers to choose from."

Ace didn't reply, his attention caught by a vendor who peddled baskets of strange fruit, both red and green, using a sing-song patter.

"Av-o-ca-do! Pom-e-gran-ate. Right here, folks, step right up. Sweet and juicy!"

Spices wafted from a mercantile shop, mingling with the odor of a nearby stall's fried fish. Red and gold poppies and chrysanthemums, a variety of squash, pumpkins, fresh and dried beans, plus odd-shaped vegetables filled a wagon. Another held baskets of green and dark purple grapes, firm pears, drifts of lemons and oranges. I breathed deep, inhaling the scents, sounds and colors, and thanking God that I'd arrived safe and alive. California was real, not a dream.

I was here at last.

To the west, I saw a shadowy blue smudge that had

to be a mountain range nearer to San Francisco Bay. So close yet so far. When this was all over, I would find the first sandy beach and wade right into the Pacific Ocean. I'd seen the Atlantic long ago as a child, when my parents had gone to New York City. I had little memory of that trip except the ocean's greenish hue. Uncle Harrison's long letters about California had been full of exciting sights, sounds and experiences. The one thing that remained in my memory, however, had been his stirring description of the crashing surf on the rocks.

Why hadn't he waited for me to arrive before going on business? I couldn't hide my disappointment that business took precedence. But I'd never wired him about the troubles I'd faced, or my worries. I reined in my impatience. Aunt Sylvia headed straight for me, plowing through the crowd without apology, her mouth set in a thin line. Charles and Kate hurried to catch up, panting for breath.

"What's this about Vallejo? Why isn't Harrison meeting us here?"

"I don't know."

"For heaven's sake, child! We can't go traipsing around the state of California, following him wherever he goes."

I bit back a sharp retort. "I'm going to check at his office—"

"But the train for Vallejo leaves soon. You won't have time." Aunt Sylvia raised a hand to block the late afternoon sun and squinted at the docks. "Where is my husband?"

"He said something about a steamship," Kate said, "right after we left the train."

"I didn't expect him to be gone so long," she said

and spoke to Charles. "Would you be so kind and see if you can find him? Hurry, please."

"Uh—"

"I'll go," Ace said with an odd gleam in his eyes. "Excuse me, ladies."

"Wait, Mr. Diamond," I called, but he didn't hear me.

Ace slithered through the crowd. I soon lost sight of his wide-brimmed hat and fringed coat. Frustration boiled inside me. I suspected he wanted a chance to confront Sir Vaughn alone. Kate must have sensed my dismay.

"I'll try to catch up to him."

She ran off before I could catch her arm. Her blue and white striped dress stood out in the crush of people, along with her feathered hat minus its bluebird. Kate raced around a street corner and vanished. I clutched my pocketbook and valise. Why hadn't we planned this all out on the train? It was too late now.

"Charles, see if you can find J Street—"

"Goodness, no," my aunt said. "We can't all split up any further. We'll wait right here till they return, or we'll never make it to the depot."

I had to agree and moved to the shade beneath a millinery shop's canvas awning. The display of hats staved off my boredom for several minutes. Charles entered the trading post next door and then emerged with a newspaper.

"This has the timetable of the Vallejo railroad. We'd better head to the depot now or we'll miss the train. Does Sir Vaughn know the depot's location?"

"Of course. He's visited Sacramento many times," Aunt Sylvia said with a sniff. "They may be waiting there now for all we know. Come along, Lily."

"I'd like to find Uncle Harrison's office first."

"That might take too long. He's been in Reno, San Francisco and now Vallejo. He never considered how inconvenient things might be for other people.."

I knew Father often complained about Uncle Harrison's lack of an inner clock as well. He jumped from one project to the next, like a bee in a meadow of clover. Charles tucked my hand under his arm and Aunt Sylvia's under the other.

"One good thing the clerk told me," he said. "The trip is relatively short."

Aunt Sylvia shrugged. "It will be nightfall, though, when we arrive. Let's hope Harrison made arrangements at the hotel in Vallejo. If there is a hotel."

"With a proper bed, a bathtub and a decent dining room," I muttered. "What about Kate and Ace, though? What if they return?"

Charles squeezed my arm. "They can take the next train. Come on or we'll miss it."

I had no choice except plod onward.

'I watch, and am as a sparrow alone upon the house top.' Psalm 102:7

Chapter Eighteen

"Lily! Be careful, child."

A family from third class surged around me, each child hugging a chicken, while the father bore a rooster enclosed in a wire crate. His wife carried two bulky strapped cases. Charles caught me when my boot heel slipped on the train's slick wooden floor. I grabbed a high-backed seat, but not before my knee twisted. Aunt Sylvia led us to a pair of seats in the second class car and plopped down with a heavy sigh. The train pulled away from the depot.

My relief at the thought of meeting Uncle Harrison deflated when I saw Tom Gentry, the drummer with his overlarge valise, sitting with two other men. He winked. I refused to acknowledge his rudeness. His presence alarmed me, and I wondered if he only pretended to be a drummer. He stroked his goatee and surveyed me from head to toe, his

215

gaze lingering on my bosom. Unnerved, I excused myself and headed to the washroom.

My shorter curls had the habit of escaping the knot behind my head, so I tucked and pinned until I gave up. The towel didn't look clean and I'd run out of handkerchiefs. That reminded me of Ace, and upset me all over again. Glum, wishing I'd stayed in Sacramento after all, I joined Charles and Aunt Sylvia.

Hunger gnawed me, but I dozed against the window while the train rattled and swayed. A shrill whistle sounded. Charles shook my arm, waking me, and I sat up straight. My vision blurry, I stared outside the window at the blackness.

"What time is it? Where—"

"In Vallejo," he said. "Your aunt has gone to find Captain Granville."

Charles lifted my valise and his own from beneath the seats. I glanced around, but Gentry and his companions had gone. Charles clasped my arm and led me to the platform. Lamps flickered on tall poles. A naval shipyard's forest of masts blocked the view toward San Francisco's sprawling hills. A misty white haze obscured the waterfront, its fingers creeping between buildings and houses. I waved frantically at a tall man in a silk top hat and called out, but the man didn't turn around. He joined a petite woman and hurried away.

Not Uncle Harrison, then. Would I even recognize him after this long?

I stood on tiptoe, craning my neck, and watched for any sign of my aunt and uncle among the lessened crowd or on the sloping, unpaved main street. Tiny Vallejo had a sleepy look, with a general store, dry goods and livery stable besides the ferry service and the Mare Island shipyard. Several nearby trees had a strong earthy odor. I pulled off a glove and plucked one oval, dusty gray leaf to examine. My eyes watered from the heavy scent and the oily residue on my fingers.

"Eucalyptus," Charles said and handed me a handkerchief. "I read about them in the newspaper on the train."

"Is that a hotel?" I asked, waving the linen toward a building on the hill top. "Parker House. It must be, let's go see. I'm tired of waiting for Aunt Sylvia."

"This might be your uncle—"

A closed carriage pulled toward the platform in a cloud of dust, led by a team of bays. The driver tipped his hat to me and climbed down to fetch our valises. Aunt Sylvia poked her head through the open window, her expression triumphant.

"I found him at last, Lily. Come along, it's getting late."

She opened the door from the inside. My excitement and relief vanished when I neared the open door. A man sat inside the carriage. Dressed like a miner with a thick beard and mustache, a plaid shirt and rough trousers, he stretched out a hand. I stared at the other which held a small derringer.

"Let's not keep your uncle waiting," he said, his deep voice muffled.

I backed into a solid body. "Get in, Lily," Charles said. "He told me he won't hurt you."

"What?"

Charles pushed me into the carriage. I twisted, lashing out at him with my pocketbook. He ducked. The stranger caught my waist from behind and hauled me onto the seat beside Aunt Sylvia. Charles climbed in and shut the door. I lurched for the door, but the man shoved me into Charles's arms.

"Keep her under control, or you won't get paid a red cent."

Stunned, I wanted to slap his face. "Traitor!"

A cloth covered my face and filled my nose with a bitter smell. "They won't hurt you, Lily. They promised," he whispered. "You'll see your uncle soon."

"How…"

My hearing faded and darkness overwhelmed me.

****

Thick-headed, my mouth woolly, I woke to jolting, rattling wheels. I drifted in and out of consciousness within an enclosed space. The carriage, I remembered that much. Another cloth with a bitter smell smothered me once more. The fumes brought strange illogical dreams that shifted like sand on a wind-swept dune.

Like swimming to the surface of a deep pool, I fought against dizziness and forced my eyelids open. Heavy timbers stretched across the ceiling above me along with ribbons of morning sunlight. My fingertips traced muslin sheets, the rough fabric of my split skirt and my tweed jacket. I rolled over and spied my boots on the floor. My valise lay on the bed's foot. I sat up, groggy and sick. How did I come to this room? Where was I? Who—Charles.

Charles had betrayed me.

First at Dale Creek, when he'd failed to reach out a hand to save me. And now he'd helped Aunt Sylvia and that rough-looking miner. I'd forgotten my uncle's telegram warning me to trust no one. I prayed that he wasn't in danger too. What did they want?

"Money," I said aloud. My voice cracked due to my parched throat.

The bearded stranger had said something about payment. Kate told me that Charles needed more money. I'd dashed his hopes of marriage, so he needed funds to replace what he'd counted on from my inheritance. Charles, who'd attended a Christian seminary and hoped to do missionary work in China, sold me to the devil. That painful truth hurt. I wept until my vision and foggy head cleared. Then I straightened. Ace's encouraging words returned.

I had gumption. I couldn't give up, so I would fight to escape. Somehow.

The stranger who'd forced me inside the carriage last night—who was he? A man who worked for George Hearst? That made the most sense, and Aunt Sylvia might have agreed to deliver me into their hands. This nightmare was real. I hoped my uncle would find me. I was isolated here, and alone, without Ace's help, without Kate, even without Charles.

But not helpless.

The bed ropes creaked under my weight when I slipped off the mattress. Once I pulled on my boots, I surveyed the room. A washstand stood against faded cabbage rose wallpaper with a gilt mirror hung above it. The quilt was folded across the brass bedstead's frame. On the other side of the bed, my valise and pocketbook lay on the floor with their contents spilled. My leather sketchbook lay in one corner, my pencils broken, my money belt empty.

Father's gold watch was missing, too. I suspected Aunt Sylvia had pocketed that when they brought me here. I crossed to the door and tested the knob. Locked. I checked the window next. A sheer drop, not a roof or a pipe or any trellis to cling to, and no shrubbery below to break a fall. This couldn't be Vallejo. We'd traveled too far from what little I recalled. Brown hills surrounded the building—hotel or house, I wasn't certain. A mountain rose further off, with smudges of green on the slopes, but not as high as the Sierras. Formidable enough.

I heard low voices from the hall. "If Hearst finds out we don't have the deed—"

"I can't help that," Aunt Sylvia interrupted. "I searched her valise and trunk from top to bottom. It's not my fault. This was all your idea in the first place."

The voices faded. I tiptoed back to the door and crouched to peek through the keyhole. A tiny pin of light, but I couldn't make out any details beyond. I paced the floor. My aunt had known from the beginning about the deed when she first arrived in Evanston. Had she been in league with Emil Todaro? Was it possible that Aunt Sylvia agreed to her own brother's cold-blooded murder?

She'd schemed to put me away in a sanitarium, and then pretended concern over propriety to follow me across country. Todaro had searched my pocketbook in Omaha, and then plotted with Aunt Sylvia to shove me off Dale Creek bridge. I'd be out of the way for good, and she could claim the Early Bird mine with the deed. But they didn't have it. Father's murder had not led to getting their hands on that paper.

Had I seen another man the night of Father's murder, or Aunt Sylvia in male dress? She was an actress, after all. Would Father have recognized her? What had he told me that day? I bit my pinky finger, trying to remember.

Something about hydraulic mining and the expensive equipment. I wished I'd paid more attention. Quicksilver, what in the world was that? And jets of water. Charles would know—that thought stopped me cold.

Oh, yes. He understood all that technology with his voracious newspaper habit. Charles knew how valuable such information could be and had used it to his advantage. That went against his nature. He wasn't brave. He didn't crave danger or adventure. Charles agreed with Aunt Sylvia's plan because he'd lost his chance to marry me. My inheritance had been his ticket to China and he had to recoup the loss somehow.

I swung my arms and flexed my lower limbs to regain my balance and flexibility. The drug or herb they'd used to induce sleep had finally worn off. I checked the pitcher and set it down with a sigh. No water to wash my hands or rinse the bitterness from my mouth. Under the bed, I found the dusty chamber pot. That helped. All the money I'd hidden in my spare boots was gone, but I found my mother's broken necklace snagged on my nightdress's lace collar.

While I stuffed all the items back into my pocketbook, my fingers bumped a hard object beneath the silk lining. Ace's stiletto! They had not taken it from its hiding place. I slid it inside my right boot.

Voices drifted from below. "—wait until he replies to the wire."

"How will we know if he receives it? My brother Harrison is crafty. He might refuse to accept it, and then what will we do?"

"Let's not worry about that until the time comes."

The door opened several minutes later. I'd resumed

my position on the bed and feigned sleep, to let them think the drug hadn't worn off yet. The hardest part was slowing my breathing, since my stomach knotted and my heart thumped in my chest and ears.

"Nothing's gone right from the start," Aunt Sylvia muttered. "We ought to let Hearst fight it out in court. Let the judge rule on the claim without the deed."

A buggy's rattling wheels drew her toward the window. I opened one eye. I heard her struggle to open the sash. The door was open. I bolted from the bed and ran out of the room. The stairs had two landings, but I didn't waste time looking back. My aunt screamed a shrill warning. I jumped the last few steps despite my burning knee. The foyer's thick rug muffled my pell-mell race to the front door. The knob slipped through my hand when someone yanked me off my feet.

Arms pinned, I kicked out and heard vile curses. I swung my head back and smacked the man's skull—then saw stars. Blinking, I ignored the ringing in my ears. A short, dark-haired maid in a white apron stared in a nearby doorway.

"Help me! I've been kidnapped, please help! Fetch the sheriff—"

"Save your breath, Miss Granville."

The maid backed away, crossing herself, eyes wide. She fled when the man spoke to her in Spanish. My captor carried me into a small side room with a long wooden table, a glass-fronted cabinet and a heavy chandelier hanging from the ceiling.

"Lupe doesn't understand English, which is why I hired her."

Once he released me, I whirled to see the black-haired bearded man. He had a familiar manner in the morning sunlight, although he wore the same plaid shirt and rough trousers from yesterday. He reeked of sweat and tobacco. When had Aunt Sylvia visited California to meet him? She must have taken the train at some point this summer.

I hadn't even questioned her when she showed up in Evanston.

My aunt walked into the room. "Stupid girl. There's nowhere to run in Walnut Creek," she said. "You'd be lost for days."

"Who are you? What do you want?" I asked the man.

"Don't you recognize me?" His voice changed when he peeled off half of his mustache and beard. "I say, that's a compliment. Quite right, quite right."

"Indeed. My husband, Rupert Chester—everyone calls him Vaughn, though—is an accomplished actor and skilled in disguises. Too bad he's not really an English baronet."

"You enjoyed being called Lady Sylvia," Vaughn said in a wry tone and peeled the rest of the artificial hair and sticky spirit gum. "A bit too much, in fact."

I watched him remove the thick black wig to reveal his gray hair. "So Ace Diamond was right. He did see you on stage in St. Louis."

"Lord Dundreary is one of my most famous roles." Vaughn bowed. "I'm surprised your friend from Texas sat through a play in the theater. He doesn't seem the cultured type."

"I should have listened to him."

"I should have listened to poor Emil."

"Emil Todaro?" I folded my arms under my bosom. "So he was involved with you."

"Oh yes. He wanted to shove Mr. Diamond off that bridge instead of you, but I disagreed. Such a pity you survived." Vaughn laughed at my shock. "Poor Emil was quite upset that I shot your father. The Colonel refused to tell us where the deed was. I lost my temper."

Speechless, reeling from his harsh words, I glanced at Aunt Sylvia. She avoided my gaze. Did she feel any sense of regret, any lost love for her brother, at such a stark confession? Emil Todaro had not killed Father. But he died for his part in this wicked scheme.

Vaughn pulled out a folded envelope. "Things have worked out after all, my love. Your brother Captain Granville replied to my telegram."

"Probably a trick." Aunt Sylvia sniffed. "I don't think Harrison will come."

"He'll come, out of curiosity than anything else. The Captain needs that deed, and he has a greedy heart. Or didn't you realize that, Miss Granville? Your uncle doesn't care a whit about you, only the deed."

"So he wasn't in Vallejo?" I asked.

His mocking laugh refueled my anger. "I arranged to have that telegram sent to you in Truckee. Western Union is so accommodating."

I chewed my lower lip. Why hadn't I listened to my instincts? Charles had played his part well and drew me into this web of deceit. Had he gotten the money he wanted? Or had he died for his betrayal? I hoped not.

"Where's Mr. Mason?"

Vaughn raised an eyebrow. "He believes you're safe with us. I paid him and sent him on his way. He took the ferry to San Francisco."

So Charles had abandoned me. Aunt Sylvia poured a glass of dark liquid from a decanter. Its cut crystal pattern caught the sunlight and sent a rainbow of hues across the room. Her hand shook when she sipped the wine. Before noon, and she needed spirits already. I wondered how much she dosed herself from Mrs. Pinkham's Elixir. The sunlight emphasized the dark circles and baggy skin beneath her eyes. Vaughn grabbed the decanter and set it back inside the cabinet.

"Keep your wits, my dear. We have to find that deed before Harrison arrives."

"I searched everything she had with her, and back at the house," Aunt Sylvia said. She sank into an upholstered chair. "Where did you hide it, Lily?"

"I don't have it."

"We came all this way for nothing?"

"She's lying," Vaughn said.

"You'll have to beat it out of her." My aunt raised her glass. "You know how stubborn Lily is."

He opened the door and said something in rapid Spanish. Lupe, her eyes haunted, carried in a tray with flat circles resembling corn cakes and a mixture of rice and beans. Her gaze darted to me and back to the others. Vaughn shooed her out before I could signal her in some way. I'd get no help from a woman who didn't understand English, and who acted deathly afraid.

Aunt Sylvia finished her wine. "If you won't beat her, I'll strip her naked. She might have hidden it inside her corset."

I clutched my jacket together. "You wouldn't dare—
"

"Oh, yes we would. Drag her upstairs, darling, and you can watch."

He'd stuffed his mouth with food and didn't answer. Either he knew Aunt Sylvia had no intention of following through, or preferred other methods of getting information. My stomach grumbled at the enticing smell of spices and corn. My aunt joined him at the table and wrapped a portion into the middle of the flat circle, then folded it. They ignored me until I inched my way toward the door.

"There are rattlesnakes in the foothills, Miss Granville," Vaughn said and wiped his greasy mouth. "And worse, scorpions and poisonous lizards. Ask my wife. Her second husband bought this little ranch long ago. Too bad he died of cholera."

"I hate this place. We ought to sell it and go back east—"

"And lose our claim? We'll get more quicksilver from the mine once we have the ransom money. We need to hire the crew again and dig deeper."

Quicksilver. That was it—I recalled the newspaper advertisement about shares for sale in a mine. Rupert Chester was one of the owners, but I couldn't remember the other man's name.

"For God's sake, Lily, sit down and eat," Aunt Sylvia snapped. "You won't get another chance today. Who knows how long we have to wait for Harrison."

"She's not getting anything," Vaughn said and scooped up the last of the rice and beans. He wrapped it and then hesitated, the folded circle in his hand. "Not unless you tell us where you hid the deed. We'll find it, one way or the other."

I swallowed, difficult with a parched throat. "Why should I tell you?"

"Because your choices are limited, Miss Granville. Tell us, or your uncle dies. It's as simple as that." He produced a revolver from his belt and laid it on the table. "The choice is yours. Now come and have a little breakfast."

Vaughn placed the food on a clean plate and slid it my way. I walked over, unable to remember when I'd eaten last. Lunch, with Ace. My heart sank at the memory of his odd eyes, the dark stubble along his jaw and upper lip, the taste of his kiss. I scraped the chair along the floor and sat down. They'd used their hands to eat, so I picked up the odd sandwich. The first bite had a pleasant taste mixed with spices. I devoured the rest. The corn, rice and beans satisfied the gnawing ache in my belly. Vaughn rose from his chair and returned with a glass of water. He set the glass out of my reach, however, and leaned against the table's edge.

"Where's the deed, Miss Granville?"

"I don't know."

"You're willing to see your uncle die?" Vaughn picked up the glass and sat back down in his chair. "I didn't expect you to be such a heartless cutthroat."

"You'll kill him anyway," I said. Aunt Sylvia stared at the cabinet with open longing. "You'll kill us both once you get your hands on the deed."

"Perhaps." He examined the glass. "If we're forced to, we will."

"You won't get away with murder."

"Or what? You'll see us hanged? Oh, your self-righteous vow. I'd quite forgotten how determined you were to bring Mr. Todaro to justice."

"He died at Dale Creek, didn't he? That was justice."

"More like pure carelessness on his part. You seemed rather shocked by his demise, from what I recall." Vaughn slid the glass toward me, but most of the contents slopped on the table before I caught it. "You were lucky the second time when that poor man died in your berth."

"You killed Mr. Robinson too?"

"Of course. You lead a charmed life, Miss Granville, but your luck's run out."

I drank what little water was left, which helped ease my thirst if not my shaken nerves. "If you do intend to kill me, why should I tell you anything?"

"My dear child. We have the quicksilver, which your uncle needs to mine his gold. He's invested too much money into hydraulic equipment for the Early Bird. I'm going to suggest a partnership. But we need that deed—or Hearst will claim the mine for himself. He did well at the Comstock Lode. Your uncle would rather die than see Hearst get it."

By his sly smirk, I knew he hadn't told the truth. "You're going to kill me and Uncle Harrison both. That way Aunt Sylvia will inherit everything."

"You see?" My aunt sauntered over to the cabinet and poured a half glass of wine. "She's too smart for her own good. We should have taken her to Bellevue straight from the funeral."

Vaughn held up a hand. "I'm willing to negotiate, if Captain Granville is willing. But he's not an easy man to deal with—"

"He's no different than the Colonel!" Aunt Sylvia glared at me. "Both my brothers cheated me, Lily. I never got any share from our parents' estate because they believed I threw my life away. I begged for help after my first husband died, but they ignored me. They wouldn't answer my letters, and treated me like scum. The same thing happened after I was widowed again. I had to fend for myself. I deserve it all. Your inheritance and the Early Bird mine."

I stared at Vaughn. "Ace Diamond will help Uncle Harrison."

"That Texas brush-popper?" Vaughn and Aunt Sylvia both burst out laughing. "You're mistaken, Miss Granville. I hired sailors to shanghai him," the actor said. "It didn't work in Utah because the men were half-drunk. But this time, Diamond will wake up on some ship bound for the South China seas."

My courage and hope failed at that terrible blow. I'd never see Ace again. Not unless he escaped the ship somehow and worked his way back home. He'd never have met such a fate if he stayed in Omaha. I felt responsible. Huddled in my chair, hands clasped, I wished I knew how to lie better. I didn't know if Father had hidden the deed or if it was still back in Evanston. Had he locked it in a bank vault back home? I had to tell them something. Otherwise, they would kill me before my uncle ever arrived.

"All right, I'll tell you." I watched Vaughn cock his head, eyes gleaming. "Father only had a copy of the deed. He sent the authentic one by courier in June on the train. Uncle Harrison doesn't need either of you. He can find another quicksilver source."

Vaughn rose to his feet and marched over to tower above me. His eyes bored into mine without blinking. "You're lying."

"It can't be true," Aunt Sylvia said, one hand clutching her throat. "Todaro said the Colonel had the real deed, that Harrison didn't have a copy at all."

Vaughn hauled me up by my jacket lapels. His crushing grip frightened me. He'd pulled the trigger and killed Father. He'd ordered Emil Todaro to push me off the bridge instead of Ace, and killed that poor man on the train. The actor was evil, pure and simple. I met his hard gaze, silent, and prayed the warmth in my cheeks wouldn't give away my fear and dread. I saw no shred of guilt or remorse in his cold eyes.

"Why would he trust a courier?"

"That's just it. He trusted someone who never made it to Sacramento. Now my uncle needs the copy to fight Mr. Hearst in court."

I raised my eyes to the beamed ceiling, unable to withstand his searching gaze. Vaughn shook me again, so hard my teeth rattled in my head, and then shoved me into the table's hard edge. I scrambled to sit once more and recover my nerves. I fisted my trembling hands in my lap. Vaughn stalked toward my aunt, picked up the empty glass and threw it in the corner where it shattered. My shivers increased but he didn't touch me again. He picked up his revolver from the table and spun the chamber, watching for my reaction, so I closed my eyes.

And prayed he'd believe me.

"Lock her upstairs again, Sylvia." Vaughn headed for the door. "I'm tired of this game playing. For your sake, Miss Granville, you'd better hope your uncle arrives today."

His threat hung over me like a death sentence.

'…we despaired even of life…' 2 Corinthians 1:8

Chapter Nineteen

I paced the upstairs bedroom once more, heartsick and worried. Uncle Harrison had arranged to meet Vaughn at six o'clock that day. Without Father's pocket watch, I had no idea what time it was except by the sunlight's track across the room. It had to be close to three or four o'clock by now, given the slanting shadows. I loosened my hair and searched my pocketbook for extra hairpins. A piece of paper had snagged on my comb's teeth.

Ace Diamond's crude 'X' crushed my spirits. It felt like years ago when I'd written the terms of our bargain and forced him to sign. He couldn't read or write—and I'd never get the chance to teach him. He might be tied and gagged on some ship right now. Poor Ace, to come all the way to California and then suffer that indignity. If Vaughn tricked me with that telegram, then Ace didn't have a chance against a band of roguish sailors.

231

We should have stuck together instead of rushing off in all directions.

"I'm sorry, I'm so sorry."

My voice sounded hoarse. I'd been given no more water or food. Not that I was hungry, but my dry throat hurt. I turned the paper over and saw a receipt from Father's tailor. What in the world — then I remembered. I'd found this in his suit pocket, the day I left Evanston. I knew he'd taken in several beaver hats in for repair and his winter coat. I tucked it inside my novel as a memento of Ace. Once I combed my hair, I twisted it into a tight knot and pinned it securely. I had to be ready when they came for me.

My straw hat lay half-crushed on the bed. I'd chosen it from an old trunk of my mother's after she passed away. Flat and black, with no brim and one gray ribbon around the crown, I'd always worn it riding. Now it was ruined.

"I'll wear it anyway," I said aloud and skewered the hat into place by its long steel pin with a pearl head. "Now I have two weapons. I can't give up."

I wondered how Aunt Sylvia could be so heartless. She was a perfect match for Vaughn, or Rupert Chester, whatever his real name was. They were both twisted, abhorrent and selfish. I pitied my aunt for resenting her brothers so much that led to blind trust in a killer.

The door banged open. I whirled around, hand on my chest, since I hadn't heard the key in the lock. Vaughn wore his 'baronet' suit with its silk waistcoat, hat and watch chain. The gold-rimmed monocle dangled from its chain, and he carried that silver-topped cane. Aunt Sylvia was not with him. Vaughn beckoned me forward impatiently, so I reached down and grabbed my valise and pocketbook.

"Leave your bags, Miss Granville. You won't need

them."

"I will not leave anything behind," I said with as much dignity as I could muster. "I'll take them to my grave."

"As you wish. Don't try anything stupid." He twisted the knob of his cane and a thin silver blade emerged from the end. "Comes in handy in a dark train."

Shivering, I walked down the steps ahead of him. Vaughn pushed me into the foyer and then thumped the stairway's newel post. "Sylvia? Aren't you ready yet?"

Her shrill voice boomed from the hall upstairs. "Coming—"

"She was never ready for her cues, either," he said to me. I ignored him.

Vaughn consulted his pocket watch and then bellowed again before my aunt appeared. She wore a rust-colored suit with brown velvet lapels and cuffs, with a yellow plaid underlay skirt that provided a puffy bustle. Her yellow straw hat held a spray of orange berries. Despite her stylish costume, she seemed disgruntled. Aunt Sylvia led the way and Vaughn followed me so that I was trapped between them. I clenched my valise and pocketbook and resorted to silent prayer. Aunt Sylvia guarded me on the front porch.

At last Vaughn appeared again driving a buggy from the nearby stable. Once the team halted, my aunt forced me to sit beside the actor. My hopes of escape evaporated when she climbed and sat beside me. A tight fit, given her full skirts, and I felt squeezed between their hard shoulders. Vaughn chirruped to the horses and guided the team away from the house.

"Here's a warning, Miss Granville. Do not try to run. It gets cold at night and wolf packs will hunt you. You might even fall into an abandoned mine shaft," he said. "We'll pick the right one for you when the time comes."

His words chilled me, despite the sun's heat on my face. Nothing looked familiar. The isolated house, built of stucco with a red-tiled roof, stood alone in a desolate and forbidding area. How far had we traveled from Vallejo? I'd been unconscious for hours, so it couldn't be close. Walnut Creek sounded like a small village. I doubted if anyone would help me there, given Vaughn's influence. Lupe had been too frightened.

Huge puffs of white drifted across the sapphire sky. The scrubby green vegetation, pine stands and the sand-hued foothills in the distance had a peaceful air. Cattle swished their tails and grazed, and flies buzzed around my face. I smelled sage and other herbs among the tall grass, reminding me of the kitchen garden at home. The buggy jounced over a rough road, careening near blue-black boulders thrusting from the banks on either side. I was grateful I hadn't eaten a normal meal, because I would have been sick from all the swaying and heavy jolting. I braced my feet until my backside grew sore.

The lone rugged mountain loomed ahead. Its sloping sides resembled a giant's shoulders, but the crown had no real head. Massive boulders of various shapes and sizes, most gray with beige or white markings, cropped up at unexpected times.

"Where *are* we?" I asked. "Close to Sacramento?"

Aunt Sylvia huffed. "It's no better here than the wastelands of Wyoming."

"A few hours southeast of San Francisco," Vaughn said. "That, my dear young woman, is Mount Diablo. The Devil's own, according to superstitious Indians."

"And your quicksilver mine is somewhere near

here."

"You'll see it for yourself. Intimately."

The buggy's hard rattling increased my headache, with stabbing pains behind my eyes and nose. "People will question what happened to me or my uncle. If we disappear, you can't claim the Early Bird mine without some kind of proof that we're dead."

Vaughn glanced sideways at me, eyebrows raised. I hadn't noticed before how pitted his skin was, due no doubt to years of greasepaint and spirit gum. "Who else knows you've arrived here, Miss Granville, except your uncle? If he fails to agree to our terms, he'll meet with an unhappy accident. You have no other family except Sylvia."

"I have friends—"

"Mr. Mason is too much of a coward to make trouble. Miss Kimball didn't have enough sense to know a charlatan when she met him. Oh yes, she told the whole story to Sylvia on the train. She can't prove she ever met you, and no one would believe her anyway."

I clung to my pocketbook. "It seems you've thought of everything."

"I've found that most people admire those who take matters into their own hands—"

"Murder isn't an admirable choice."

"Your father committed suicide, Miss Granville," he said. "Sylvia informed the police that her brother had been despondent. You were out of sorts, if you recall, the day after the Colonel's death."

"People won't accept your story of an accident." I glanced at Aunt Sylvia, but her eyes remained closed. "Uncle Harrison's a well-known businessman. He has far more friends and associates than my father did. He can't just disappear."

Vaughn guided the buggy's team to a smaller side road. "Sylvia, you never told me how amusing your niece can be in a conversation. I would have loved to debate her over philosophy or politics during that boring train ride."

"It was bad enough, sitting for days with nothing to do," my aunt said and yawned. "The last person I wanted to hear was Lily. She's as self-righteous as my brothers."

"You never answered me about covering up Uncle Harrison's death," I said, but he laughed. "I don't find it amusing."

"He's often gone for weeks or months at a time. And don't you know that money talks, dear girl? Judges are quite fond of their vices. A little bribe here and there goes a long way and helps the system thrive."

I fell silent. It was no use talking to either of them and changing their plans. They were set on gaining what they wanted, no matter what the cost. Despite the inconvenience or any danger to themselves. Clearly they didn't consider me a danger. I had the stiletto in my boot and my long hatpin. They hadn't forced me to strip naked, although they'd have no qualms of picking over my corpse. But I intended to stay alive as long as possible. I'd fulfill Ace's admiration and go down fighting.

We traveled into higher foothills, meandering around more frequent outcroppings and rock piles, but the dusty road continued upward. Green swards fell away on the left, with sloping bare rock to the right. Odd looking holes, some large, most small, pitted the surface. I saw other holes as big as caves further ahead at higher points. Vaughn stopped the buggy. I coughed from the raised dust. The road ended and a rough path led around several large boulders.

"Soon we'll be rich at last," Aunt Sylvia said. "I've spent years in cold hotel rooms, musty beds, traveling all over the country by train or stagecoach. No more of that. I'll pick and choose the roles I want, in New York and Chicago."

"Yes, dear. You will."

"And you'll arrange to promote my triumphant return?"

"All in due time. First find a company who will take you," he pointed out. "Your reputation for missing rehearsals hurt your chances in the past."

She sniffed. "Like you said, money talks."

"You'll have your money, my love. Soon." After looping the reins around the whip socket, Vaughn thumped his chest in self-satisfaction and breathed deep. Then he climbed down to survey the rocks. "Come along, ladies. This is a perfect setting for intrigue."

"What time is it?" I asked, peering around me.

"Time to get you out of sight. Captain Granville will arrive soon, if he does." The actor drew his revolver and checked the bullets. "Climb down, Lily. Don't spoil our little party by being stubborn."

"I'd rather wait right here. Uncle Harrison might not believe I'm with you."

Vaughn grabbed my arm and hauled me out, oblivious to my protests, the scrapes on my hands or my awkward sprawl on the ground. "Leave your valise. That will be proof enough that we have you. Safe and sound, up in our quicksilver mine," he said. "Take her, Sylvia. And don't dawdle along the way."

My aunt stared at him in fury once she climbed from the buggy. "What? I can't go up there in these clothes!"

"I won't have you spoiling things by getting angry

with the Captain."

"I promise I won't."

"That's what you said in St. Louis, and we were both fired." He pulled me to my feet and shoved me against the buggy's wheel. "Stop arguing, Sylvia. Just go."

She whimpered like a child. "I have my best shoes. You take her and tie her up in the mine. You'll get there faster."

Vaughn pointed toward the sloping path. "I'm sorry you'll miss our tragedy's last act, my love, but you must stay out of sight. The Captain won't agree to anything if he sees you, and you can't deny it. Once your brother's dead, then we can celebrate."

I'd backed away during their argument and sized up the buggy. Sir Vaughn would shoot me to prevent escape that way. He stalked and caught my arm, clearly suspicious of how I'd managed to inch around the back, while Aunt Sylvia searched her skirt pocket. She brought out a small caliber derringer and then prodded me forward.

"Follow the path over there, Lily. And no tricks."

I snatched my pocketbook from the ground first and marched ahead. My boots slid on the loose stones and gravel. My aunt's French-heeled shoes gave her more difficulty with the pocked holes along the path. Scrubby oaks offered little shade from the blazing sun. Thistles and a bush with inch-long thorns snagged our clothing. Her bustled train caught several times, and she tugged it, grumbling and cursing under her breath. I passed high stems of feathery brown grass and then halted, in a mix of revulsion and fascination. A huge hairy spider traveled along the rocky ground, its swift movement amazing.

"What is it now, Lily—oh, oh! A tarantula. Ugh, I

hate those awful things."

I blocked Aunt Sylvia's aim with her pistol. "It hasn't threatened us. There, it's gone already. I've never seen a tarantula before."

"You've never been bitten by one either."

"Are they poisonous?"

She swept around in a wide circle, avoiding the spot where the spider had disappeared into the brush. "I don't know or care. Go ahead, keep climbing."

I obeyed. The path soon became steeper and I used my hands to keep my balance among the rocks. I glanced back at Aunt Sylvia, but she still held the derringer ready. Somehow she hadn't lost her footing. I tried to catch my breath, hesitating to slow our progress and my eventual fate. She prodded me hard between the shoulders.

"Once your husband has all the money along with both mines, he might arrange an accident for you as well. Find a younger wife—"

"Shut your mouth or I'll break your jaw."

Her fury left me in no doubt of her serious threat. I'd hit a soft spot beneath the dragon-like veneer she presented to the world. Perhaps Vaughn had cheated on her with other actresses. He seemed the type to charm women into his bed.

Aunt Sylvia pointed to a clearing between high rocks. "Over there, go on. And if I hear another word out of you, I'll throw you in the canyon."

I reached a grassy area and stumbled, since my foot caught in a hole. I half-slid into a hollow full of sandy weeds. Pain stabbed the palm of one hand. I saw a tiny horned lizard and snatched it up before it could scuttle away. Its nubby beige and brown skin blended so well against the ground, I'd almost missed it.

"Clumsy girl," my aunt grumbled. "Wait, don't move."

I obeyed, praying that she hadn't noticed my furtive movements. Instead she turned, shielding her eyes from the sun. I heard the rattling of buggy wheels somewhere below and a cheerful shout. An answering call echoed. I couldn't tell if Uncle Harrison had arrived or if someone else happened to be roaming the area. I hoped and prayed the latter. It would give me more time, for one thing, and provide a witness to prevent another murder.

No other sounds came to our ears. No gunshots. No rattle of wheels.

Aunt Sylvia sighed. "Let's go on then."

I rose to my feet. The lizard clung to my pocketbook with its sticky pads. I hoped it wasn't poisonous. Despite my sturdy boots and split skirt, I had to grab slender shrubs to keep my balance in a shallow gully. I didn't look back to see how Aunt Sylvia managed. My heart caught in my throat. I saw a narrow ledge against a cliff face. A deep ravine fell to the left. I had to time my chance and hope for the best opportunity.

The mine had to be somewhere ahead. She would no doubt shoot me in the muffled darkness. I knew Aunt Sylvia resented missing out on witnessing Uncle Harrison's demise.

A trickling stream with reddish brown banks flowed well below in the canyon's bottom. With one hand on the cliff face and my gaze on the path, ignoring my clenched stomach and thumping heart, I started forward. This time there'd be no iron rail for me to catch if I fell. Farther ahead, a cleft in the hillside led to another open clearing. Massive pine timbers flanked a narrow opening. Several wagons and wood crates stood before it. I slowed my steps. Took a deep breath, and then plucked the lizard from my pocketbook.

Whirling, I threw the creature at her neck. I ducked low, a wise decision, since Aunt Sylvia fired the gun in the air. She screamed, clawing her chest, and then fired again. The loud shots hurt my ears, but the second bullet ricocheted off rock high above my head.

Arms flailing, she lost her footing and tumbled into the ravine. Her screams echoed. At last she rolled to a stop in the rocky stream bed. Silent, she didn't move. One limb stuck out at an odd angle. Within moments, I heard other distant gunshots and a blood-curdling yell from afar.

Panic seized me. Vaughn must have killed Uncle Harrison. I would be next, I was sure of that. I fled toward the mine. The open wagon offered little cover. The wood crates were half-broken and too small. Even crouching behind them would not give me security. Choking fear gripped me when I approached the weathered gray timbers. Splinters hung from each side. Someone had marked symbols in crude chalk. I placed one foot on the plank that stretched into darkness and stopped. Nausea crashed over me. I fought it down.

I had to go inside. Or die.

A shout echoed behind me. I recognized my aunt's shrill yet weak voice. She hadn't died from the fall. If Vaughn rescued her, they'd come after me for blood. The two of them would never forgive or forget.

At the sharp blast of another gunshot, I plunged inside.

'Thou hast laid me in the lowest pit, in darkness...' Psalm 88:6

Chapter Twenty

My eyes adjusted to the darkness within a few minutes. That surprised me. I'd expected to grope blindly inside toward my fate. The boards lining the entrance soon ended in reddish brown rock. Chunks had been hewn away at various points. My boots scattered gravel stones further into the dim tunnel. An odd smell lingered. I couldn't identify the source or the reason for it, but it had a sharp metallic bite.

I stopped after counting to fifty when the walls narrowed. The ceiling crowded my head. My chest tightened so hard, I couldn't breathe. I closed my eyes, willed my lungs to expand. It didn't work. Panic struck hard.

I was alone, in darkness. Suffocating.

The cellar's shelves marched above me, full of dusty jars and heavy stoneware. A musty scent filled my nostrils. My stomach rebelled and I bent over, saw a dead rat. Its eyes gleamed and its bent claws sent me screaming backwards. A stack of boxes toppled onto my head. That hurt. I cried, called out for help, crawled my way to the cellar steps. The door stayed shut. Tears blinded my eyes, and the slivers of light faded. Mother.

I had to find Mother. I couldn't die down here alone.

Each slick step under my pudgy hands gave me courage to reach for the next. My knees hurt, my pinafore had black smudges. Would she mind so much? More tears blinded me. At last I reached the door. Locked. I pounded with my little fists. No one came to fetch me.

Furious, I rose to my feet inside the mine. My head cleared when that awful memory drained away. How could I have forgotten? So long ago, my cousin had exacted a cruel revenge. I told Mother that I'd seen him steal a necklace from her dressing table. Gilbert's father had whipped him behind the stable. And months later, at a family picnic, he enticed me away with the promise of strawberries and cream. Instead, he'd locked me in the cellar for hours.

I drew in several ragged breaths, eyed the mine's walls and hesitated. I couldn't stay in here to hide. That memory was too fresh, too raw.

Too painful.

Instead I unpinned my straw hat and left it on the entrance's rotting planks. Then I gulped fresh air and sunshine outside. Its warmth boosted my courage. I didn't see anyone, and stood a moment listening, but no sounds came to my ears. I debated the road leading downward, but knew Vaughn would guess that and follow me. Too easy. Instead, I chose a snaky path between two large rocks. It reminded me of the Devil's Slide and that drummer—Tom Gentry. He'd been innocent of my suspicions. A laugh bubbled up inside my throat.

If people climbed that monstrous formation, then this couldn't be as difficult. Vaughn might assume I'd gone farther into the mine. He didn't know my fear of facing the darkness. After that five mile long Summit tunnel, and the awful memory of the cellar dredged from my past, I would take my chances out in the sun and high places.

I panted for breath. My parched throat was agony but I kept climbing. My pocketbook banged my knees and against the rocks. I nearly fell backwards when a root came away in my hand, but I managed to grab a sturdier one. One large hole above beckoned me. I reached it and squirmed halfway inside before I heard a voice below me.

"Stop right where you are, Miss Granville."

The hammer cocked on a revolver. I turned around. Vaughn aimed at my head. He'd lost his hat, and a trickle of blood marked one side of his face. He waved the weapon.

"I see you managed to thwart my dear wife. She's badly injured—"

"She deserves it after what happened to my father."

"So un-Christian of you to think that. Come down at once."

"You're going to shoot me anyway."

A bullet nicked the rock where my hand had been an instant before. Its lingering whine tightened my chest. I'd called his bluff and he answered. His next shot would not miss. I braced myself, my pocketbook dangling, but stayed where I was.

His tone impatient, Vaughn cursed like a drunken sailor that hurt my ears. "I said climb down, Lily. Now."

I inched my way around one foothold. "Where's Uncle Harrison? Did you kill him? I see he shot you first."

"Get down here and quit asking questions. Hurry

up!"

I'd made it more than halfway to that large hole, and wished I'd been able to climb faster. Now my sore hands scrabbled against the rock while I slid another few inches.

"What if I fall and break my neck?"

"I plan to do that for you, don't worry," Vaughn said, glancing back at the path. "Let go, stupid girl, and slide down. Move!"

Gauging the distance, I let go but kept my knees bent. He leaned forward at the same time that I drew the stiletto from my boot. My speed increased. I thrust it upward to defend myself. He reeled back. Shock widened his eyes.

His own momentum had driven the weapon deep into his abdomen, where the stiletto's handle protruded. Vaughn raised his revolver.

The gunshot deafened me. I grunted when the actor's heavy weight crushed me. The stiletto's handle bit into my neck. I'd expected to feel a burning pain, somewhere, or warm blood flowing from the bullet. I shoved against Vaughn. He didn't budge. Pinned to the sloping ground, I realized my eyes were closed and opened them. Sunlight. No pain bloomed inside my body. I closed them again. Still nothing.

The heavy weight disappeared and rough hands pulled me to my feet. I opened my eyes. One blue and one green eye stared back.

"You're alive. Ace!" I touched his stubbly jaw to make certain.

"You ain't hurt?" He folded me into a tight bear hug. "I thought you were dead, Lily. Scared the daylights outta me, seein' that son-of-a—I don't regret it. No way, no how."

"Regret what?" I asked weakly. "Not being shanghaied?"

"Are you sure you're all right?" Ace dragged me away from Vaughn's body and then hugged me again. "Thought I'd never find you."

Safe in his rock-hard arms, with his soft buckskin coat and a fierce heartbeat thrumming beneath my cheek, I slid my arms around his neck. Then I kissed him. Soft, and then joyously, so grateful that he was here. He matched my excitement, twirled me around and laughed. I joined him. Thanks to God we were both safe and alive. His hat had fallen to the ground and I noticed another stitched wound above his cheekbone. He sported a cut on the corner of his mouth.

I kissed that spot too. "Look at you. Such a disreputable outlaw."

"Mmm." He kissed me again, his hands rubbing my back as if making sure I was real and not a dream. "I aim to please."

Laughing, I breathed deep to drink in his familiar musky scent. "Vaughn told me he hired a gang of sailors to jump you in Sacramento."

Ace brushed my cheek with a thumb. "They put up a good fight. But they didn't know Texans fight as dirty as any old salts."

"Where's Uncle Harrison? Is he hurt?"

"Got winged in his arm. I tied it up for him before he high-tailed outta here to fetch the sheriff. Dunno how long that's gonna take."

My heart sank. Uncle Harrison had not waited to make sure I was safe. Perhaps he assumed I was already dead. I wasn't sure I cared anymore. I hugged Ace again, nestled my head into his shoulder in gratitude. I owed him my life, twice. I didn't want this moment spoiled.

Ace drew me toward Vaughn and nudged him with a boot. The bullet hole was a little off dead center in his back, barely visible. I stepped aside while he leaned down and flipped the corpse over. Ace stood again.

"Whoa. You stuck him good, Lily."

"I didn't—I mean he came at me and I was sliding down."

"Don't worry about it," Ace said and hugged me again. "He'd a-killed you."

"I thought he did shoot me," I said. My voice was hoarser than before.

"Can't believe I shot him in the back," he said in disgust. "I didn't have a choice."

"I'm not sorry. You said you didn't regret it."

He looked troubled. "I winged him first. I'd never missed at that close a range before," Ace said. "Guess I was still mad as all get up about those sailors. Lord Van led me straight to them and I took the bait. All that sittin' on the train dulled my thinkin'."

"His real name was Rupert Chester. An actor, just like you told me," I said. "You were right about St. Louis. I'm sorry I didn't believe you."

"It's over now. Your uncle will be back soon with the sheriff."

"We can't leave Aunt Sylvia down in the ravine. She's still alive."

"There's nothin' we can do for her yet," he said. "That's a twenty foot drop at least. We need a rope and some kind of litter. Hope the Captain brings a few other men."

"All right."

Ace kept a tight hold around my waist until we reached the narrow ledge. "Aunt Sylvia?" I called. "Can you hear me?"

She didn't answer. Maybe she was too angry with me. I had no strength to climb down, and she still had her derringer. Ace led me along the ledge and then the sloping path, slowing at the steeper sections. At last we reached the clearing where two teams waited patiently in the sun. Ace tossed a heavy canvas cloth aside from the larger buggy and rummaged around the floor. He brought out a metal flask and unscrewed the lid.

"Sounds like you need water."

I sipped, the liquid so refreshing despite its warmth. "Thank you. Tell me what happened back in Sacramento."

"Easy now, we have time. You been through a lot," he said and found a smooth rock where I could rest. "Here, your uncle left this too. Go on, you need it."

I took the thin hip flask from him and then choked down the fiery brandy. "What about the Early Bird? Did Uncle Harrison believe Vaughn had it?"

Ace sat beside me and placed my hands between his own. "Your uncle said he had a copy locked up in a bank vault, but Vaughn didn't believe him. Then the Captain got all hot after we heard that gunshot up in the rocks. Figgered he tricked us."

"He planned to kill us both."

Ace opened his revolver's chamber and reloaded, then snapped it back into place. "The Captain didn't want me tagging along. Told him I didn't take orders from anyone."

"I'm glad." I set my pocketbook on the ground. "What about Kate?"

"She's waitin' back in Sacramento with Mason."

"Charles?" That stunned me. "Vaughn told me he took the ferry to San Francisco."

Ace shook his head. "Mason showed up all of a sudden at your uncle's office, talkin' crazy. Said he'd trusted them, that Vaughn and your aunt promised they wouldn't hurt you. They only wanted to talk to you or so they told him. And Mason said they'd fund his mission trip if he made sure you left for Vallejo with your aunt."

"Did they pay him then?"

"Nope. Knocked him out cold and left him on the roadside. Said he walked back to Vallejo and caught the last train back."

I glanced up at the blue and white expanse above my head. Poor Charles. He'd made a mistake and was lucky not to pay with his life. I was certain his betrayal would lead to my death. Shame filled me, remembering Aunt Sylvia at the canyon's bottom. I'd known about her fear of lizards and used that to benefit myself. I was no better than Charles. That weighed heavy on my heart and soul.

But I'd had no choice. Like Ace, who had to shoot Vaughn in the back.

"It's so strange," I said, huddled against him. Ace drew me close, one arm around my shoulder. "This is a beautiful place, but so deadly."

"You cold?"

"No. But a bath and clean clothes would make everything perfect."

In less than a week, I'd lost both a father and a formidable enemy. I also gained two loyal, wonderful friends—Ace Diamond and Kate Kimball. Grateful to be alive, I drank in the distant blue smudge to the west, the green shrubbery and red-brown sand hills. Reveling in that joy, I watched Ace slap dust from his hat. He clapped it on his dark head with that boyish, mischievous grin.

"I'm lookin' forward to that bonus. Triple if you're feelin' generous."

"More than generous. I'll show you." That kiss lasted far too long and I had to grab his hands from roaming. "Behave yourself like a gentleman, Mr. Diamond."

"Gonna take a lot to turn me into one, Lily."

"You never told me your real name," I said. "Is it a family name you hate? Or something Biblical, like Ezekiel or Abraham?"

"Nope."

"What, then?"

Ace ducked his head. "Just plain Jesse."

I liked the sound of that. Jesse Diamond. It fit him well. I was no longer Lily Rose Delano Granville, spoiled and sheltered, who delighted in shopping sprees and conveniences a wealthy family could afford. I'd changed. And I intended to make a fresh start.

"I have one thing to say," he said. "Your uncle made it clear that you'd be going back to Evanston, Lily."

Surprised, I touched my sunburned nose. "He did? I suppose I might, one day."

"Take my advice then."

"Oh?"

"Steer clear of theater people." He hugged me when I laughed. "I'm serious."

"All right," I said and kissed him. "I'll keep a spur handy, Jesse."

'But why dost thou judge thy brother?' Romans 14:10

Chapter Twenty One

My damp hair curled around my shoulders while I untangled a stubborn knot. "That bath was wonderful, Uncle Harrison."

"We can't appear in court without that deed!"

He pounded his fist on the dressing table. Ever since I'd enjoyed a long soak and changed into clean underclothes and my traveling suit, my uncle paced the hotel room at Vallejo's Parker House hotel. Distance and time had changed him over the years, his fond letters a memory. He was consumed by business now. I hadn't sensed any emotion except relief that I'd survived, along with the deed, or so he assumed. Once he learned the truth, he lost his temper.

"Where did John hide it? Are you sure you searched everywhere?"

"As much as I could. Aunt Sylvia said she searched my baggage several times. I didn't expect you to search my pocketbook like a thief."

"I'd like an explanation for this. I found it in your

251

book." He held up the scrap of paper. His brown eyes flashed reproach. "The last thing I expected to see when I returned to Mount Diablo was you and that Texan. Kissing like a married couple."

"He saved my life." I slammed the hairbrush on the table. "I would appreciate a measure of privacy when it comes to my personal things."

"Your father warned me about your temper."

"He didn't warn me how much you've changed. Money, that's all you've talked about since we returned from Walnut Creek. I left Evanston to find Father's killer. I thought Todaro had stolen the deed, so don't blame me if they never found it."

Uncle Harrison slicked his thin brown hair back. "Without it, we'll lose the investment in all that hydraulic equipment. I hate to see George Hearst get the best of me," he said. I snatched the paper from his extended hand. "Let's not quarrel, Lily."

That stopped me cold. His words reminded me of the argument I'd had with Father over Emil Todaro. "I didn't start this, uncle. You did."

"I never meant that—"

The loud rap on the door startled us both. Uncle Harrison yanked it open and then tried to close it, but a dusty boot blocked the wood. Ace shoved him aside and stalked in, clearly furious, his cheeks flushed and his eyes narrowed. He tossed a handful of coins on the rug.

"Take your money, Lily. I kept my end of the bargain, better than you deserve."

"What?" I felt like a fool, my mouth hanging open, and swallowed hard. "I didn't give you that money."

"Get out, Diamond, or I'll call the sheriff back,"

Uncle Harrison said.

"You do that."

"Lily, come out of this room. Don't force me to drag you, either," he said. "We're going back to Sacramento immediately."

I counted to ten, eyeing the two angry men, the canopied bed, the heavy curtains at the window, the Oriental screen with my filthy clothes still draped over it. "In the morning, yes."

"I'll hire a steamer if I have to, but we're leaving. Right now." My uncle crossed to the fireplace and rested an arm on the mantel. "This man fought against the Union. I won't allow any dealings between you."

I glanced at Ace. His hair was damp and combed straight, and his jaw clean-shaven. That touched me. "I take it my uncle paid you a bonus. Ten dollars, is that what I see there? Not even triple the fee I paid you last week."

"Triple?" Uncle Harrison snorted in disgust. "He's a gambler, Lily. Sylvia told me all about him before they took her to the doctor."

I stared at him. "And you believed her? After she tried to kill me, and plotted to kill you with her husband?"

Ace stabbed a finger in my direction. "I ain't taking his money or yours, Lily. Not when the Captain said I wasn't fit to lick his boots clean."

"I was mistaken," my uncle said. "You aren't fit to lick a dog's—"

"Stop this, both of you!"

I stepped between them. Ace's taut chest beneath my hand relaxed a tiny bit. I withdrew, sensing the Captain would tear his throat out if he touched me in return. Demanding either of them to apologize would be useless. I

253

knew my guardian would never leave me alone with Ace in a public square, much less a hotel room. He'd already reminded me several times that I had no choice but to obey his wishes. He was my legal guardian. That left a bitter taste in my mouth. I'd spend the next year in a virtual prison until I turned twenty-one in October.

With no special coming-of-age celebration with Father.

"Don't say anything more to him, Lily," my uncle warned. "I want him gone, and I don't care if I have to pay him fifteen hundred dollars. The Colonel—"

"Is dead. My father and I didn't always agree," I interrupted, fighting tears, "but he never dictated terms to me."

"You need it, that's clear enough." The Captain retrieved a small leather book from his inner coat pocket and bent over the table. He flipped several pages and then scrawled out a message. "Take this to my bank, Diamond, or whatever your real name is. They'll honor it. Three thousand dollars, and that should be rid of you for good."

Ace folded his arms in silence. I snatched up the crumpled paper from the table—the receipt I'd written that Ace had marked with an X. I turned it over in my hand and read a tailor's jotted bill for services. Two hats, one coat and leather work, which cost twenty five dollars by itself. An enormous sum.

For leather work? "Oh!"

Grabbing my pocketbook, I dug until I found the small sewing kit. I unfolded the silver scissors and then hauled out my sketchbook. The lower edge was wrinkled from being crushed at some point. *Treasure all that is precious to you...*

I snipped the waxy thread of the book's interior stitching. Ace and the Captain stood behind me, watching in silence. I freed the leather's edge, tugged it loose and then pulled out a thick vellum sheet hidden beneath. I withdrew the folded paper and smoothed it open. Thin cribbed writing and gold scrollwork marked the corners. The seal of a notary public graced the bottom. My cheeks grew warm and I cleared my throat. Tears filled my eyes.

The Captain pulled it out of my hands and read it aloud, his voice triumphant. "'Know all Men by these Presents, that John Elijah Granville of Evanston, Illinois, and William Harrison Granville of Sacramento County, California, in consideration of the sum of Five hundred dollars, paid by W. H. Granville, the receipt whereof is hereby acknowledged, hereby gives, grants and conveys to said W. H. Granville and J. E. Granville, their heirs and assigns, the following tract of land.'"

"It's the Early Bird deed," I said weakly. "I had it with me all the time."

My uncle folded the paper again and deposited it in his inner coat pocket. His eyes burned with self-satisfaction. "You'll be quite the catch for every young bachelor in the state of California, Lily. Take your bonus, Diamond. You're lucky to get that."

Ace glared at him, ready to spit. He didn't glance my way, only snatched the note the Captain held out and left. I dashed out of the room after him.

"Wait! Please, wait. Jesse."

He stopped. Silent, Ace circled to face me in the lamp-lit hallway. I dashed away tears with my fingertips, aware that the Captain watched us from my room's doorway.

"Well?" Ace held up the note, his tone harsh. "Does this end our bargain?"

I met his steely gaze. "Only if you want it to end. I don't."

His voice softened. "Is that right."

"I need time. That's all."

"Time." He drew in a deep breath and then folded the paper. Ace tucked it away inside his coat. "I'll give you all the time you need. But you oughter know, Lily Granville, that I aim to win you, rich or poor. And remember, I ain't a patient man."

I smiled. "Take my advice until then, Mr. Diamond. Steer clear of muleskinners."

"I'll keep that in mind."

He tipped his hat and strolled the rest of the way to the stairs. I watched until his fringed buckskin coat and dark hat vanished and walked back to my room. The Captain prowled the hall in fury. After dealing with Aunt Sylvia and her husband, I refused to be anyone's puppet.

"You can't be serious about Diamond, Lily—"

"Whether I am or not is none of your business."

"It is, for the next year. I have to act as your guardian."

"To protect my inheritance, yes. My personal business is my own," I said.

He raised an eyebrow. Muttering a hasty excuse, the Captain stalked across the hall and into his own room. I locked my own door after him and leaned against the wood. I had much to think about, given the Early Bird deed and Captain Granville's radical change from a caring, compassionate hero. Had that only been a childish impression? This competitive and ambitious man was a virtual stranger.

Ace was not a gentleman, not of my social class and perhaps not even a Christian. His vow to win me warmed my heart, but was it based on ambition or real love?

I had yet to discover if I could return the latter. I needed time. Time to recover from the long journey on the train and the terror on Mount Diablo. Time to find my bearings in California, and whether I wanted to return to Evanston or Chicago. Time to decide my future.

Thank God time was on my side now.

About the Author

Meg Mims may have been born in the wrong century. Her love of historical fiction started early, with visits to Michigan's Greenfield Village and any museum at hand. She's published articles on her blog and in magazines about the transcontinental railroad, lighthouse keepers, a 1909 dance pavilion and holiday traditions over the past few centuries. Meg is also a watercolor and acrylic artist and photographer. From a young age, she had a taste for classics such as Jane Eyre and Gone With The Wind, books by A. C. Doyle and Agatha Christie, along with J.R.R. Tolkien and Ursula LeGuin. Now Meg devours historical, cozy and PI mysteries. Her award-winning fiction always has a dead body or two, plus an independent-minded heroine and a sense of justice being served in the end. She lives with her husband, a drooling black cat and a make-my-day Malti-poo, and enjoys visits to her favorite tea room with Sweet Pea whenever she's back home.

Astraea Press
Where Fiction Meets Virtue
www.astraeapress.com

Made in the USA
Lexington, KY
13 April 2012